Tetrahedron

Nicky Linville

ISBN: 0692737405
ISBN 13: 9780692737408

Introduction

JIM SUTTON DROVE the gravel road cautiously looking for holes and ruts. Shallow or deep was on his mind as he splashed each depression in the wavy surface. Mud was sticking to his tires and then slinging off in different directions. He felt the thuds of some of the soft projectiles hitting the bottom of his car. The mud seemed to never end.

He turned on the radio to cancel the monotony and the sounds of the thuds that were hitting the bottom of the car. The news announcer on the local AM station said, "The jail in Lincoln County is taken over since this morning by the prisoners. Our latest information reports three guards are held hostage. Negotiations by the jail officials and the prisoners are beginning. There are no reports of any deaths or injuries at this time. Stand by for more news on this station as we receive updates."

The light orange mud was getting deeper, and the car began to slide sideways. Jim was able to correct the sway and continued on the road. The old corrugated sided house with the rusty metal roof began to appear behind the trees and overgrowth in the yard. The driveway showed a small place to park, but the grass had overgrown much of the gravel on both sides. The post oak trees were still alive, and the overgrowth declined under their immediate shade.

The windows were still intact, and the cedar posts holding up the porch still showed where the limbs had been removed. The posts were mere cedar trees cut and skinned of their bark with the amputated limbs showing small sharp stumps. His memory of the old house was drawn to the inside, a horse shoe floor plan with no hall. He remembered the living room going straight into the kitchen. The side door on the living room went into a front bedroom.

The front bedroom had a door to the back bedroom. Both the kitchen and the back bedroom had back doors to the outside. The only thing that kept you from walking in a square circle in the house was no door between the kitchen and the back-bedroom wall. Also, the walls and ceilings were boards nailed over two by fours without insulation except for the unfinished drywall in the back bedroom, thanks to his oldest uncle who decided to renovate his little part of the home.

Jim was on the run and had planned that his grandmother's abandoned home would be a great place to hide.Often, he would beg his parents to allow him to stay at the home with his grandmother and uncles who always seemed to enjoy his company. The house was also near the cold, clear Turkey Creek in Tennessee. At least, it was clear when the spring rains were not causing it to flood. The creek was too small to navigate but actually held bass, crappie, perch, and catfish. All he could eat in the way of fish and small game would be available. The car was stolen and had to be hidden. If rats and mice had moved into the house, snakes might be a problem. Otherwise, it might be a good place to hide while the spring rains made it almost impossible to navigate the old road without a four-wheel drive.

Stopping in the driveway to throw what clothes, food, and supplies he could take hurriedly from the prison onto the board porch, Jim started the car and drove to the dip in the road where the flooded creek was washing rapid, deep muddy water over the remains of a wooden bridge that had half collapsed years ago. He got out of the car while the engine was still running, turned the front wheels the direction of the muddy water, pushed on the brake pedal with his left hand while leaning into the car, and with his right hand placed the car in drive. He released the brake, and the car inched into the water. It traveled a short way into the deep and washed down into the bushes surrounded by rushing water. Only a small portion of the roof was able to be seen for a few seconds, and then, it disappeared into the muddy abyss.

Jim knew the rain would wash out even the car tracks and took no caution to hide the big holes his feet made while walking back to the house in the deep mud.

He picked up his small amount of supplies from the porch, stomped the mud off his shoes on the porch as best he could, opened the front door slowly with his free hand, and entered the old farmhouse. No guns or weapons of any kind were in his makeshift luggage, but he was raised in these Tennessee hills and hallows. He would look for safety pins and other things that could be used for fish hooks. Maybe a fisherman left some tangled line on the creek banks. Anyway, he could find food. He had some matches, and the old wood stove in the living room looked rusty but usable. He would have to be cautious about making too much smoke, but moonshiners in the area make smoke that nobody investigates for worry of being shot. He remembered that his Uncle Ted had been shot with a 22 rifle two decades ago by a moonshiner.He walked all the way home and showed the family the small bullet hole in his lower left abdomen. A small hole no bigger than a small pea killed his uncle before the family could get him to the small town hospital.He thought; a woodstove fire should be limited and only at night to further limit suspicion.

While inspecting the contents of the home, he noted that mice and rats had eaten the stuffing out of the old chair sitting near the south living room wall window in the home. The living room had some cots and bedding, maybe left by some of his kin that had used it for a deer camp during the winter. In the kitchen, the floor was slanting down toward the back door, and a snakeskin lay near a small hole that penetrated through the outside wall. This was home but not a wonderful place to live. Leaning on the right hand front corner of the light green board kitchen wall, there was a folding card table with folding metal chairs. It did not alarm Jim due to this being a possible deer camp used last winter.

Jim reentered the front living room and eventually explored into the small bedroom at the back of the house where his Uncle Samuel had slept. The room was never painted, and he looked long at the plaster that still covered the nail holes in the drywall while remembering his uncle and then the family. It was beginning to get dark, and to Jim's surprise, a rusty oil lamp with what looked like oil still in it was sitting on a small wooden table by the iron bed frame. No mattress was on the rusty latticed springs. Jim lighted the lamp with a match he had stolen during the escape. As darkness began to blacken the small bedroom window, the light looked eerie as the shadows from the lamp's smoky glass cover showed about the walls. A legend had been told by his Uncle Samuel about the back door on the bedroom side of the home; he was his oldest uncle and often told of something knocking at the door at midnight.As told, the light would travel by no apparent means to an old tree and go out. If the door was locked, the door would shake as if someone were trying to break in. When the door was opened, the small light about three foot off the ground, would go to the old tree as if it wanted someone to see and follow. Later, Samuel would dig up a large strong box of twenty-dollar gold pieces reportedly worth over one million dollars. Some say that is how Samuel made his fortune in the late 1990's. However, Uncle Samuel was also known as a great liar. Often, he spun tales out of thin air; however, he was very rich when he died.

Jim remembered listening to Samuel's and his other uncle's ghost stories around the old stove that sat rusty in the living room. He continued looking around the bedroom and walked to the small closet that jutted out into the room and stood on the left side of the back door. Pulling back the dusty thin cloth curtain, he peered into a small cavity filled with dried foods and full water bottles. He thought, what is going on? Fear began to encapsulate him, and a question loomed in his mind. Is this someone's home?

CHAPTER 1

First Contact

FEAR SOARED AS the double windows in Samuel's bedroom showed the shadowy darkness of late evening because Jim had just heard four consecutive knocks on the bedroom's door.

"Do not be afraid Jim. I have been expecting you," came the voice from the other side of the creaky green stained six panel door. The porcelain knob surrounded by rust began to turn. Jim looked around for possible weapons, but none were noted in the time it took for the unlocked door to open. On the other side stood a man in camouflage from head to toe to include his face that was covered with camouflage netting.

"Turkey season," the man proclaimed as he entered the room without signs of worry. The man began to pull the netting from his face and then removed his thin netting style camouflaged gloves. The stranger stood at least three inches taller than Jim, about six foot four inches as Jim could guess and looked like a Swede that practiced body building. His short hair was blond, his body was stocky without fat, but his face carried a pleasant look- a contradiction Jim thought. Jim's feet were size thirteen wide, but the man looked like he wore about a sixteen boot.

"I don't suppose I could take you," Jim said.

"Let's not see," the man said. "My name is Charles Dorgan for today and maybe this week, and you are Jim Sutton."

"How do you know me?"

"That will all be explained later. Did you have much problem breaking out of jail?"

"Not really. I want you to know something. I am innocent, and I was rail-roaded," proclaimed Jim.

1

"I know that. I am a psychologist by trade. It is fairly easy to tell when someone is a liar, a criminal, or a good person."

Jim managed to swallow a little despite his thoroughly dry throat, "What are you here for Charles?"

"Oh, to see you and to explain some things to you. I know where we can find a couple of chairs in this place?"

Jim, while still in shock from the sudden visitor, began to try to place his brain back on subject and remember the chairs in the kitchen.

Jim took another long look at Charles and said sarcastically, "You look much like Swedish descent. Shouldn't you be named Spin, Ollie, or something like that"?

"Yes."

"Yes, what?"

"Yes, my real name is something like that," said Charles as he began to walk toward Jim. "Come, let us go to the kitchen to the table and chairs." Charles pulled a small flashlight from his pocket and twisted the top until a faint light came on. Charles said, "We can find our way to the kitchen with this flashlight. We can leave the lighted lamp in here if you wish." Both Charles and Jim knew to leave the lighted lamp in the bedroom but for different reasons.

"Fairly wise," said Jim.

"Yes, limiting yourself to one room makes for an easy target. It is good to split the lights and confuse people after you. I thought you would greatly approve," said Charles.

Charles was walking partially sideways behind Jim who was walking backwards. Jim said while starring Charles in the eyes and continuing to back up toward the kitchen, "Yes, fifty percent chance of escape is better than no chance of escape." Getting through the kitchen door was awkward. Once through, Charles walked straight to an oil lamp, took out his lighter, removed the glass cover, and twisted up the wick as he held the fire near the burned tip. The shadowy, flickering light filled the kitchen. The folding card table with the folding chairs sat in the corner. Charles placed the lamp on the floor and set the table and chairs in place. Then he placed the lamp on the table being careful not to touch the thin, hot glass cover. Charles sat down in one of the folding chairs careful not to disturb the lamp.

"Jim, get yourself a chair and sit."

"I don't want to sit. I don't know you. Your bigger than I am, and you are armed."

"Oh, so you see the bulge in my coat. It's a 22 long barrel single action revolver."

Jim looked nervously at Charles, and then the coldness caressed his body, mind, and spirit. For the first time, Charles was seeing the very soul of the man in front of him, a man who could kill now without hesitation or worry. The coldness in Jim's eyes shook Charles.

Charles blurted out as he sat not daring to take his eyes off Jim, "It is yours! It is loaded with rat shot for snakes and rats. I do not like snakes and rats, and I do not like cats either."

Jim said coldly, "Fine, give it to me then."

Charles opened his coat and carefully pulled the long barreled pistol from the shoulder holster and handed it butt first to Jim.

Jim took the pistol without a word, looked into the cylinder, and found the crimped end of the 22 shells. It was loaded with rat shot. Jim took a deep breath, looked at Charles, and said, "I'm sorry, you had me worried".

"I hope I never see that look in your eyes again."

"I did not mind you having that 40 caliber in your right zipped coat pocket. It is an honest gun anyway. But, the 22 said it might be my demise."

"How did you know it was a 40 caliber in my right coat pocket?"

"Barrel width causing the gun to look larger than a 9 mil but smaller than a 45."

"Speaking of 45's, if you look in my pack outside the bedroom's back door, you will find your 1911 forty-five caliber pistol."

"You obviously don't know that felons can't have guns."

"They are not to break out of jail either, but you look pure to me Jim."

"You're confusing me. Pure?"

"Yes Jim, pure."

Jim motioned to Charles, and Charles handed him his flashlight. Jim then backed out of the kitchen. He went to the bedroom's back door and opened it slowly. The small flashlight showed a small camouflaged bag and a dead Eastern

Bird turkey that lay on the ground while a large pump shotgun leaned against the wall near the single rock step to enter the room.

Charles began to lighten up and said, "You do know it probably looks like we are dancing without music with you backing and me following and all. Here, let me get that for you. I know you are expecting a bomb or some type of booby trap. I assure you that I had plenty of chances to kill you when you were sinking the car or going toward the front door."

Charles reached down into the darkness with both hands picking up the bag with his right hand and the turkey in his left. He laid the turkey on the floor beside him and proclaimed, "That is our dinner; I get tired of dried dinners very quickly." Then he opened the bag slowly with both hands and held the opening up at an angle where Jim could see the inside with the reflection of the oil lamp. On the bottom of the bag lay scattered red and brass shotgun shells and a 1911 pistol cradled in a black fabric holster.

"You certainly know how to pick them. Do you mind if I hold it?" asked Jim.

"I do not mind. After all, you have the 22."

Jim had forgotten the 22 was in his left hand which he then slid into the front of his cloth belt. He looked at Charles and for the first time gave a nervous smile. "With the rat shot, it is nothing but a club."

"Well, are you going to take it out of the bag?"

Jim reached his hand into the bag feeling the finely worked Zebrawood flat grips of the 1911. The gun fit his hand perfectly. He pushed the button on the side and released the magazine. The lamp reflected off the stainless steel magazine and the top of the six 45 ACP full metal jacket rounds, shiny and new. Placing the magazine into his pocket, he then pulled back the slide looking down into an empty chamber while he turned the barrel toward him in one motion. The barrel reflected the dull stainless steel when turned toward the fire of the lamp. The sights were made for targets with white dots in the back and a reflector in the front. The slide was tight. The weapon was one of the best pistols he had ever held in his life.

"What is this worth Charles?"

"About five thousand dollars. Here is another thing you might want." Charles handed Jim a target clipping with 3 shots within the diameter of a nickel. The target had the initials RJ, FMJ .45 weight 230 grains at 50 yards. "Thought you might like to meet RJ of the quality assurance person who tested the gun."

"That is some direct quality assurance. RJ, whoever he is, put 3 full metal jacket rounds in a nickel sized group at fifty yards. It is well made. Why give it to me?" asked Jim.

"It establishes trust between us. It is also your favorite type of hand gun except for certain revolvers."

"Both weapons are fantastic," replied Jim.

"Is there anything you do not notice about weapons?" asked Charles.

"Charles, there are very few if any."

"Now, can we go sit down? Bring the bag to the kitchen. We have some talking to do." Jim placed the clip back into the 45, unbuckled his cloth belt, and placed the pistol holster on it. The weight of the gun stretched the belt down on his right hip. "Well, it does have too much weight for this belt," said Jim.

"I have a pistol belt for you in my luggage. Come on."

Jim and Charles sat across from each other with nothing but the eight-inch barrel 22 single action and the lamp between them. Charles asked Jim, "Are you settled now?"

"I think so. I forgot how much the floor slants downhill."

"OK, I am about to reach in my pocket and pull out a couple of harmless things."

Jim feeling more relaxed said, "OK."

Charles pulled a wooden triangle and a wooden tetrahedron from his left coat pocket.

Charles handed the two pieces of wood to Jim and said, "Look at the triangle Jim and note that all the sides are the same length."

"An isosceles triangle," said Jim.

"Yes. Triangles have three points. However, one more point can mean three additional triangles and a solid tetrahedron. Since you used the word isosceles, it would be an isosceles tetrahedron if all the lines are equal."

"First of all Charles, have you ever answered a question directly in your life? Second, why the geometry lesson?"

Charles explained, "Because, these four equidistant points make up the tetrahedron, there is a lesson here in human endeavors." Jim fingered the small wooden tetrahedron between his right thumb and forefinger. "Note this Jim, if a point is turned upward, let us say it is the leader." Jim then turned the figure until another point was upward. "It is a change in leader instantly, and yet, the form is not lost. Also, the only way to destroy a triangle or tetrahedron is to break its lines. It cannot alter its angles like a square, rectangle, or a box. If the correctly picked people are the points, the tetrahedron is mostly indestructible."

"So, who is to be the leader on top?" asked Jim.

"You are, I am, and there are two others who will be when appropriate."

"What two others?"

"Jim, I do not want to weigh you down with too much information too soon, but there are two others that will be joining us in our endeavors."

"What endeavors?"

"The endeavors that you were skillfully broken out of jail to accomplish. "

"Again, what endeavors?"

"When you first saw me, I could see in your eyes that you thought I meant to kill you. Actually, I am here to try to keep you, myself, and the two others we will be working with alive. What we are about to do is very dangerous Jim, and we may not survive. We will be given supplies and some assistance as needed and a new life if we succeed."

"What if we fail?"

"Cremation and never heard of again."

"Charles, I am going to ask you a question, but I bet you will not answer it directly. Who are the other two?"

"The answer takes a leap of faith Jim. One is the most violent woman I have ever known. The other is a physician."

"Do they have names, and when will they be arriving?"

"Fake names and tomorrow Jim."

"Why are they not here now?"

"That is my fault. I wanted time to spend with you alone."

Jim looked at Charles and jokingly proclaimed, "You are scaring me."

"You would not accept too much truth and change. You have fidgeted since you met me, watching my every movement. You placed the magazine in the 45 pistol and placed a round in the barrel before putting it in the holster and placing it on your belt." Jim suddenly set up as if being caught doing something very wrong. "Do not worry Jim; I knew it was only a caution. You even thought of taking me out fearing for your life. Three people at once would have probably set you over your threshold. You are in shock that I showed up on this night. Do you not even wonder how I knew you would be here?"

"That is easy. You had a bug in the car I stole."

"Actually, there was no bug. As you are a weapons and tactical expert, I am an expert on human behavior. I deduced you would be here. When I heard the news, I merely timed myself to get here a day before you would arrive."

"How long did you surmise that I would be here?"

"The past year. I began a year ago studying you."

Jim looked at Charles and said in a stern voice, "So, I'm the one you studied for a year just to meet me in a small run down house in Tennessee. No more round about answers. Why am I here?"

Charles looked back in the dancing lamp light and explained succinctly, "to stop mass murderers from mass murdering. Do you remember the two hundred plus bodies in the desert on the Mexican border buried in shallow graves? It happened about three years ago. The graves had the bones of children, young adult men and women, and even the bones of babies."

"I remember the headlines. I read about them before I was framed."

"Jim, they were not bodies; they were skeletons robbed of their organs, their corneas, their skin, and other precious parts for sale in an underground market."

"So, we have to kill the business people making money off this misery," Jim said as he looked at the 22 caliber pistol between them. He proclaimed, "That is an assign's gun even down to the smooth bore to keep the round from being traced."

Charles noted Jim's continued stare at the pistol and said, "It is not for assignations Jim; it is a gun simply to shoot snakes and rats in this house. You see, we will be living and hiding here for a while."

"Who are we working for?"

"First, I want to answer your other unspoken question. We do not assassinate unless it is necessary. We are to use our wits and our talents to close the cartel and bring the criminals to justice. The answer to the second question is the US government."

Charles saw Jim stare directly at him and lift his right eyebrow while he asked a question, "Is the pay good?"

"Look at all we have already- a nice home nestled in the woods with all the snakes we can eat; the list goes on."

"Charles, tell me what pure means."

"It means you are innocent, as far as myself and the government believe, but I do not count. Also, you are dead."

"Dead!"

"Yes, you are dead. You ran off the road on the flooded Turkey creek and you drown as the car sank in the rapid muddy water. We have the whole thing recorded and will doctor the recording appropriately."

"Who are we? You know Charles, you are freaking me out. How did you or all of you know I would sink the car?"

"I studied you. Again, my specialty is human behavior."

"How did you know it would flood?"

"We did not know, but we would have come up with another plan if it did not flood. The flood just gave us good opportunities."

"My father will be devastated. It will be really bad for him and my sister and brother."

"And, they will be targets if the right people learn about you. They are safer if you are dead. Maybe someday you can be resurrected, a simple mistake concerning your demise. But currently, you are dead."

"I met you about a half hour ago. Before I met you, I was just an escaped criminal, and now, you're telling me that I am both innocent and dead." Jim smiled while looking at Charles and proclaimed, "That's it; you are a horrible man who has been studying how to destroy the rest of my sanity for a year. Why should I believe any of this?"

"Believe what you want. I have a gas grill in the back room closet and a dead turkey to clean and cook. I will find something to go with the meat. During that time, you can find a wash kit in the front bedroom closet and some plastic bags with water. Wet wipes are there to. You will find a razor with shave cream in the kit also. I have some toothpaste and a new tooth brush for you in the right side pocket on my bag. Feel free to wash up. If you wish, I can heat you some water on the gas grill."

"Cold will be fine."

Jim took the new toothbrush and paste from Charles' bag and began to walk through the kitchen door into the living room. Charles spoke, and for the first time, he allowed Jim to see the full view of his back, "Jim, remember that a tetrahedron has four points and is made up of four triangles. It is a solid three-dimensional structure, but if just one point is missing, you lose three sides and it becomes a two dimensional, flat triangle. We will be a team Jim; we cannot lose one person, or we could all be killed or worse fail our mission. I am not confused Jim; we must all work together. Remember that when you meet the others tomorrow."

"If nobody shows up, I will know you are probably a liar or from another planet."

"Go get cleaner and then set up a cot with blankets and pillows. Yours will be in the living room by the stove, and mine is already in the front bedroom. Watch for snakes and rats in the back closet. I will get this bird stewing."

Jim disappeared into the living room after retrieving the water, soap, shave cream, and razor and began to set up to wash himself. After Charles had retrieved the small gas stove from the back room closet, he began to set it up along with a small gas bottle near the opened small kitchen window. Both began to do their separate work. Both were on edge. Both kept their weapons near and loaded.

CHAPTER 2

The Arrivals

ABRUPTLY AWAKENING, JIM was startled as the front door opened and sunlight flooded the room. He suddenly proclaimed from the blinding sunlight, "Now, I remember the front door faces east. I can't see."

Jim's eyes strained as he stood up suddenly from the cot he was so restfully sleeping on a second before. His eyes then looked at what would be chest high on an average man and then suddenly moved down to see the figure of a small woman in the door. He could barely focus and fought sleepiness to clear his head. He stood in white underwear with brown stains from the muddy water, a pair of black socks on his feet, and a black toboggan that puffed up to a short tube looking tower on top of his head that leaned toward the left.

"So, you're the tactical expert," came the squeaky voice from the small woman in the door, "But, I never expected such a fancy dresser."

Charles entered the room from the kitchen in the back and began to laugh while Jim was grabbing the green wool blanket to cover himself. As his arms encircled the blanket around him, the short lady looked on. She was about four foot nine inches by Jim's guess and had an impish nose that turned up. Freckles covered her face, and Jim could not tell if her hair was red, brown, or blonde. Her large brown eyes were beautiful and piercing.

She walked inside, dropped her backpack, and then proceeded to walk over to Charles. As she passed by Jim, she stuck her hand into the blanket about where his navel would be and scratched Jim's abdomen lightly. Jim in surprise said with a gasp, "don't do that!"

The lady simply ignored Jim and jumped up into Charles arms with her legs wrapped as far as they would go around his waist- "kiss me you big hunk of man." Charles looking at her while she moved her left cheek in place pecked her jaw with his lips.

"I guess that will have to do me for now," she said.

Then, she climbed down Charles and headed back to Jim, and while extending her right hand said, "Hi brown shorts, my name is Candice Edwards."

"My shorts are brown from the mud and the water. I could not wash them last night."

"Sure they are. I mean from the mud and the water. Or else, maybe I scared you when I suddenly appeared and caught you sleeping."

"It was a long day yesterday. I'm still not over the shock."

Candice looked at Jim and smiled sarcastically, "I can help you cope with your stress, and maybe Doctor Do can help you with your bowel problems."

"After meeting Charles and you, I know where I am now. I registered in the Hotel California, but I could have sworn I was in Tennessee," proclaimed Jim.

Charles looked at Candice staring up at Jim with her big brown eyes set on his face. "Do not let him get to you Candice. You will need to control your hormones."

"It's the brown shorts and the blanket Charles and that little fat pouch that his navel sinks into."

"I knew I shouldn't have slept in the living room. I was afraid of what might come in at night and violate me. What do you do anyway Candice?"

Charles said, "I can answer that. She is IT, and she can call Russia with some bailing wire and a wet shoestring."

"That is not true Charles. The shoestring has to be dry."

Jim looked into her face with the freckles and turned up nose. He realized her age was early thirties, about his age. She was covered with cute, and he had always been a sucker for freckles. He realized also that she was wearing no makeup; she was naturally beautiful. "I see why you are dangerous. You are perky and beautiful."

"You're supposed to think that and not just blurt it out," Charles proclaimed in a half joking voice. "She already knows she is beautiful."

Jim tore his eyes from her face and said, "But you know, I like taller and more muscular women."

"And, I like men without bowel and bladder problems."

"Would you stop with my shorts? It is mud and water!"

Charles said, "Both of you should stop. Dr. Do is coming. I saw him walking down the road trying to step on the dryer spots."

Jim asked, "What is wrong with the Doctor?"

"Loud, bombastic, and full of himself. About five foot ten but built like a tank. Do not let him tell you about blowing your own trumpet," said Charles.

Doctor Filbert Calhoun stomped the mud off his feet while the other three listening on the inside thought the old boards on the porch might break. Nick, knowing they were Yellow Popular, had a personal hope the porch would hold. Dr. Calhoun came through the door with a quick stride while slamming the door behind him. The old east window shook in its frame as the door rattled the room. Quickly, he made a bee line for Candice with outstretched arms. Candice tried to turn to run, but he caught her from the back and picked her feet off the floor. Jim heard the air leaving her body in a strong forced exhale from the hug.

"I dare you try to get away from me; you're my one true love," yelled Dr. Calhoun.

"I tried to run because I want to live," Candice said in a squeaky, near breathless voice.

Charles walked over to the doctor with his right hand out. Dr. Calhoun placed Candice down gently on the floor, bypassed Charles hand, and grabbed Charles around the waist in a bear hug. Even Charles lost some breath by Dr. Calhoun's embrace. Then after two hard pats to Charles back, he broke from Charles and started toward Jim with determination. Jim backed up so fast that he fell backward over the cot barely missing the left front stove leg with his head. Dr. Calhoun, not being stopped by mere canvas and aluminum tubes, came over the cot lying on its side right onto the floor with Jim.

"What the, hey watch it; who are you?"

"I am Filbert Calhoun, and you must be Nick."

"No, I am Jim."

Jim realized that Dr. Calhoun had him in some kind of a wrestling hold with his iron like legs wrapped around Jim's legs and the doctor's arms encircling the shoulders with his hands in a deadlock at the back of Jim's neck.

"My mistake Jim. I trust you are well." Dr. Calhoun then broke the hold and allowed Jim to stand.

Candice looking on as the doctor helped Jim to get up said, "thank you Jim. You took a lot off Charles and I by being here."

Jim stood up trying to get the blanket around his near nude body again.

"Obviously, I came at a bad time," joked Dr. Calhoun.

Jim got dressed as breakfast was being cooked by Charles and Candice. Doctor Calhoun was doing something in the back bedroom that consisted of partly singing, grunting, and something that sounded like cursing.

Jim finished dressing in the front side bedroom and then proceeded to the back bedroom where he saw the good doctor spreading some kind of a pad from his backpack on the rusty bed springs and then taking out toiletries and a small plastic wash basin.

"Do you need any help?" asked Jim.

"Yes. I just turned fifty years old. Can you transplant a prostate?"

"Why? You got problems?"

"Yes, I do. This is my last mission. I am beginning to look for bathrooms more than bad people. I should have been a urologist; they never run out of work, and they're going to make a fortune off me."

"Would you tell me all you know about this mission?"

"Oh, I jumped ahead. I didn't mean to. You have not been fully briefed yet." Doctor Calhoun raised his voice so that it rang through the small house, "Hey guys, how much does he know?"

"Very little," came back Charles' voice trying to boom as much as Doctor Calhoun's.

"Well tell him some things before I put both feet in my mouth."

"You tell him. You're back there with him," came Candice's squeaky voice trying to get as much volume as possible.

"Listen Minnie Mouse, that is not my job. My job is to practice my malpractice on you when you get hurt."

Jim looked at the doctor as he was busying himself placing his razor, soap, comb, and other items in order. Feeling he would get very little information about the mission from the doctor, his mind turned to the word malpractice that held some deeper meaning to him. He asked, "What do you mean by malpractice?"

"Oh, it's nothing to worry about, I haven't had a real medical license in years."

"You're kidding."

"Nobody asks for one when they're shot and bleeding.'

Jim immediately left the room walking the square horseshoe through the front bedroom, the living room and then into the kitchen where Candice and Charles were laughing about some private joke.

Jim screamed at the top of his lungs and caught the startled eyes of both Candice and Charles. The doctor even left the bedroom running as well as he could to the kitchen. Jim stood deadly quiet only turning his head and looking directly into the startled eyes of each person. Then he laughed out loud an almost hysterical laugh.

Charles was startled as was the others but found some words, "Why did you just do that?"

"I was nothing more than a prisoner yesterday waiting to do some hard time. I dodged and drove a long way only to find I was expected by a weirdo who shows up at the back door that is supposedly haunted. Then a woman scratches my stomach, and an unlicensed doctor told me that he would cure me but tried to kill me in the living room. Now, you wonder why I screamed. I have no idea what is happening, but I thought a good scream and hysterical laugh would just fit right in with the other actions that I have witnessed in this house."

Charles looked around at the startled faces of Candice and the doctor, laughed, and proclaimed, "He figured it out himself."

Candice began to laugh as she moved in and placed her arm around Jim's waist. "Welcome to the Hotel California. Hardly anyone noticed that it moved to Tennessee. You seem to fit in well."

Charles then looked serious and proclaimed to the other three, "No, I mean it. He has figured it out."

Jim looked down into the eyes of Candice with a serious stare, "Candice, I was in the military, and I was in war. I know about replacements. Who did I replace?"

Candice looked at the doctor who was no help and then to Charles who nodded in agreement.

Candice began to speak softly and sadly, "The name he had last was Joseph Woods. He was with us on our last mission, and he died just as we had cleared the area. Nobody even knew that he had been shot; he kept it from us until we got to the boat. He did it to help us."

"Where was he shot?"

"That is secret. I can't tell you that."

"I understand that, but I meant where did the bullet enter his body."

Doctor Calhoun then said, "It entered the upper right quadrant of his abdomen. It nicked his liver from all indications. He was slowly bleeding to death. Probably a low velocity bullet from a pistol."

Jim looked at Candice who already had tears in her eyes and said, "Liver shots are very painful- even if it was just nicked. He must have been a good man."

Charles took his turn to continue explaining, "He was one of us, you know that one for all and all for one thing."

Jim looked down again at Candice whose left arm was beginning to feel out of place around his waist and asked an out of place question, but he needed to know, "Were you two an item Candice? Did you love him? "

"I loved him like a brother Jim. I loved him just like I love Charles and Doctor Do. He was one of the three brothers I never had."

Jim looked at Charles who seemed to know more about behavior than anyone in the room. Jim also began to be aware of the eggs, the gas grill and the make shift biscuits ready to bake. This was a breakfast, a home, a place he had known love before from his grandmother and uncles.

Jim's eyes turned hard when he asked Charles, "How good is it to fight an enemy with people you really care about?"

"Jim, it is the best until someone is lost. You invest so much, and then, there is a hole that cannot be filled."

"That hole Charles, am I here to fill that hole?"

"Jim, you were picked from over seven hundred candidates. You were picked because you were innocent, because of your character, because of your record of actions under fire, and because we voted on you. It was three to zero to bring you in."

"So Charles, I am stuck here."

Candice pulled her arm away from Jim's side and began to go over toward the cooking area and prepare breakfast again. The doctor sat down within easy ear shot in the living room, and Charles turned his back on Jim and began breaking eggs into a bowl as he spoke.

"I hope you like scrambled Jim. Jim, you are not a prisoner here. There are some agents guarding this road that look like turkey hunters out on vacation. No

Jim, you are free to go after you hear us out. You will meet some scraggly looking big man tomorrow who will place two contracts in front of you. He will answer most of your questions. One contract will stipulate that you go with us on this mission, and the other will be your way out."

"If I refuse, do I go to prison?"

"No Jim, you will be placed into a witness protection type of program where you will be hidden until this assignment is finished. Then you may or may not be sent back to your family, depending on what is going on. Either way, you will not go back to jail or to prison. But, one thing is certain if you stay or leave; you will have to contract that you will not try to find those who killed your wife and grandfather."

Jim pulled one of the chairs from the card table and straddled it from the back. As he rested his chest on the back of the chair, he asked seriously, "What are my chances of surviving this so called mission?"

Candice then spoke without turning around, "The last mission was easier, and one of us was killed."

"So, there is a fairly good chance that I will be killed."

Charles began to answer questions not verbally asked, "Jim, if you die, you will be cremated and your ashes scattered. You will have no grave and no stone. There will be no funeral. Your family will never be told that you did not drown in the flooded Turkey Creek while you were making your escape from jail prior to your transport to prison. Your family will be told you were cremated due to the increased decomposition of the body when it was finally located. However, not even the ashes will be from you. This, in one way or another, is what each of us face."

"Thus is the story of Joseph. So, you don't even know where his ashes are right now?"

Charles turned and looked Jim in the eyes, "No Jim, it would be classified anyway. Nor does his family know. As far as they are concerned, he was already dead. We may have our problems Jim, but we do this for a reason. None of us are blind going in. We are those few who do great things, but only a select few ever know.However, we do save lives in the long run."

"Tell me all you know about the mission."

Charles turned back to his eggs and said, "That will be tomorrow with the contracts. The strong man will make sure you understand what you will need to know to make a good decision. Nobody here will judge you either way. Okay, no more questions for now but get ready for a bunch of answers tomorrow."

Candice exclaimed as she was composing herself after thinking about Joseph, "fair enough. Now, get to work and help us fix this meal. I will guarantee it to be good."

Jim suddenly felt lighter; his main questions had been answered, and he believed Charles when he said he would not go to prison. Either way, a new life awaited him. Jim rose from his backward chair and began walking slowly toward the portable sink where he would wash his hands and pronounced as he walked, "I hope it is good. That turkey last night was somewhere in the category of not edible and nearing poisonous."

Charles said in a lighter voice, "We take turns cooking, and those who complain get more turns. You are two days straight in a row now. Would you like to try for three?"

"No, but I can cook. Do you actually have food here?"

"Okay. That's three."

CHAPTER 3

Candice and Nick

NIGHTTIME CAME, AND Jim began to set up his cot again by placing the provided green mat back in place and tightening it down with the green straps. Then he placed the thick green wool blanket over the pad and placed the bottom sheet on so tight he could literally bounce a quarter off it. He noticed out of the corner of his eye that Candice was dragging her cot from the corner of the living room toward him, and he looked up in surprise when she began to set up her cot right beside his. He asked while fighting shock, "What are you doing?"

"Why honey, don't you think married people should sleep close to each other?"

"Married!"

"Yes, you might as well know that, on this assignment, you are my husband."

"Husband! What about all that brother stuff you were talking about in the kitchen?"

"I don't know you that well, and by the way, it is your job to turn off the lamp when I get into bed. Now, turn around and pretend you are doing something while I get dressed for bed."

Jim turned around looking at the horizontally placed aged green painted warping boards in the wall. After getting tired of staring at the wall, he bent down and set up his wind up clock that he had dug out of the supply closet. Still waiting to hear Candice get settled, he checked his 45 pistol for dirt and dust. Then, he heard the shuffling of covers and the creaking of the cot. Candice was in bed.

"You like that weapon? I picked it out."

"You did a good job. What does this marriage require?"

"Oh, it is like other marriages; you do what I need, and you get no sex."

"That's what I thought, but you look about thirty-one to thirty-three to me. Your cuteness will not always give you control."

"Yes, but it's working now. Besides honey, I have our rings." Candice reached over with her right hand and while taking Jim's left hand in her left hand, she deposited a white gold band with a small embedded diamond into his palm.

"Nice ring." Jim looked at it in the lamplight; placed it on his ring finger, and it fit perfectly. "I am not surprised you knew my ring size. Actually, I am beginning to get used to having a gut jerk every fifteen minutes or so since I have been here."

Candice began to take a more serious tone. "I know you hate change, but there are some things I need to tell you."

"Now what?"

"Doctor Do didn't make a mistake when he called you Nick. You will no longer have the name of Jim. Your name is Nick, and nobody will call you Jim again except to test you. You will be expected to ignore the name like nobody is even speaking to you."

"So, what is my full name?"

"Nicholas Richard Lippincott."

"Why did you do that?"

"Well, I picked it out and don't feel bad. My name is now Candice Lippincott."

"Great, I hope you give me the exact spelling."

"I will Nick. I just want you to know the circumstances if you decide to stay tomorrow."

"Who's betting on me staying?"

"How did you know that?"

"Come on, who is betting on my joining the tetrahedron?"

"Only me."

"So, it is two against one."

"Something like that."

"Tell me something. Do you want me to stay?"

"All of us want you to stay. If a tetrahedron loses one point it goes from a solid structure to a flat two-dimensional triangle, lose two points and you only have a straight line, lose three points and you're all alone. I want us to be solid again."

"I don't want to die until I see justice done. I want those things that killed my family to be hung upside down in the wind, so their naked bodies will slap against thorn trees."

"The three of us are like you Nick. All of us have similar stories. All of us lost people special to us."

"Were any of you in jail or prison?"

"Only Doctor Do. He was the best surgeon ever until something happened. If you stay, you will learn things about us like we know about you. We do that so we can tell if someone has penetrated our disguises. But enough of this, would you like to see my ring?"

"Sure, why not?"

Candice placed her left hand so the ring would reflect the light of the oil lamp. It was the same as Nick's except smaller, white gold and a small diamond embedded in the front.

"I guess you picked both of these rings."

"I did. Aren't they great?"

"Is there anything else you would like to surprise me with Mrs. Lippincott?"

"Yes, I would like to remind you that you need to turn out the living room light."

"Do you have a small flashlight that will help me get back to the cot in the dark without falling over you?"

"You do not need one. The light from the bedroom should give you enough light. Charles is usually up all night reading or something. He hardly ever sleeps except he rests a little on Friday night to Saturday night. By the way, I know you are an atheist, but Charles is very religious. He does not eat pork or shellfish either."

"So, that's the reason we eat nothing but eggs and biscuits for breakfast. You know, he does not cook well."

Charles voice came from the front bedroom, "You know that I can hear you."

"I spent a lot of time in this house while I was growing up. Doctor Do can hear us in the back bedroom. The walls are boards without insulation that seem to resonate sounds like a fiddle."

Nick got up and blew out the lamp and walked back to his bunk by the shadowy lamplight that flickered from the connecting but opened door to the front bedroom and asked as he made his way to his cot, "Charles, were you up all night last night?"

Doctor Do's voice came loud from the back bedroom; "He does not sleep during the night. I think he is really a vampire. He will go for days sometime without good sleep. It is a medical miracle, and I noticed some bites on my neck during our last assignment."

"Listen, I am tired, and my wife has just given me some disturbing pillow talk. Is this the part where we say good night John boy?" asked Nick.

Candice reached her small hand over and placed it on Nick's chest. "Good night Jim." No reply came back.

"Okay, good night Nick."

"Good night honey," came back Nick's sarcastic voice in the semi darkness.

"You have a big day tomorrow. We all have a big day tomorrow. Besides, I may win my bet."

"Can I bet?"

"Not this time. Now, go to sleep."

"Yes dear," Nick said.

"Now, that's better."

CHAPTER 4

The Decision.

NICK AWOKE TO sunlight again hitting his cot from the opened front door. He noticed Candice was out of her cot, and the covers were neatly pulled up with the pillow fluffed and perfectly placed. Her small pistol sat on the tight blanket about the center of the cot. He also heard rattling coming from the back bedroom. Groaning, he made his way off his cot, grabbed his blanket to cover his body only clothed in toboggan, shorts, and socks, and began his short journey to the back bedroom. As he entered the first bedroom, he noted that Charles looked asleep with his Bible on his chest and other books laying around him.

Nick walked cautiously into the back bedroom where Doctor Do was lying in his bed looking irritated as Candice was lying on top of the boxes halfway inside the supply closet with her feet sticking out and up. She was rifling through the stacks of dried food, water, and other things.

"What are you doing my lovely field wife?" asked Nick.

Doctor Do answered the question without hesitation. "Charles made the mistake of telling her last night that a coffee pot was in the back of the closet. Evidently, it is a special one that can be used on top of the gas grill. Did she wait on me to help her this morning? No, she woke me up moving everything in every direction in hope of getting her fix."

Candice's voice came muffled from the supplies surrounding her head. "I want my coffee. If there is a pot in here, I will find it. Now, help me get this mess out of my way."

Suddenly, a muffled scream of glee came from the bottom of the closet. "I found it. Nick, go fix breakfast. I will be there in a minute."

"Okay. But, my eggs may not be rubbery, and my biscuits may not have to be licensed as lethal weapons in most states."

Doctor Do chimed in, "Nobody ever died from Charles cooking. Well, at least if they did not have an underlying condition."

Candice pulled herself out of the closet over the debris looking up at Nick with dirt on her face and her reddish, blondish, brownish hair mostly in her face.

"With her looks Doctor Do, I guess you know why I had to marry her?"

"My good man, just being her soul brother is a fantastic task. If you are smart, you will take the tribulation one day at a time."

Nick looked at her as she raked back the hair from her face exposing her big brown eyes as she sat in the middle of the pile she had created. "You do know that snakes are still in this house," said Nick.

"That's their problem. I will try not to hurt them if they will leave me alone."

"Yes, coffee is worth risking snakebites," said Doctor Do.

Nick turned his head toward Doctor Do, "Can you cure Timber Rattlesnake bites?"

"I don't know."

"What do you mean you don't know?"

"Nobody ever made it to me with one of those."

Candice began to rise from the scattered food and supplies while saying, "Nick, I am hungry, and I want to get my coffee going. I'll be in the kitchen after I clean this up."

"Oh no, my dear sister," said the doctor. "It will be good just to get you out of the bedroom where I only have rats and snakes to worry about. I will clean it up."

"Oh alright, I'll go into the kitchen to help with breakfast."

Nick walked over to the boxes and rummaged through them until he found the packets of powered eggs and sausage. "Did we use all the real eggs yesterday?"

"Yes, my love," came the squeaky voice moving through the house toward the kitchen.

"What about this sausage?" asked Nick as he left Dr. Do's room and made his way toward the kitchen.

Candice spoke as she entered the kitchen and was brushing herself off with her right hand as she held the coffee pot in the left, "They're okay; there's no real meat in them. The shelf life is longer without meat."

"So, it is mystery meat," said Nick.

"Yes, nothing is as it seems in this house," proclaimed the doctor in a sarcastic loud voice from the back bedroom. "The meat is much like your marriage Nick."

"I understand. Well, I hope you will be liking breakfast this morning, but what if I cook it and don't like it myself?"

"Complaints are complaints even if it is about your own cooking. You'll be required to cook the next time. That is, if you stay."

After breakfast, Charles relaxed as well as he could in the folding poker chair. "Breakfast was better but not what I would call good," he proclaimed.

Nick looked at Charles and jokingly said, "My food bridges the gap between non-poisonous and edible. However, I changed my mind about your cooking. It leans more to the dark side. When we first met, I said you could kill me. Now, I know it could happen with your cooking."

"Well, I am not going to sit here and be insulted. I am about to leave this house and take all the company with me."

Slowly, all began to rise when someone knocked on the door.

Candice looking at Nick said, "He's right on time."

"Who Candice?" asked Nick.

"The closest thing to a boss we have. He will introduce himself. We need to leave." Then all left Nick and disappeared through the back kitchen door.

Nick answered the front door, and a gentleman dressed in camouflage looking like a hunter faced Nick. The man was big, had a no nonsense expression, and carried a camouflaged 12-gauge pump shotgun in his right hand and a large camouflaged back pack in his left hand. The man was about sixty years old with thinning bluish gray and brown hair covering his head. His large blue eyes were staring at Nick as he stood his shotgun in the corner and began to cross the room. The man's face looked stern and even ugly in its expression. Nick had met people who called themselves powerful before and bragged about the power of life and death, but this man did not need to brag. He was powerful.

The man sat at the table and motioned for Nick to sit straight across from him. Nick noticed the worn leather briefcase as the man pulled it from his oversized backpack. The strong man was muscular, fit, and appeared like he could handle himself in many situations.

He held out his hand over the table. Nick placed his right hand in the man's right as he looked him in the eye. The handshake was firm but not hurting. Nick thought this man is honest and trustworthy.

The man said in a relaxing voice, "This is a very serious time for you. We will have a discussion. You will then do some reading. You will sign one of two contracts, and it will be entirely your decision to stay or to leave."

Nick listened as he explained about the mission. "Nick, I have been in this business for a while, and this is the worse assignment that I have seen. I cannot give you a great deal of details, but people have died where you are going, if you decide to stay. This tetrahedron volunteered for it. There are other tetrahedrons, but you are neither allowed to ask about them, nor are members to be interchanged or recruited from other tetrahedrons. I gave you a chance to meet your teammates before I came here. You will be working exclusively with them. You were recruited to replace the fallen member. I will not answer any more questions about him; you already know what your teammates were allowed to tell. Anyway, I will explain the mission. You can ask questions after I finish."

Nick leaned back a little and took a deep breath. He already figured out at this level that names meant nothing, so he was not bothered about the man not introducing himself. He looked at Nick and began to speak about the head to near the tail operation that would involve neutralizing a bootleg human organ distribution cartel that was also an illegal drug network operating out of Mexico to the tail that went through different routes through the United States. Nick was told that this tetrahedron would be closing down the head and that the tail would be someone else's problem, but the tetrahedron was responsible to gain the information of those who did business with the cartel outside of Mexico. The FBI and local authorities would then handle all the tail: the doctors, nurses, other medical personnel, law enforcement officers, businesspeople, workers, and all others involved in the illegal distribution network. After the long explanation, the man closed with, "I repeat, you are being recruited because tetrahedrons are not allowed to know about each other and members cannot be recruited from other tetrahedrons. You will also find that I will repeat some things as I just said. It is a mainstay of adult education techniques."

Then the strong man spoke to Nick about the evidence concerning the selling of body parts by the cartel. "Nick, you have heard about the two

25

hundred skeletons in the desert. They were robbed of their most valuable organs. Some were children. Some were even infants. Some were pregnant women, and there were many young men. We have found four other deposits of human remains in Mexico, each having more than two hundred skeletons. The four other deposits were not allowed in the news because we do not want this information to be publicized, and it is the job of this tetrahedron to stop this. Also, there may be more than five body deposits in an American dessert. Now, what are your questions?"

"What happens if I ask to leave?"

"You will not go back to jail or be transported to prison, but you will not be allowed to return to your family either. As the others told you, you will be placed in a protection program much like a witness protection program. You will go back to prison if you tell anything to anyone about what you know about Tetrahedron. Also, you will go back to prison if you try to find those who murdered your wife and framed you."

"Thank you for your directness. Is this place bugged?"

"No."

"Are you bugged. Is this being recorded?"

"No."

"Why are we cremated if we are killed in action?"

"Bodies have evidence. We try to never leave evidence."

"How secret is Tetrahedron?"

"Echelons above special forces and even Delta Force."

"Why four people?"

"Four people are our best working team. If you think about TV shows and movies, the ones with four main characters always are more interesting and more complete. If you accept, you will be a member of a complete group. A tetrahedron always has a point upward. That point is always the leader. In this case, all are leaders, and all are followers depending on the circumstances. The tetrahedron cannot waver. The only way to destroy it is to break a side like destroying a relationship or kill a point. As you were told, either way one point lost makes the design two dimensional and a single triangle. If two points are lost, it becomes a straight line. Three points lost and it becomes an individual with only the depth of the individual. And by the way, were there three musketeers or four in reality?"

"Why did you pick me?" asked Nick.

"Your personality and other characteristics closely match the others in this team," stated the strong man.

Nick stated, "Charles has some kind of a religion that I am still trying to understand, and I do not know what the doctor and Candice believe. I am an atheist. All of us have different professions. How are we similar?"

"Nick, it is not about religion or even about professions. We like to interlock professions. Nick, it is about character, core beliefs and values to include honesty, integrity, and sense of duty to mention a few. All of you align in these areas. You believe in a sense of order and that lies, theft, murder, and other such things break that order. All of you have that same sense of right and wrong in one way or another."

"What is the penalty if I say I will stay and then quit?"

"From your personality profile, you would not do that, but if you did, you might get three people killed, even if you quit during training. Once we begin, we only have so much time even if it takes several months or even a year to prepare. Then, the mission must be carried out with what we have. It is too late to get another tetrahedron ready if you begin training and then quit. We must know today, so we can pick another if you decline. Also, if anyone quits after the training is started, they will go to solitary confinement until the mission is complete. The danger of a leak, after you or any other member of the team know too much, would be too great."

Nick could think of no more questions as his mind was struggling to take in all the recent life changes. He looked at the strong man opposite him and declared, "I have no more questions."

The strong man picked up his leather case from the floor, opened it and took out a leather bound notebook holding two contracts and placed both on the table in front of Nick. "The contract at your right hand says you will stay; the one at your left hand says you will leave. You are required to read both, and I am required to stay and answer any questions about what is written. If you sign the same contract as the other members did to stay, there will be two men who will come to this house and give you the finished mission statement with need to know details. After that, you will be expected to stay and will be expected to understand you will be locked up if you decide to stay and then change your mind."

The strong man sat still looking as Nick began to read the notebook sized pieces of paper printed in bold ink at a sixteen font. The contracts were straight forward about rights and responsibilities. Nick leaned back after reading both and said, "I have no questions, but I do have some requests before I sign. Can I write them out? If the requests cannot be done, I will understand."

The strong man took a shiny golden pen from the back pack and set it down exactly between the two contracts. Then he looked annoyed but said, "Do not write anything but your name on the contract." And with that he pulled a small writing tablet from the leather brief case. "Make it brief. I will look at the requests and see if they are feasible. I make no promises." Nick picked up the pen and began to write on the small memory pad. The three requests were succinct and barely covered two of the small pages.

Nick laid down the pen, looked at the strong man and asked, "Will this make a difference?"

The strong man read Nick's writing and proclaimed, "I see no problems." Then he folded the paper and placed it into a small pocket in the briefcase.

Nick again picked up the pen, signed one, and got up and left the table. The strong man arose from the table, walked to Nick and shook his hand again, walked to the door, and stopped long enough to place the leather case back into the camouflaged back pack and pick up the shotgun he brought. Looking back, the strong man stared at Nick for a few seconds without speaking, but his eyes communicated to Nick some kind of approval. Then, the man walked outside on the porch and closed the door. Nick turned around to see three faces looking straight at him from the kitchen.

"Where did you go?"

Candice said, "couldn't be here when you signed." She was holding two small white bags.

"What's in the bags?"

"I won the bet. I got a bear claw from Charles and a donut from Doctor Do."

"How did you know I was staying?"

"Well, you did not go with the man. Besides, we already knew. That is why both of these are stale."

"What would Charles and the doctor have gotten if I left?"

"A hundred dollars each from me."

"So, it was dollars to donuts?"

"Yes, something like that."

CHAPTER 5

The Long Night

NICK AWOKE SUDDENLY with a deep sweat and an overriding feeling of anxiety in the middle of the night and noticed on his field clock that it was 1:46AM. Candice had her small left hand on Nick's chest and was looking at him in a stare. Charles was up as was the doctor, and Charles lighted a lamp in his bedroom. The shadowy light was flickering and sending shadows of Charles getting dressed.

Candice removed her hand and said, "Nick, you were screaming. "

"I was having a nightmare."

"Tell me about it."

"I don't want to talk about it."

Charles and Doctor Do walked from their bedrooms into the living room. Doctor Do proceeded to the kitchen and pronounced, "I'll make the coffee. If Candice makes it, we'll be up for days."

Candice had on full pajamas while Nick had begun to sleep in t-shirt and running shorts. Their gaze turned to Charles as he said, "Your presence is required in the kitchen."

Nick looked at Candice and asked with fear in his voice, "What is this about?"

"It's about you not sleeping well the first night after you signed the contract," said Candice.

Nick looked from Candice to Charles and asked, "Do you think I can't do it?"

"Not at all sir. But you need to come to the kitchen," declared Charles.

Candice took Nick by the hand with deep affection, stood up from her cot, and said, "Let's go."

"It was just a bad dream."

"I know, but we have to address it," Candice replied.

Charles sat across from Nick with the doctor to his right and Candice to his left. Nick looked at Charles and said, "I guess you are the top point this time."

"No Nick, you are actually the top point. Talk to us."

"About what?"

"About anything. We will start from there," proclaimed Charles.

"I guess you want me to start with the dream. You seem awfully concerned about it."

"We are," said Candice.

Nick leaned forward, wiped his face and sleepy eyes with his hands, and began to describe the dream. "A dead man was in a room. It looked like he had been shot. I wanted to run out the door, but a woman stood near the wall in a black dress facing the wall. She was middle aged but muscular and attractive. She would not look at me or the dead man. I ran out into a hall outside the room, and a small man held a razor blade on a stick. He looked like a shyster. He wore a floppy felt hat, had on a suit and tie, but he was dirty and smelly. He had an evil grin on his face. I thought I could get by him, but when I hit his right arm where he held the razor, his arm was so strong it knocked the air out of me. I could not get by him. That little nasty man was much stronger than he looked."

Charles looking at Nick asked, "So, what does the dream mean to you?"

"I don't know Charles. Is this one of these psychologist things where you keep asking me questions?"

"Not really," proclaimed Charles. "If you wish I will give you an explanation, and you can see if it is correct."

"Okay, why don't you do that while we're all up at 2 o'clock in the morning?"

The more Nick's voice got loud and sarcastic, the more Charles' voice got soft and meaningful. Charles had a deep announcers voice, and he held language in high esteem. He knew Nick was hurting and took no offense. Instead, he looked at Nick with understanding eyes and began to speak.

"Your dead man is the body of the crime. The lady standing against the wall is lady justice, but she could not look at the atrocity that was being committed. When you entered into the hall, a dirty little man stands in your way in a dirty suit. That is your mind's interpretation of the law. He was small and slimy, but he was stronger than you thought. Therefore, you went to jail, stood trial, and was about to be placed into prison for a crime you did not commit while the real killers are free. They spent so much time on drumming up charges on you, no justice was done. How correct is my interpretation? I could be wrong."

Nick's eyes were large as he starred back at Charles. "Alright, you got my attention. What kind of a psychologist are you?"

"I'm a Christian psychologist, and you are covered in brown."

"What are you talking about?"

Candice chimed in and explained, "He sees colors, kind of like auras around people. I know this one; brown means guilt."

"Okay," said Nick. "How do you see colors?"

"It's a gift. Red is anger, yellow is fear, and brown is guilt to mention three," said Charles.

"How many colors can you see?"

"Several. Do you feel guilty?"

Nick looked over at Doctor Do and asked in a pleading voice, "Are you going to be any help to me here? You have not said anything. And another thing, why do they call you Dr. Do?"

"Oh, I get to speak now. Well, I am a Doctor of Osteopathy, not an MD. Anyway, I prefer you call me Doctor Do when we're together. Are you familiar with DO's?"

"Yes, I am," said Nick. "While in the Army, I hurt my back one time while stationed at Fort Benning, Georgia. The hospital's ER had a doctor of osteopathy. He manipulated my back, and the pain went away. It was at that time in my life I realized that I loved doctors, especially DO's."

Dr. Do continued, "In this business, names come and go, but nicknames stay forever. Candice started that mess. I was put off at first, but now I find it endearing. It is just another cute thing she does. Besides, what do you mean you love doctors?"

"I love doctors, nurses, dentists, and anyone else who can keep me healthy. My main business was putting a high-powered bullet into a person at a long distance. But, your business is to heal and help people."

"But, your business saves lives in the long run."

"I hope so."

Charles cut in to the conversation, "How about Christian psychologists? Do you love us?"

Nick looked down for a few seconds knowing the diversion had not worked well. "How are you doing what you are doing?" asked Nick. "You are scaring me, and I'm not easily scared."

"So, you do feel guilty?"

"Yes, I do feel guilty, and how many times have each of you had sessions in the wee hours of the morning like this where you were the top point."

Charles said, "five. Candice waited and answered with "four". Doctor Do looked around the room and then with stern eyes pronounced a guilty "okay, ten!"

"Ten?" asked Nick.

"Yes, for a long time I thought if somebody died, even if I did all I could, it was my fault. I had to learn that I could only cure and do so much. The guilt had to go."

"So, each of you have done this?" asked Nick.

Candice spoke, "We hit problems as they come. If you get a snake bite from living in this rat hole, would you not expect all of us to do our part to take care of you? Of course, Doctor Do would be the top point, but I could see that you got to an ER. Charles could help Doctor Do with the medical stuff. Both are quite good. Why would you not expect us to help if your mind and spirit are hurt?"

"Okay, but how often is Charles correct with his color stuff?"

"We're not quite sure that it works or how accurate it is, but so far, it has been one hundred percent," Candice explained.

Nick leaned back and took a deep breath; then, he straightened his back and said, "But, Charles said that I am the top point in this excursion."

Charles said, "You are. We are only here to help, but you have to heal yourself."

"Heal myself of what?"

"Your PTSD or otherwise known as Post Traumatic Stress Disorder," said Charles.

"Okay, now you are scaring me again."

"I am not trying to scare you. I am trying to get you to see something, so you can begin to fix it."

"Okay, let's say I have PTSD. I'm in charge of this. Let's say I wanted to stop this whole proceeding right now."

Doctor Do looked at Nick and began to explain, "Then, you would place yourself and all of us in danger. You were a Ranger in the Army and a sniper, and we know you did some secret stuff also. We know no details of the secret stuff. But, you know the hardest time for a soldier is not the battle but midnight to 2AM the night before. You also know that what is broken prior to combat will not be fixed during combat. It will only get worse."

Nick said angrily, "I understand. I am broken. Why did you want me?"

Candice looked at Charles and Doctor Do and both nodded in permission. Candice knew she could get too emotional but felt she should make her point. "I have killed four people. Your record says sixteen."

Nick had a look of guilt on his face as he corrected her. "The number is nineteen. I don't want to ever talk about the other three."

"Okay Nick, I believe you. But, were any of them murder?"

"No."

"All of us here have killed. We did it because we had to kill," said Candice.

Charles slipped in then with the statement; "But, that is not why you feel guilty; is it Nick?"

"No, it isn't."

"Tell us about it," said Charles.

"It is hard to put into words."

"Let me ask you a question then."

"Okay, ask it Charles."

"When did the bad dreams start?"

Nick looked in deep thought, pondered a little while during the silence and then proclaimed, "It was sometime during the trial."

"During the miscarriage of justice?" asked Charles.

"Yes, during that mockery of a trial, I started having bad dreams. I hated sleep because I knew I would wake up startled and sweating."

"And you did not have bad dreams here until tonight?"

"No, for once in years, I slept through the night the first two nights I was here. Then tonight, it slipped up on me again."

"So, how did you feel when you first arrived here?" Charles continued.

"After I got over the initial shock. I felt something peaceful about all of you. I felt peace. And with cuteness sleeping beside me, I felt close to someone.

Doctor Do seems to be fun inside, and yet, I know he has seen much disease and evil in this world. I feel like I am at the right place."

"So, what changed?" asked Charles.

Nick looked at Charles, and for the first time, it became clear. He said in a meaningful voice, "the contract."

"Yes, you signed away your freedom?" asked Charles.

"No, it was my choice. I don't think it is about freedom."

There were a few minutes of quiet as all at the table looked at Nick expecting him to speak. Finally, he blurted, "I am at a loss again."

"May I propose another interpretation? And, you tell me if I am correct," said Charles.

"Sure, you have been mostly right so far."

"Okay, I see two main things that are hurting you- not only guilt but betrayal also. What could have betrayed you?"

"Why did you say what and not who?"

"Okay, were you betrayed? And, if so, what or who betrayed you?"

"I don't know."

"You are an atheist; I am making a point, and I am not judging you," said Charles. "However, you believe in a system of order. A system of order to an atheist should be the law."

"The law betrayed me?"

"Look at your dream. Is that little dirty but unreasonably strong man the law to you now?"

"I think you're right."

"So what betrayed you?"

"I believe the law betrayed me."

"Are you sure?"

"Not really, I don't know."

"Nick," asked Charles, "Did the law change, or did someone use the law wrongly making a mockery and travesty of true justice and mercy?"

"It was a mockery and a travesty as you say."

Nick looked at Charles, then Doctor Do, and then Candice and noticed that Candice had tears in her eyes. Nick quickly looked back at Charles to find stability and not break down. Then, he proclaimed in a shaky but relieved voice,

"Murder is still murder and wrong. Lying under oath is still wrong. Stealing is still wrong."

"So, the law is still good?" asked Charles. "And, good is still good, and evil is still evil?"

"Yes," proclaimed Nick. "I look at the people here, and I see people willing to risk their lives to stop the murders of children and others. All of you give me hope."

Charles said, "So, the law is still good, order is still good, and some people are still good? Nobody is perfect, but some people have good in them."

"Yes, and I think I can go back to sleep now. I want to thank all of you. I know it's not over, but I think I can sleep now."

"I think you are correct," said Charles.

CHAPTER 6

The Mission Arrives

CHARLES WAS FIRST to the door while the others were trying to awaken. Candice was sleeping on her right side with her left hand on Nick's chest. Nick was awake and looking down at her hand.

Candice wiggled the fingers of her left hand and spoke with her eyes still closed, "I won't put it there anymore if it bothers you."

"No, I like your hand there. Charles is at the door. I think the visitors you warned me about are here," Nick said in a sleepy voice as he yawned.

Charles opened the front door to show the two figures standing in the glow of the sunlight.

Nick squinted his eyes and proclaimed, "Does everyone know the exact time when the sun is coming through the door?"

"They are earlier than usual," said Candice.

Charles yelled, "They are early!" toward Doctor Do, and a sleepy and muffled reply came from the back bedroom.

"Yes, they are early, and we are both half-dressed and half asleep," proclaimed Charles.

Charles looked at the pseudo newlyweds struggling between sleep and awake as he moved toward the kitchen to get the four folding chairs.

"Can they come back later?" asked Nick.

"Not on your life. Really!" said Candice. "Besides, this won't take long."

Doctor Do appeared in the doorway to the living room while Charles was in the kitchen rattling the chairs. The two men without speaking stepped back on the board porch and turned their heads away looking out over the field in front of the house with both staring down slightly to avoid the sun in their eyes.

The four finished dressing hurriedly and then sat in the four kitchen chairs in a slight semi-circle in the living room. Candice, sitting next to Nick on the far-right end of the curved line of chairs pronounced in the loudest squeak she could manage toward the porch, "OK, we're ready."

The two men dressed in mixed camouflage and looking like hunters walked into the living room and placed their guns upright near the door.

Nick quickly assessed the guns they carried as short barreled, fully choked, and looking like two and three quarter inch shell shooting twelve gauges. These were guns seasoned turkey hunters would use. Someone had studied that overwhelming power often compromised accuracy and that using a three-and-a-half-inch magnum shotgun shell did not usually give good patterns at a distance. Also, the hunter would often anticipate the pounding kick and miss the target. Nick thought that whoever was orchestrating this was good at making details believable.

The two men looked at the four members of the tetrahedron, and the man on the left hand began to speak first. "This is your agreement. Because you have all agreed to accomplish this mission and are under contract with the United States government, the penalty for trying to quit at this time is solitary confinement in prison until the mission is completed. After that, your fates will be decided on an individual basis." The man then simply quit speaking and stood emotionless. Nick thought that man who had just spoken could kill me and never worry about it.

Then, the right-hand man began to speak, "This is your mission; you are to reside in Mexico in the areas so designated in the written briefs, and by using clandestine means, you are to permanently close the Garcia Cartel. If any of you are captured or killed, the United States will disavow any and all of your actions. If your bodies are retrieved, you will be cremated, and there will no contact to anyone not authorized to know where your ashes are distributed to include your family, friends, and members of this tetrahedron.

Expenses and your payments are covered in your briefing papers. This is a black budget item. Any speaking about secrets to include budgeting will result in prison terms in solitary confinement. You will be responsible for your own escape if the mission is accomplished or collapses. However, peripheral assistance can and will be provided as necessary by assistants, especially from a designated ship in the area. From the ship, you will have access to assistance from helicopters and various weaponry that can be used by approval from a higher authority. To protect their safety, you may only be informed of some of our assisting forces or designated personnel on a need to know basis. Other than telling you about Commander Morales of the police who is also in your briefing as a possible friendly associate and honest police officer, we will answer no questions about other possible associates at this time. Airstrikes and other such possibilities will be done only on a needed basis and will be used only in the interest of the United States. United States military, police forces, or other entities will be used only if such measures can be cleared by echelons of authority above this tetrahedron. This was inserted by our leader as a simple statement to be quoted to you- 'you are to cut off the head of the snake'- or more fully explained, you are to neutralize the leaders and gain and distribute valuable information about the Cartel's operations, so federal, state, and local law enforcement in this country can kill the body that extends throughout the United States."

With that, the two men picked up their guns and walked out.

Nick looked at Candice and proclaimed, "Well, I thought they would never leave. So, how bad are they?"

"We never know, and the last time, they were different men. We never saw them again," said Candice.

Charles got up and began carrying his chair back into the kitchen. Doctor Do asked Candice if she would take his chair back as he was moving fast for the back door.

Nick looked over his left shoulder seeing Doctor Do as he was opening the back-kitchen door and said without emotion, "hope everything comes out alright."

"It's hurry up and wait," said Doctor Do as he was clearing the steps and trying to close the door at the same time.

Charles walked to the kitchen door that connected it to the living room and was looking around the kitchen hearing something. He heard feet and then saw a shadow disappear under the legs of the gas stove. He walked in the living room where Candice and Nick were straightening up their cots and making things neat and said in a whisper, "Nick, I need to borrow your pistol- the 22- now!"

Nick slipped the 22 from his back pack and handed it to Charles butt first with the barrel turned downward. Charles quickly turned and sneaked back into the kitchen and pulled back the pistol's hammer as the shadow began to take form. Candice and Nick had sneaked in behind Charles, and as Charles raised the weapon to aim, Candice yelled, "Don't shoot!"

Charles startled from behind jumped as the cat jumped from the floor to the table knocking over the coffee pot breaking the glass pitcher. The large light gray haired cat with a pug nose then jumped again on the stove and showed his canines while hissing.

Candice was too stunned to speak; her coffee pot was broken; it would take a day to get another one.

Nick started walking toward the cat as if he had known it all his life. Charles yelled, "Be careful; it is wild!"

Nick placed the back of his index finger on his right hand on the animal's left cheek. The cat rubbed against his finger, and as Nick was pulling away his hand, the cat reached out with its left front paw and pulled his hand gently back to his head. Candice proclaimed, "It's tame." She started moving toward the cat saying "nice kitty" at which time the cat looked toward Candice, bowed in the middle, and hissed.

"Well, I guess he's your cat Nick," said Candice.

"He just doesn't know you yet, but he is tame," pronounced Nick.

Charles looking on in amazement asked, "Nick, how did you do that?"

"Animals know me. They are not afraid. I think sometimes they see things that we don't."

"Well, that is impressive," said Charles. "But, I must tell you. I hate cats, so he will have to stay outside."

"He probably prefers outside. I'll fix him a little home on the porch, but he should be allowed in the house some. He will be much better than rat shot against rats and snakes."

Charles barked, "You don't understand, I put cats in the same category as rats and snakes. Besides, Candice probably doesn't like him either because he broke her coffee pot."

"I love him and don't you hurt him," said Candice.

Nick picked up the gray cat, and it moved up his left shoulder to get a good view of the others. Nick looked at Candice and said "ouch" as Candice looked on.

"He does not know how to be carried.I will put him down on the porch. Do you think you can find a can of tuna or something for him?" Nick asked Candice.

"We do have some tuna or salmon or something like that in pouches. I'll bring one out."

Candice disappeared toward the back room closet as Nick took the cat outside and peeled its claws from his left shoulder and upper back. "I think I'll call you Gray Kitty Cat."

"You have a special talent for pet names," said Candice as she walked out the front door and onto the porch. "At least, it's not smoked." She handed Nick a foil packet of salmon.Also, she brought a box and an extra blanket from the back.

Nick thanked her and went about fixing the cat a bed by folding the blanket several times and then fitting it into the box. The cat looked at the bed and began again to rub up against Nick's hand as he held it out. The cat began to purr after a short time. Nick placed the food in front of the bed, and the cat began to eat.Candice had disappeared back into the house, and after a few minutes, she returned with a plastic bowl filled with water and sat it down near the cat.

"Well, I think we have seen after his immediate needs," said Candice.

"Thank you," said Nick. "Cats are nice to have around when snakes and other vermin are about. I will sleep better tonight just knowing that he is prowling around the house."

The night was cloudy, moonless, and extremely dark. Charles' lamp was flickering as he was trying to read his books scattered about on his cot. Charles spoke and read Spanish, so some of the books and articles were in Spanish. Suddenly, he closed the book he was reading, stood up from his cot abruptly, and announced in a loud voice, "OK, we need to talk!"

Nick felt it was about his reaction to the two men and their summary of the mission. Also, he knew that Charles hated cats as much as a person who is scared of snakes. Nick was thinking about his defense responses as Candice began to scramble from the bed. She looked like a little girl holding her blanket in her left crooked arm as her mouth opened in a wide yawn. She began her way toward the kitchen.

Dr. Do was half tripping while pulling on his pants, and his shirt was rolled up above his little pouch of a belly. He was yawning also while staggering and weaving toward the kitchen. Nick looked at Candice and asked, "Is it about me?"

"No dearest. From the tone of Charles' voice, I think it is about him."

The four met in the kitchen. Charles asked Candice to get some water and snacks as the other three sat down around the table. Candice worked efficiently as Charles began to talk. He pronounced, "I'm on top."

"OK," said Nick. "What's wrong? Is it because of what I said after the men left who gave us our mission? I assure you I took them seriously."

"No Nick," said Charles. "This is about my fear of what I am seeing in the spirit. Nick, I see things as we have talked about before, but when I see spiritual balls falling, it means the emotions are widespread.This is about orange balls of mixed fear and anger, and this scares me tremendously."

Nick caught Candice's eye as she had just finished placing the water and what snacks she could gather on the table. Then, Candice looked at Nick as she walked to her seat at the table facing him and spoke, "It's what Charles does sometimes. He sees emotions as colored balls. Like the colors we talked about before, fear balls are yellow, and anger balls are red. When you mix the red balls of anger and yellow balls of fear together, they make orange. So, it goes."

"I know. We don't know if this works, but it is at one hundred percent so far." Nick continued in a sarcastic voice. "Am I right?"

Charles looked at Nick and stated, "You are correct Nick, but there is more to it than that."

"What do you mean?" asked Candice.

"This fear is mechanical and is something like I have never seen before, and there is a lot of it."

Dr. Do began to speak while fighting sleep, "Fear is emotional, not mechanical, unless it is produced by some artificial means. Am I making sense? I think I'm not quite awake. Candice, is there any way you can make coffee? You got me hooked on it now."

Charles confessed, "I try not to walk in fear, but this one is very frightening."

Candice looked surprised, "Charles, I have never heard you admit to fear before. This must really be bad."

"I can handle it, but I may need to speak about it at another time. Nick, the others know already, I have severe PTSD."

"I figured as much; you stay up till all hours; you patrol and watch everything in the house, but at least, you seem to be more comfortable around me lately," explained Nick.

"You noticed that?"

"Yea, I can't ride in a back seat, and that is something that I don't understand," said Nick.

Dr. Do spoke up, "I can answer this one."

"OK," said Candice. "Can we please quit talking without saying the tacit premises? I am having trouble filling in the blanks to the conclusion."

"It's easy to figure," said Dr. Do. "Nick sees the problems each of us happen to have, and he is wondering why we are here. After all, we have gone on at least one Tetrahedron mission, and he figures we are all well off financially. Besides, with our talents, we could all get other jobs."

Candice looked at Nick whose hands were sitting on top of the table, reached across, and placed her hands on top of his. "Is this true Nick? Is that what you are thinking?"

"Yea, why are all of you here? You survived at least one. You were probably paid millions. Dr. Do has at least one physical problem with his plumbing; Charles has PTSD as one thing he admits to." With that, he choked before he got to Candice.

"Go ahead, say what is wrong with me, but remember, I sleep beside you."

"I had rather not say. I'm afraid," confessed Nick.

"OK chowder head, you know I want to start a family. I want children. I may borrow some sperm from you and get artificially inseminated. Would you be interested?"

"I might."

Charles looked around to each person starting with Candice to his left, then Dr. Do, and then Nick and spoke slowly and deliberately, "If my fear endangers any of you, I will have to be taken out. I could not live with myself anyway if any of you got hurt because of me, and it is too late to get replaced."

Candice looked at Charles sternly and said with a firm voice, "OK, I will do that for you if you will take me out if I lose it."

"I cannot do that."

"Nor can I you," said Candice.

Nick began to speak, "There are too many options. We have to begin planning. I like a minimum of three plans and an open mind going in. We are honest with each other, and we are learning each other's strengths and weaknesses. This fear and anger thing is not good, but we can surmount anything. But, nobody answered as to why you are all here for this mission."

Dr. Do began to speak, but Charles stopped him by lifting his right hand. "I will tell him. My wife was Hispanic, a Mexican. She was visiting her relatives and disappeared." A tear dripped from Charles right eye, and his voice began to break as he tried to remain strong. "Her bones were found in a grave pile. We knew it by DNA."

"Oh crap," said Nick.

"I know Nick. You should have been told. I am sorry."

"Charles, I would have still volunteered."

Candice looked at Nick with admiration in her eyes and began to speak to Charles. "Charles, we came here for you and for those others in the grave pile and all the other grave piles. You said you could not bring her back, but you wanted it to stop."

"You are correct, but what if one or all of you get hurt or killed? This last vision tells me it is worse than I thought, and I thought it was bad,"declared Charles.

Dr. Do spoke up, "Why don't we concentrate on what mechanical emotions are tomorrow? Charles, we would have volunteered if you were not involved. The guilt needs to go. We are not doing this for you. It is the cause. Besides, I think more of myself when I am trying to save the world. Also, nobody else I know has your mental capabilities even though you scare me most of the time. You are the best for this mission even with all your mental luggage."

Candice stood up, moved to Charles side, and placed her arms around his shoulders. She kissed him on his left cheek and then pulled the left side of his head into her chest. Charles moved his arms backward and hugged her and said, "The best people I know are with me right now. Nobody is ever to remind me that I said that. OK?"

All three said "OK", and Charles got up and started back to his bed. His light flickered until Dr. Do reached his bed and Candice and Nick laid down in their cots. As Candice placed her left palm on Nick's chest and as Nick got comfortable on his back, Charles' light went out. Charles slept.

Candice awoke with a start due to the sunlight from the east window to the right hand side of the front door. Her left hand was cold and lying on a pillow and not on Nick's chest. Propping herself up on her right arm, she looked over the cot to see that Nick's pistol was lying on the floor intact in the holster. She thought about him being with the gray cat outside. Charles began to stir, and she heard a yawn from his direction. Then suddenly it hit her. Nick was gone. She called out to Charles as Dr. Do came from the kitchen holding something that looked like a hot biscuit. The aroma hit her nose, but even the smell was not pleasant to her.

Dr. Do came and stood by her cot, "I figure he left about 2 to 3AM."

"Did he say anything?" asked Candice.

"No. I woke up about 3:30 to pee." Dr. Do saw someone moving in the yard through the wavy glass of the side window. "Charles!" said Dr. Do in a loud voice as he turned his head toward the general direction.

"Yes," came Charles' voice that sounded hung over. "What do you want?"

"Did Nick tell you he was leaving?" asked Dr. Do.

"No, was he supposed to?"

"Charles, sleep doesn't agree with you. I prescribe you go back to vampire status," said Dr. Do.

"Ok Dr. Do, could you please leave the living dead alone?" asked Charles as he tried to get out of bed.

Candice looked startled. "What time is it?"

"It's 6:36," replied Dr. Do.

Candice's angry voice seemed to squeak through the whole house, "He is gone. That thing is gone. I will tear him apart if I ever see him again. Where will they move him to? We told him about Charles' wife, and he is gone."

Charles sounded sleepy and craggy, "Will all of you please stop? He is somewhere, not here, and I do not feel anything bad about this. In fact, I feel good about the whole thing. Actually, I feel much better about his leaving than the pain in my head right now. How long must we discuss this?"

"He did not tell me where he was going," squeaked Candice in anger. "He better not have left without at least writing me something that says goodbye. I hope he's healthy when I find him, so I can make him sick."

As Dr. Do continued to look out the window, he began to relax; he turned to Candice and said, "He'll be back soon."

"How long?" asked Candice.

"Thirty or forty seconds."

"How do you know that?"

"Candice, he's walking onto the yard."

Candice stumbled over the cots as she made her way to the side window that Dr. Do was looking out. She pressed her nose against the window pane, and there stood Nick holding the gray cat straddling his left arm. Nick was rubbing the cat's stubby face with his left finger tips while he was signaling something in the road with his free right arm.

"What in the world? He has someone backing a trailer," proclaimed Candice. She looked up the road and two more trucks were hauling livable fifth wheel camping trailers. The one pulling up in the rear looked extra-long as if the back were an open area.

A man got out of the truck and signaled Nick to move while he was signaling the trucks with their trailers onto the driveway. The beep, beep, beep of the truck backing began to resonate into the small cabin. Candice looked on in surprise as Nick walked through the door.

"Dear, what have you done?" asked Candice while trying to keep a calm voice.

Dr. Do pronounced, "Who cares. I can live in one of those and not worry about snakes and rats. Aren't they beautiful?"

"No dear, you don't get off that easy. Why did you leave me in the middle of the night and go somewhere and do something without my knowing? How much did you spend?"

Nick looked at Candice and smiled and then grimaced as the gray cat crawled up on his left shoulder sinking his front claws into his back.Nick said in painful voice, "Gray Kitty, we have got to work on that."

"You think he can claw your back. You have to sleep sometime," pronounced Candice.

Nick placed the gray cat gently on the floor, and the cat ran toward Charles.

"Don't come in here," said Charles.

"Oh, he's going to my room," said Dr. Do.

"Why would you say that? I mean it gray cat; do not stop here."

The cat went into Dr. Do's room and began to finish eating a small snake that he killed at the beginning of last night.

"Oh by the way, it is only a chicken snake, but Gray Kitty killed it right at the foot of my bed," said Dr. Do.

"I told you he was good," proclaimed Nick.

Amid the confusion, a sleepy Charles began to arise slowly and place on his pants.

"I see your butt Charles; it looks pretty good, and I may need a new husband," sang Candice.

"I don't care; you can look all you want, but I am saving myself for someone special. Someone taller, slower, and less perky," said Charles.

Nick continued to look outside as the trailers were being parked and balanced. The whole ordeal was being handled by people who knew what they were doing. Minutes would see the tasks completed and the trucks on their way. One trailer was at the back of the house setting perfectly in the small area between the house and the decomposing board smoke house; the other angled from the back to the right side of the house, and the toy hauler stretched out along the right side of the house extending almost to the middle of the gravel driveway.

After the last truck pulled out of the yard, Nick took Candice by the hand and asked, "Do you know what a toy hauler is?"

"Yes honey. I do. I also know where your most vulnerable parts are on your body."

Ignoring her last comment, Nick continued, "I got the idea when you said I could be living in a four-star hotel or five star, something like that. Come on, I want to show you our new temporary home."

The toy hauler was thirty-six feet long and most of the rear end was open area. The large bedroom and one bath was up three small steps toward the front. The small kitchen lay just behind the forward bedroom wall and was directly in front of the side door located on the right side of the trailer. Nick had a table for four planted on the left middle side. The two back doors swung out, and a ramp could be pulled out for cars, motorcycles, four wheelers, or other types of man toys that could be pulled in and strapped down in the large back open area. Therefore, the trailer was a toy hauler.

Candice and Nick entered the door on the right side of the trailer and immediately turned their heads toward the open area. Looking back in front of her was an actual open kitchen with sinks, refrigerator, and an espresso machine. The four-seat dining table was bolted to the floor. The folding chairs were stashed and tied near the small bar jutting from the kitchen cabinets. Her eyes then moved up to the narrow steps with a door atop. She stood at the bottom of the steps holding to the metal guard rails looking, and there in the room only a few feet above the floor was a king size bed, actual built in cabinets, a full-size closet, a small bathroom with a commode, shower, and small sink, and to her amazement, there was something that made her not even think about Nick being gone and not telling her. There, above the stairs, was an actual small washing machine and dryer stacked one on top of the other.

She turned to Nick with tears in her eyes and said, "You did this for me; you're the best fake husband I ever had, but how are we going to work this?"

"Oh, electricity tomorrow. All the trailers have gas heaters and electric air conditioners. Septic tank and field line are already here. All we have to do is tap into the septic tank. City water is not available, but a company is coming to check out the well. If push comes to shove, we can have a big refillable water tank, but the well used to have good water. It may take a little while to get everything up and running, but at least, we'll be sleeping in a real bed tonight."

"Oh, it's beautiful Nick," said Candice. "We'll have to have some fake sex tonight to celebrate." And with that, Candice went flying up the steps to her new bedroom, closed the door, and locked it from the inside. Her voice came from inside the room as she said sarcastically, "Now, if you don't mind honey, I am about to actually sleep on a good bed. If you do not wake me, I may let you sleep with me tonight. Now, go and get something else done."

Nick opened the trailer door leading to the outside to find the gray cat looking up at him from the ground. He patted the door facing with his right hand, and the cat jumped up onto the floor of the trailer. Then, he walked to the porch and got Gray Kitty's blanket while the cat looked around the inside of the trailer. Nick returned to the trailer with the blanket, doubled it twice, and laid it on the floor as the cat looked on. The cat stepped onto the blanket and began to circle until the place was just perfect. Gray Kitty laid down, curled up, and closed his eyes. Nick planned to keep the door cracked, so the cat could go outside if he had business.

The doors on the other two trailers had closed long ago. He knew that Dr. Do and Charles had chosen their own. It was quiet, and all his new friends had beds. However, he had a cot in a rat and snake infested house.Everybody was probably asleep with the temptation of actual beds too much to overcome. Everybody had the potential for a good rest except Nick, who stood in the toy hauler looking at the gray cat who began to purr and snore at the same time.

"Well, I guess everyone is happy now," whispered Nick to himself. He stepped out of the toy hauler and gently closed the door on a stick that he found; this ensured the gray cat could get out easily. Later, he would get a litter box. Then, Nick made his way to his old cot in the cabin living room, laid down, and went to sleep.

Night had come, and Nick awoke in darkness with the gray cat nestled by his left arm. He began to get up when he realized someone was sitting on Candice's cot. The voice was deep, and he immediately recognized it as Charles.

Charles asked, "Well, how did you arrange to get the trailers?"

Nick replied in a sleepy voice, "I wrote it on a couple of pieces of note paper before I signed the contract. I gave it to the strong man."

"Do not let that cat come over to me."

"OK," said Nick as he wrapped his left arm and hand around the cat's body. The cat settled his head near Nick's elbow and began to purr. "But, you sound like something is wrong."

"There is nothing wrong with the trailers. I love them, but there is something wrong with Candice."

Nick asked in a worried voice, "What is it?"

Charles stood up in the dark and walked over to a folding chair using his little flashlight and sat down with a big sigh. "It is about Candice. She feels good, but something is wrong. I am worried about her relationship with you."

"Why isn't Candice here?" asked Nick.

"Because, I am worried. It is about her colors. I will say it this way. She cares very much for you. "

"Are you worried that I will hurt her? Let me tell you I have no intention of doing that."

"I know you also care for her very deeply," said Charles.

"Are you afraid we will have sex?"

"No, that is inevitable. But, she will pick the time and place. I need to tell you this. Candice is not all she appears to be."

"Charles, she is wonderful. I have never met anyone more perfect."

"That is because, my good man, your nostrils are open. I want to make this as clear as possible. She is hard as bricks on the outside, but inside, she is a masterpiece of love, honor, and some kind of dedication to those she loves that goes into the spiritual level."

"Charles, can you please spell out what you are thinking?

"I need to ask one question. If she has to be sacrificed for the good of the mission, can you do it? I am afraid she could not sacrifice you."

Charles turned off his flashlight and was sitting in the blackness of the room. Nick looked in the general direction trying to make out some of his form and answered a definitive, "no". He continued, "But, before you judge me, I could not sacrifice you or Dr. Do either. "

"That is what I thought. You would not leave any of us behind."

"No," said Nick. "I would not. Does that make me unfit for the mission?"

"No, it makes you human."

"Are you about to recommend that I be taken off the team?"

"No, I would need to take myself off the team for the same reason," said Charles.

"Then why did you ask me?"

"I did not know for sure. But, we can adjust everything to our feelings. I do not like speaking to someone without the group, but I want you to know that all of you are my family now. I want nothing to happen to my family, and that love can be dangerous. By the way, I asked both of them permission to speak to you alone."

Nick looked in Charles's direction and wanted to cut to the chase. "Why are you on this mission Charles? I mean you have PTSD, and you are very close to this case. Why are you here?"

"I thought it unwise for me to come on this mission, but Candice and Dr. Do asked me to be a part of it. I think that I am too close, but they want me to be with them. Also, they say they do not want two new members. I am the only one who speaks and reads Spanish well, but that may not be so important."

"After meeting you, I feel the same way that you do about the group. You have some powers I have not seen before. Are you trying to become a martyr for God or something?"

"Nick, getting martyred is not my goal. Actually, I desperately want to live. I want to continue on and see more things. Also, there is only one woman that I ever loved enough to marry. She is dead because of the madness that I still cannot comprehend. Since she was killed, I continue to use anger as a drug. My anger is red and hostile, and it somehow consoles me at night when I cannot sleep. You believe in order and especially the law. The law is set up in this country, so others cannot take revenge on their own. I want that revenge. I dream about getting even, punishing people, and killing the guilty in the worse ways, so they die slowly and painfully and scared out of their wits. I know the speech about how I would stoop to their levels and such. But, I want them scared and dying. Yet, I cannot for the life of me understand why anyone would kill women and children especially for organs and profit."

"Charles, did you ever think it is good that you cannot understand the people who do such things? If you could understand, would your mind be in a place where it should never be?"

"Yes, it would. After tonight, I promise not to speak with you about such things again without the group."

Nick began again, "Do you trust me Charles?"

"With my life. I never doubted you, even before I met you."

"And, I trust you with my life also. But, I am not getting the gist of this conversation. Why did you really need to speak with me?"

Charles said, "I see a color from you that bothers me. It is something that I have only seen in killers that have no conscious. I see that, under the right circumstances you could turn cold blue, a light blue, that means your conscience is no longer in control of you. Would you tell me about that?"

"I will tell you, and I assume you are wondering if I have murdered someone?"

"Something like that."

"I have not murdered. There were two times in my life before I experienced combat that I was about to kill, and I found myself cold and without feelings if you must know. I do not think combat is a fair comparison of actions."

"Would you tell me about those two times before combat?"

"Sure, but nobody died. The first time a car got after my date and myself on a dark night, much like tonight, in Tennessee. The weather turned cold suddenly in the early spring. We had on summer clothes. I was driving a fast car, but this car was faster and had Alabama tags. I was throwing them off well until I went down a dirt road that dead ended into a graveyard in the woods. There were three boys in the other car."

"What did you do?"

"I had been quail hunting and had my automatic shotgun in the back floor board. I thought I was about to be late for the date, so I pushed it up under the back seat. While waiting for their car to stop, I loaded the shotgun with the two shells that I had left in the glove compartment. It was a rural area, and nobody thought twice about having a long gun in the car. The car was a two door, but it had a back seat. I rolled down the back window on the driver's side and placed the gun stock on the armrest. The two shells were loaded with one in the barrel, and the safety was on. I got out and asked twice if the boys had the wrong car. Actually, I was trying to distract them while I waited for all three to get in front of their car lights. Whoever had a weapon of any kind would be shot first. The next target would be the largest or the one who looked like he could handle himself in a fight. The third I would have to beat off with the gun like a club. With the shells having only lightly loaded bird shot, I would have to get them in close to do maximum damage."

"You saw all that in seconds?" asked Charles.

"Yes. Not only that, I had no fear, no remorse, and no plans beyond killing all three."

"What happened?" asked Charles.

"They saw the gun and ran. The car filled up with the three boys faster than I could aim, and it was backing down the dirt road before I could drop to one knee and steady myself. I'm glad they were cowards. My father used to say, 'they were cowards and the other was proud of it.' I was very proud of it."

Charles looked attentive and in deep thought. He turned his eyes toward where he thought Nick was in the darkness and began to speak, "Yes, I know criminals need one hundred percent control. Even ninety-nine percent, and most criminals will run. It is part of their predatory nature. You already told me that you have not murdered anyone. Would you tell me if the second incident involved you alone or was it someone you loved or cared about or maybe felt responsible for that was in danger?"

Nick began again, "I pulled a knife on two men to protect my first cousin. They had us cut off on a dead-end road near the lake where we were fishing. Like most criminals, they ran at the first sign of my fighting back."

"I think the two incidences are very related," said Charles. "In the military, how did this work for you when your buddies were attacked?"

"Cold and calculating. It is like a coldness comes over me, and I can think clearly and decisively without caring about anything else."

"How do you feel afterwards?"

"Nothing. I feel nothing concerning it."

"I know you care a lot about Dr. Do, and I believe you like me also. However, your feelings for Candice go much deeper."

With reluctance in his voice, Nick moaned, "agreed".

"Now, I think that I have identified what was bothering me. Will you be able to control yourself if it comes to Candice? There may be a time when you will need to listen to Candice or even Dr. Do or myself to keep from doing something when your spirit is cold. Will you listen?"

"I hope so. I know what you mean."

"Nick, I believe that things should be brought out to look at and know what can happen if certain issues occur. This is not combat, and you cannot kill in most cases on this mission. You may have to endure things that are very hurtful without getting angry and going off on your own. In your case, try to avoid being in the predicament that will put you over the edge of reason."

"I will watch it. I never think about it Charles. I try to do only what needs to be done."

Charles looked toward Nick with begging eyes that could not be seen by Nick and said, "I know. Your coldness can be an asset or a nightmare; it depends on how you control it. Personally, I am afraid my anger will get out of hand. If it does, I am asking you personally to stop me from endangering the people I care about."

"I will stop you, but I will not kill you. As cold as I am, I could not live with that. But knowing you, I think you can handle it when the time comes. "

"Nick, there is one thing that you must remember; I am not the man I was in the first mission; I am much less."

"You look big to me. Actually, your silhouette looks big. Can we turn the lights on now?"

"Yes, I think you might want to come to my trailer. We can light the lamp and stay in this magnificent rat hole, but would you not like a warm shower?" asked Charles. He turned on his small flashlight and moved toward the door, opened it, and directed the light from the small flashlight outwards; however, the light cut only a few feet into the deep darkness. Charles was smiling as he walked over toward Nick and proclaimed, "There is some water in my trailer tank for you to shower." He placed the beam on Nick's shoes, so he could see how to walk to the trailer.

"Candice is so apologetic that she used all her water, "said Charles. "I think I had a minute and a half shower trying to save you some of mine at her request."

"I want Candice to use the water, but I bet she didn't know she had two tanks in the toy hauler."

"No, she knew. Both tanks are empty. She feels terrible."

"Oh well, did she light the water heater?" asked Nick.

"Oh yes, and she took the shower of a lifetime to hear her tell it."

"Thanks, but I may not shower tonight."

"Oh, my dear young man that I have grown to like so much yet has not a clue as to why she wants you to shower. She does not want her new clean sheets dirty."

"Didn't she sleep on them without a shower?"

"This is not about her. This is about you, and unless you want to sleep on the floor and not beside your fake wife tonight, you will need to shower."

"OK," said Nick as he continued to follow Charles to his trailer where warm water from Heaven lay silently and wonderfully yet in limited supply.

CHAPTER 7

Preparation

A MONTH WENT by, and a folding table with books and plans was in the middle of the large room in the toy hauler. The pace was grueling. The makeshift bookcase against the wall opposite the kitchen area in the toy hauler was full of books and booklets, reference pages, DVD's, CD's, and maps with lots of lose papers stacked on top. Each member now had laptops and stations with mounds of finger drives and many other kinds of research information. Also, Spanish programs were being played nightly, and the members were trying to incorporate Spanish into their speech.

The best thing about being believable was to be imperfect. Spanish, except for Charles, would not be perfect. Dr. Do would be an older man with real prostate problems. Charles would have a medical record with PTSD due to prison time that was not deserved; his fake criminal history was written out for the Mexican government and police officials review. Many things were made up by the group and entered into permanent files into computers. Fake ID's, birth certificates, and debit and credit cards were made by Candice and began to be carried in Candice's purse and in billfolds by the men. At night, fake social security numbers had to be spoken, and the false stories of childhood had to be told by each person and reviewed for accuracy. The four people who were never born began to live, and each person began to identify with their characters. Expressions changed when childhood traumas were recited. Sadness occurred with stories, and tears would come into their eyes when they told about made up personal traumas. Everybody knew that one slip of the tongue could be deadly for all involved.

Also, there was self-defense. Everybody agreed that Candice was the best one to teach fighting and killing hand to hand. This was not because she was the strongest or even the most agile, but she had a tendency to read movements and to keep her opponent off guard and off balance as she moved quickly and efficiently around them. She was never head on but took an oblique step to make her opponent turn. During the turn, she would hit, stab, or break a knee with a stick. Padding was worn and blows were pulled to keep from damage, but Candice was the best to keep sparring partners off balance and use the opponent's strength as a disadvantage to them.

Charles was responsible for teaching Spanish classes for one hour each day, and Spanish words continued to be spoken by the other three as much as possible.

Plans were made, studied, evaluated, and then remade. Candice and Nick would generally fall in bed at late hours, and Candice still slept with her left hand on Nick's chest as he slept on his back. They never kissed or made love. However, there was no tension, but their emotions seemed to deepen for each other.

Dr. Do was taking a blood pressure drug now meant to help relax his prostate, and peeing was still a challenge sometimes. The flow was sometimes difficult to start and then difficult to stop. He planned to be realistic in his history of the illness. Also, the last semblance of a real name had disappeared. Dr. Do was no longer called by that nickname but was now known as Dr. Calhoun all of the time.

Charles was usually reading when he had time and always clear and concise about plans and potential problems; however; in contrast, he encouraged others often and seemed to always have time to discuss real feelings with the other tetrahedron members. Plans were developing at a steady rate; broken Spanish was continued to be learned, and Candice was getting people into shape only to show each person how to use the opponent's strengths to devastate and control. Charles and Dr. Calhoun were trained in self-defense by Candice before, but all this was new to Nick who liked to come in fast and hard and from the front. Candice even allowed him to come at her full speed one time to teach him about his mistake. Nick found himself lying defenseless face down on the now padded floor of the living room in the old house. Also, the timbers of the old house would shake as each person would take great falls.

Nick had the odd jobs. He had to pick or even make weapons that did not look like combat weapons for the urban and city areas where they would be living when assessing and stopping the cartel. Also, he had to figure out the best places to put caches of weapons, food, and other supplies in escape routes. He was pouring over maps of the areas and satellite imagery to pick the most plausible, safe escape routes if needed.

Everything could be well, but any part of the plans could go wrong. There could easily be four people coming out without a scratch or four dead nobodies that some US officials would claim they knew nothing about. It was chancy and difficult.

Each member was different like four strings on a violin, but the music was beginning to be pure and in harmony. The different members with their different beliefs, knowledge, and expertise were blending together into a powerful team. Nick called it being able to understand tacit premises to make quick and accurate logical conclusions, and he also taught them how to communicate with simple hand signals and with touch. Charles called it spiritual partnerships as he continued to critique each person's Spanish. Dr. Calhoun grunted a lot and looked at Nick and Charles with distain when they expounded upon the reasons why all were getting alone so well, but he continued to take care of the three-other's general health. Finally, Candice just went about her way making gourmet coffee in the mornings for all, cleaning all their clothes, and complaining when her trailer home got mussed up by one of the men as she devised computer software and systems specific for the mission. She did not think that men should not clean and care for their own clothing, but no one was allowed to touch the shrine of the washer and dryer. Also, to enter the bedroom of the toy hauler, one must be clean and without the blemish of soil, and shoes must be removed. Otherwise, she just simply called the group her family and began to place down some kind of roots in the small trailer camp where her people were living and thriving. Yet, the thought of losing just one sometimes paralyzed her. Certain things had never been this important before; she was becoming a homemaker.

Everything told, Nick was beginning to realize what the others already knew. Their imperfections were their camouflage, and their humanness was their shield.

The months continued, and the spring turned to a hot and muggy summer which slowly gave way to fall. The maple leaves began to turn their orange, reds, and yellows on the hills surrounding the camp appearing like distant patch work quilts. The time was growing short on preparation; the months had gone by quickly, but looking back, the time seemed to drag during the grueling days. It was time to act.

Chapter 8

Arrivals

THE SPY SHIP, disguised as a large research vessel, lay just over the horizon in the Gulf of Campeche near the northern coast of the Yucatan Peninsula. The ship was big enough to have a large helicopter landing site and a hanger below. It had a civilian style helicopter latched to the deck with its four propeller blades tied back like a woman would tie back her hair. A blue, black, and gray camouflaged Seahawk SH60 without any military markings was hidden under the deck on the large elevator. The civilian helicopter had a dark blue nose and was painted a light blue over the rest of its body.

Currently, the seas had one foot waves with a twelve-knot wind hitting the stern of the boat as assessed by Nick due to the white capping as he glanced out the small, round starboard window. In order to avoid the salt spray, Candice and Nick were sorting their supplies in a closed room near the short front deck of the ship. The supplies were taken out of the shipping boxes for the final check. It was a tight fit all around in the room. Ammunition was piled in waterproof boxes. The weapons were zipped into airtight bags with water absorbing patches and placed in camouflaged aluminum small coffin like containers that had narrow but tall wagon wheels and a pull handle. They had the appearance of solid camouflaged kid's wagons with large rubber wheels. Also, the one by one by three foot boxes held, in addition to the weapons and ammunition, an assortment of dehydrated foods, water absorbing pouches that purified water, water purifying straws, first-aid kits with various medications, various explosives, and fitting rain gear for emergency clothing. Each cache box held enough for a week of living in the forest. A week should be gross overkill for the time it would take the ship crew to analyze the situation and then get within helicopter range for a stealth pick up, but Nick always prepared for the worse type scenario.

No one wore uniforms on board the ship; the crew dressed in plain clothes and sometimes were seen on the deck in shorts, deck shoes, bathing suits, and even the pilots of the helicopters, while on missions, wore simple civilian looking flight suits. All personnel knew each other by name, their pseudo rank, and were never allowed to salute anywhere on board. The ship did not exist on any paperwork as anything military except on the highest levels of secrecy. It held a small submergible for research fixed on cables on the deck, but it` also held weapons disguised as part of the ship to include surface to air and to ground missiles and various machine guns. Hand held fire arms were stored in an arms room, and two small torpedoes lay hidden and ready behind circular doors on each side of the bow. The doors were almost invisible to the eye. Some of the crew were actually studying sonar's biological effect on fish and marine mammals with the greater emphasis on sharks. Three of the crew were marine biologists assigned to answer any questions to any foreign officials who wished to inquire, but if pirated, she could pull out a myriad of weapons and reek fire very quickly on any boat, ship, and aircraft that tried to take her over or harm her. Personnel on board would never get a metal or any recognition, and the thirty-two-person crew was neither Navy nor any form of military. All the well paid handpicked personnel were sworn to secrecy and would face prison time if they said anything about the ship to anyone not connected to the mission. The Captain and crew did use the fake rank structure to have order, but all were really above top secret civilian government employees who believed that people's body parts, drugs, and other illegal items coming through channels to the United States were acts of invasion and war. Also, the ship could be destroyed along with the helicopters by the crew if necessary to maintain secrecy, and the crew would be able to escape in small emergency motorized life boats that would signal pick-ups from friendly ships or aircraft. Everybody in the tetrahedron knew this ship was a great asset and even their lifeline when things went bad. Each tetrahedron member greatly appreciated the work of every individual on board.

CHAPTER 9

Making the Caches

THE CIVILIAN LOOKING helicopter made a whining sound as it dropped off Candice and Nick at the first stop as a civilian clothed flight assistant was continuously looking at the ground for activity. Then, the helicopter disappeared in the distance of the Yucatan Peninsula forests. However, it was not unusual to see flights touch down due to drug trafficking. The pilot and crew knew the allotted time to check and hide the cache that contained the weapons, food, water, and emergency supplies. Then, Candice and Nick would hike at least two miles through the forest to the pick-up point. Candice and Nick acted with clockwork precision checking, wrapping, locking, and burying the small coffin looking containers. A quick hike with a check on the global positioning system that Candice carried would place them at the correct ten digit coordinates. Sometimes simple is better or at least just as good as Nick moved another bead down the string attached to his shirt every so many steps as he held in front of him a simple compass.

Nick was amazed at the dead looking trees and the dryness of the vegetation around them. He knew it was about the third month of their usual seven-month dry season. Many of the trees had already lost their leaves and appeared dead. He saw some broader leaves on the ones who were still hanging on.

He focused on a black looking bird for a few seconds as he looked around for possible predators and snakes. Candice noticed and pronounced, "They call it a jay, but it is actually a type of crow."

"Well, that is interesting, but what about the leopards?"

"They are endangered and very rare. With your way with cats, they might let you pet them."

"Well, it only takes one leopard to not like me, and I am dinner. What about the snakes?"

"Oh, they are here," said Candice."It is good we are wearing snake proof boots. Remember the coral snakes are in this area. Don't pick up anything without your gloves on. I have already seen a Variable King Snake running away from us through the leaves."

Nick spoke sarcastically, "I am so sad that I missed that. I hate snakes. That is the orange one with the black band stripes with yellow head and tail."

"Why is it you know indigenous snakes so well, but you do not know birds?"

"Birds don't kill you."

"Good point."

They traveled from the first cache to the pick-up point while looking for deadly wildlife to include snakes. Also, they recorded the sink holes in the area. As they stood on the one-meter placement with the GPS position reading the exact ten digit coordinates, they heard the helicopter. It suddenly appeared over them and dropped cables. Each stuck a foot in the bottom rings on the two cables, clipped the rings on their safety vests in place, and held with both hands as they were winched up and hauled on board. This process would be repeated four additional times today for a total of five caches, and this meant five alternatives of escape if push came to shove.

Candice and Nick arrived back to the ship where they would be taken back across the gulf to Corpus Christi. There, they would catch a flight to Cancun. The trip through the Gulf of Mexico, to Corpus, and then to Cancun would take about two days.

They arrived at the five-star hotel in Cancun, and Candice made a memorable face of disgust when Nick tipped the limousine driver and the bell hop fifty US dollars each. Also, she looked a little embarrassed when room service arrived with the most expensive dishes that Nick supposedly liked. Again, she looked like she was quietly steaming at the size of the tip. Nick insisted to the bell hop that fresh flowers be delivered every day to the room and then called to inform the concierge that his classic two seat sports car convertible would be arriving tomorrow. She reported to call him upon the car's arrival.

Candice was enrolled in a university doctoral program in ornithology. She had always liked birds and had a real minor in biology from her BS degree. Also, she had a hobby of bird watching. Otherwise, her two fake master degrees were recorded as done on line.

Doctor Calhoun and Pastor Charles Dorgan were working for the Intercontinental Mission and Health Services as volunteers. Doctor Calhoun would work at a makeshift general medicine clinic in a small village about ten miles to the south east of Valladolid and was seeing patients with various illnesses. His pseudo diploma placed strategically on the wall declared completion of his general surgery residency. There were several volunteers in the free clinic, but the two that helped the most was a nurse anesthetist who was also a surgical nurse and a well-liked Mayan orderly named Antonio.

Charles set up his ministry in the same village and was helping people to build and repair their homes while others helped him occasionally with refurbishing the old stone church. Both men were in their element as was Candice in hers. However, Nick had the most difficult role. He had to become a millionaire reformed playboy who had found the woman of his dreams. An older couple living in Nashville, Tennessee would answer any call concerning their make believe son. Nick learned how to be rich by observing different actual rich descendants on record. He studied the videos, books, and stories concerning real rich people with old money. The fake history would reveal that Nick did not give up his womanizing and generally bad behavior until he met Candice who came from more humble beginnings. Nick would retain many of his old habits except his womanizing that was done away by his love for Candice; he would take Candice anywhere for her studies and interests. Or, so the story goes.

Candice was on top of the tetrahedron first. She had her bird surveillance equipment that consisted of long lenses on cameras and videos, sound gathering devices, recording equipment, and most importantly, her two fuel driven drones with four propellers each that could be fitted with cameras. She would not have to climb cliffs or trees to study certain birds. Her main job was communication of tetrahedron members and surveillance of the suspects. The drone guidance systems were also state of the art and could be flown through most trees and brush without being wrecked. She worked on her studies a little the first day in the room; otherwise, she fussed around her hotel suite with equipment that would alert both Nick and herself to intruders through the door and even through the windows where they were staying on the third story. Once she was satisfied the room was safely secured, she began to relax and called toward the large living room where Nick appeared asleep on the plush sofa.

"Nick, wake up, and let's get a shower."

Nick got up from the couch and began to move toward one of the large baths in the suite, "not asleep, but I could have been. I'm so tired. Part of me wants to get clean, and part of me doesn't care if my teeth rot out of my mouth."

Candice also made her way to the other bathroom in the suite and used the hot water until she felt clean and relaxed. After their long simultaneous showers, they met on opposite sides of the king sized bed covered with silk sheets. Nick was in his silk pajamas, and Candice simply wore a jersey with shorts. Nick laid down on his back on the right side of the bed while Candice laid down on her right side facing him and placed her left hand on his mid chest and said, "no bugs by my equipment."

"What is the margin of error?"

"They would have to have something I do not know about. It is possible but not at all probable."

"It's been a long day. Doc and Charles are in place. Tomorrow, I need to try to get noticed being rich some more."

"Nick, are you sure you're not enjoying this?"

"It is difficult to act this way. It takes a lot of study and a lot of acting lessons. Unlike you, Doc, and Charles, I do not feel real comfortable in my role."

"You do look good doing it though. You are scaring me how well you are acting rich. Promise me that you will not act rich once this is over."

"It's this silk I don't like. It feels like I will slide off the bed."

"Well, it does look good on you. How did you like the meal?"

"A burger and a beer are better; can we sneak some in?"

"Nick, maybe there is some hope."

"I know it's a small thing, but what is the subject of your dissertation?"

"Oh, I think it will be on the life habits of the Keel-billed Toucan. Can you guess the color of their bills?"

"It is a wild guess, but I would have to say their oversized bill would be green with orange on the sides and red on the tip," said Nick in a sarcastic voice.

She gave him a solid pre-cordial thump on the chest and said sharply, "You cheated. You've been reading my notes."

"Yes, I admit that I read some of your notes, but I like the pictures the best. Are you sure you are not more interested in the Turquoise-browned Motmot?

Candice looked strongly at Nick and proclaimed, "OK chowder head, quit reading my notes. Besides, I am dreaming lately about a rock house in Central Texas with a bird feeder in front of the kitchen window. I really want to see a Painted Bunting. The extra studies and dry research are ruining my bird watching."

"I still like the pictures the best," said Nick. "There sure are some pretty birds in this place. I hope we don't have to eat any of them if we go into survival mode. Anyway, I bet you that I will be asleep before you. I had no idea how hard it would be to bury everything and get here in two days. My sore places have sore places from actually working instead of exercising."

"I know," Candice said as she yawned.

Both began to breath rhythmically. There was quit and slumber. Candice and Nick were asleep.

CHAPTER 10

Reverend Dorgan

REVEREND CHARLES DORGAN invited several of the villagers and the new doctor to his once abandoned stone church for meals and praise as he called it.

At first the older women and some of the children would show at the doors of the church to beg for money and food. Reverend Dorgan never gave money but did give out food and sometimes used but clean clothing to anyone who came to his church.

Often, Charles traveled the roads to towns to purchase much needed medical supplies for Dr. Filbert Calhoun's clinic and hospital. Both he and Dr. Calhoun seemed to like working for the Intercontinental Mission and Health Services.

Candice and Nick planned to begin their surveillance of the country using the bird watching to cover their real intentions. Room service delivered their breakfast at 6AM. After breakfast, Nick was quickly loading the black SUV making room for cameras, laptops and tablets, hiking gear with food and water, and the two drones with their fuel just to mention some of the supplies.

Candice saw Nick slowing to think about what else needed to be loaded and whispered, "Nick, did you get the medicine?"

"Oh yes, my sick pills are in my shirt pocket. What do you think are in them?"

"Nick, please do not worry. They are not poison but something to make you look sick."

"Yes, malaria pills that make you look like a malaria flare is happening. Boy, does the doctor have a flare for me. So Candice, I ask again; what is in these pills?"

"The doctor said it was a whopping dose of niacin plus some other things. Remember not to take them until it has rained hard for at least a half hour, and remember to take them on an empty stomach."

"OK Candice, but next time, you get the sickness."

"I don't think so. I look too healthy and spelt to be sick."

"Really, you use a word like spelt? I plan to start exercising after my seven course meals. I can be spelt again."

"Sure Nick, but in the meantime, we need to check the list."

The SUV was loaded, and they were traveling from Cancun to the small village located about ten miles from Valladolid. About five miles from the village, they stopped to release one of the fuel driven drones with a movie camera on board. Candice placed the permission paper in the windshield that allowed her to study but not harm local wildlife and then pulled on her pack. Nick checked to ensure they both had binoculars and canteens. The prize was footage of the toucan, but other exotic birds would do also. Candice needed to get at least some study footage to the university. As the drones went through the trees guided by Candice on her laptop, Nick looked through his expensive binoculars to see if he could spot any large forest birds.

Both had listened to weather predictions on TV, radio, and internet stations. The rain could occur at this time of year but would be torrential and last only about an hour usually. They attempted to calculate the time of the downpour. The heavy rain began just as the local weather people had predicted. Candice quickly pulled back the drone and made it land a few feet from the SUV. Nick began the countdown as they walked through the rain slipping and sliding as if they were ill prepared. They got into the four-wheel drive SUV and found the mud on the forest road was good competition for their tire's traction.

As the slipping SUV continued to find some ground here and there, Candice asked, "Do you see the size of these mosquitoes? I think they are bigger than any I have ever seen." Candice was on her tablet and had just mentioned an insect. This was code for we are bugged. "You know, the insects here are bigger near the coast. Maybe I am thinking about that. However, I think I was able to scare them off with the repellant." Candice always welcomed computer bugs knowing that she could identify and block them, but the bugs also carried the potential to be traced back to their source. She started the trace.

Nick knowing now that the listening devices used by whomever was trying to listen had been stopped. Listening bugs were no longer being scanned by Candice, and she began to speak freely.

"Nick, it began to rain at 9:16. I think we can time this just right. At 9:44, take the two pills. I placed malaria into your recorded medical history with several visits in the past to ER's because of flares. You caught it on one of your playboy travels."

"Let me review my new disease. The pills begin working in fifteen minutes with fever and sweats. I am to act very tired and act as if I have chills. I want a code word if my acting becomes unrealistic."

"Are your chills worse is the question I will ask to tip you if anything is wrong."

"Sounds good."

The torrential rain continued, and Nick swallowed the two pills. The SUV was still spinning but making progress. It's all terrain wheels were well covered with mud as they finally arrived at the clinic. The weather, as planned if weather cooperated, would not permit them to drive to a clinic in the nearest city without much difficulty.

The small stone hospital, with an attached patient clinic, looked old but clean on the outside. Inside, Dr. Calhoun was speaking to the young couple whose son was just diagnosed with an infected appendix. He was trying to explain about the surgery to them in broken Spanish. Some young looking Mayan man was speaking over him at times to help the poor couple to understand.

Nick's symptoms arrived just in time with instant flushing, fever, sweating, and an unsuspected severe headache. He felt terrible.

Candice helped Nick to the clinic as the young Mayan man waited at the opened front door. The man looked at Nick who was dressed in nice clothing and driving an expensive luxury SUV and began to speak in broken English, "My name is Antonio. I am helper orderly. May I help you?"

"Yes," said Candice. "My husband is very sick, and we got caught in the rain this morning. Can we see a doctor?"

"This is free clinic. You sure you want be seen here? There is hospital in Valladolid about ten miles that way," and he pointed down the road.

Candice looked at Antonio and said, "My husband will make a good contribution to the clinic if he can just see a doctor. Do you have a doctor?"

"We have doctor here. He is a surgeon. I ask him if he see you."

Antonio disappeared behind the door that closed off the makeshift waiting room from the rest of the clinic. Candice and Nick heard Spanish spoken so fast they could barely make out the words. A female voice answered the question.

"What did she say?" asked Nick.

Candice jokingly replied, "I think she said Dr. Calhoun is either in the bathroom or in surgery."

Antonio came into the waiting room and motioned for Nick and Candice to follow him. Nick stood up slowly, looked like he would faint, and began to heave. Candice stood up suddenly and started to ask him about his chills but realized that Nick was not acting. He was a bright cherry red on all points that could be seen on his head, neck and hands.

"I think this is my worse flare so far," said Nick as he was trying to walk straight. He began to sweat profusely.

"Just hang in there. Maybe the doctor can give you something to help you," said Candice.

Antonio ushered the two into a small but clean exam room and closed the door. Both noticed the Saltillo tile was uneven but clean and shiny. An occasional small human hand or dog footprint showed in the tile since it was primitively made by laying the clay in the sun allowing the children and animals to walk over it as it dried. In about an hour, Dr. Calhoun came through the exam room door looking preoccupied and noted that Nick was sitting on the metal framed exam table with Candice seated to his left side in a small metal chair. Dr. Calhoun grabbed a clip board with a charting template and began to hurriedly get a history.

"I am Dr. Calhoun, and I see your name is Nick Lippincott. How long have you had this?"

"It began this morning."

"How are you feeling?"

"I feel terrible. I'm having chills and fever. It feels like the malaria flares I've had before except this feels like the worse one." Nick continued to speak, as rehearsed about the disease and previous treatments to include his memorized past medications.

Dr. Calhoun finished the history and began the physical starting with the temperature, blood pressure, and pulse. Then, he moved about hurriedly as he listened to chest, abdomen, and checked the circulation in Nick's neck and feet.

"It is indeed a repeat malarial flare," pronounced Dr. Calhoun.

"Can you help him?" asked Candice.

"I am prescribing some medications to help get you through it. You can pick them up in this pharmacy in Valladolid," said Dr. Calhoun as he handed the prescription slip to Candice. "I wrote the name and address of the pharmacy on the prescription. The roads should be better from here. Now, if you will excuse me, I have an emergency surgery to perform. It worked out that I could see you while they prepped the patient." Then, Dr. Calhoun walked to the closed exam door, opened it, and looking back called for a nurse to complete all paperwork and see the couple out of the clinic.

The three, while standing in the hallway, saw the double doors open to the nearby operating room showing a sterile well lighted room in the rear of the clinic that was attached to the small adjoining operating suite by a well waxed hallway. As the strong smells of cleaning agents passed Nick's nose, a masked female spoke in Spanish toward the surgical staff; her voice was slightly muffled from the surgical mask. Nick noticed she had beautiful hazel or green eyes.

"The patient is prepped and ready," she pronounced in Spanish. Nick noticed behind her two figures in gowns, masks, and gloves were busy setting up instruments.

Antonio answered back in Spanish as he appeared at the other end of the clinic with the patient on a gurney. Antonio was always coordinating everything in the clinic from about 10AM to midnight each day and was trying to accommodate the rhythm of the clinic to the interruption caused by Candice and Nick's sudden arrival. Dr. Calhoun, knowing he needed to get to his surgical patient as soon as possible, quickly dismissed himself, entered the door, and began to walk toward the small room where he would wash and gown. As Dr. Calhoun walked quickly toward the small wash room in the surgical suite where he would ready himself for surgery, Candice asked quickly through the slowly closing door, "What can we do for you?"

Dr. Calhoun was walking hurriedly and spoke over his shoulder, "Intercontinental Mission and Health Services. You can find them on-line. Now, if you will excuse me, I am in a hurry."

Candice and Nick got into the SUV, and Candice began to drive while slipping and sliding again but less than before. The road toward town seemed a little better. When they arrived, the pharmacy was modern looking, and the drugs were delivered promptly. Then, they began driving toward Cancun on the better roads. The SUV was muddy but running well. Nick was beginning to feel better. He woke up Candice's tablet, and it showed a little orange and black beetle in the upper left hand corner lying on its back and not moving; this was Candice's computer bug alert on all the tetrahedron's computers, tablets, and phones. A dead bug meant no one had bugged the computer. Nick made a positive remark about insects.

While driving, Candice pulled a black looking device from her shirt pocket and handed it to Nick. "Nick, Dr. Calhoun slipped me a thumb drive; it is secured of course. It's from Charles and is about the roads, police, and information about Dr. Calhoun's clinic and also Charles's ministry. We can listen to it now. We may be bugged at home, and I will code and hide it later in the hard drive."

"Good, which one of us do you think will make it into the cartel first?"

"Well, I doubt if the cartel will want a minister or even a volunteer doctor, but a playboy with lots of money might be a good bet."

"I am thinking more about drones and surveillance equipment. I think you will get in first."

"I understand one thing Nick. They definitely have to find us and have their own ideas about how we can help."

Nick plugged in the thumb drive and turned up the volume so both could hear about different road connections, clinic personnel, and other data.

When they arrived at the hotel, Candice and Nick took the stairs and checked for bugs in the suite. Candice encoded the data from the thumb drive while Nick stayed inside the suite continuing his acting sick. Sleep would come easy due to their working and hiking in the forest. It could be any day that one of them might be contacted in some way by members of the Cartel. Still feeling some effects from the pills, Nick planned to unload their supplies from the SUV tomorrow.

During the days to come, Candice and Nick continued to watch the birds while assessing roads and areas for criminal traffic and for possible escape routes. Hidden internet contact methods kept them in contact with Charles and Dr. Calhoun. All four waited for the first hint of a cartel contact.

CHAPTER 11

First Cartel Contact

THREE WEEKS PASSED with Candice going into the forests attempting to get pictures and videos of various birds in their natural habitat. After arriving home from a successful day of collecting bird data and pictures, Nick began his usual routine business of unloading the equipment from the SUV to include the two four propeller drones. He disconnected both the video camera from one and the camera used for stills from the other and placed the drones, cameras, and accompanying equipment into the appropriate water proof aluminum cases.

Candice went upstairs to check the suite for bugs, bombs, and to begin her routine surveillance of the area outside the apartment. She seated herself by the window, so she could glance occasionally at Nick working. She felt fear in the pit of her stomach as she noticed a red limousine parked along the road with two people staring in Nick's direction. She pulled her cell phone and pushed a combination of buttons. She noticed Nick signaling back by stretching his back as he got the vibrating message. She checked her surveillance equipment hidden in her tablet and small printer; the suite was bugged. Her surveillance equipment showed listening bugs only, and no cameras were detected. Since the signal had reached Nick, she knew he would be doing the plans practiced in case this occurred. Meanwhile, she was attempting to find anything that could be troublesome or deadly. She took the sound equipment that she used in her bird studies and pointed the small metal umbrella toward the luxury auto. The men were speaking Spanish, and she began to record the conversation.

The large red limousine with a separate back compartment had dark windows and was parked near the hotel on the opposite side of the road. Candice noticed the man behind the steering wheel seemed slim faced with a black mustache. The other looked older with a rounder smooth shaven face. They had on suits that appeared from a distance to be made of a dark wool and silk fabric. Their ties were black. The back window opened slightly for a few seconds with what appeared to be cigar smoke coming from the window, and she saw a man at first glance wearing what appeared to be a gray expensive suit, white shirt, and red tie with all appearing to be silk and tailored as best she could assess. His face looked chiseled, and his hair looked dark. She had learned to assess as much as possible at a glance.

While Nick continued to act busy with the equipment in the SUV, Candice continued to look at the roof tops and windows using infrared and heat sensitive spy glasses to detect possible snipers. She plugged the cameras fitted with scopes into the self-made laptop and began to take pictures of buildings and streets nearby and then out to as far as the buildings would allow her to survey. Nick was stretching backward occasionally looking at the rooftop of the hotel where they were staying for possible snipers or other problems since Candice could not assess directly above and below her window. She moved back farther from the window in order not to be seen but found no signs of snipers or surveillance equipment hidden in the windows of the buildings within her line of sight.

She continued to look at the limousine as much as possible and noted the men in the front seat looked to be body guards and also appeared to her to be amateurs and possibly thugs due to their being vulnerable to attack. Also, the spy equipment that someone had placed in their hotel suite was antiquated by her electronic analysis.

She analyzed the conversation in the automobile on her interpretation software. Nothing was said that denoted immediate danger. She heard no sounds emanating from the back seat and believed the glass might be bullet proof and the chamber soundproof. She awaited Nick to come upstairs and set-up any equipment to take these three out and make a mad dash if it were necessary. Nick had hidden weapons in his SUV but would not have time to reach them if shooting began. Her biggest fear was the men kidnapping him for ransom; he was almost helpless in his current position. Each member of their tetrahedron had a chip embedded into their skin, so they could be traced by her and allied equipment. By the push of three buttons, Charles and Dr. Calhoun would see and know as much as she and Nick knew about the current situation, and the plan by designated number that could be used. Also, Charles and Dr. Calhoun could alert them with their data and plan for escape if the mission became too dangerous.

Nick began to bring the equipment into the suite via the elevator. He was closely watched by the two men in the red automobile, and as he walked into the suite with two of the aluminum cases, Candice continued her assessment by scanning local texts, internet, and face book traffic.

Nick entered the suite and asked, "How are your mosquito bites?"

"Not too bad for the two bites I got while I was trying to find that stupid toucan."

"Why did you pick that bird anyway?"

"I like toucans. I think they are unusual looking. I don't know. Why do you like fancy cars?"

"Because, they perform well, and they cost a lot of money."

"Well, I like toucans because they are pretty and unusual."

"Can I see the bites?" asked Nick.

Candice replied "sure" as she pointed to the corner lamp in the living room of the suite and to the right of the headboard of the bed.

"Are you treating them with something?"

"No, I plan to leave them alone for now. They're not bothering me as much as they were."

Nick made for the bedroom where he picked up his two over-under shotguns and checked the shells for various colors on their primers. He brought two over-under shotguns and two side by side doubled barreled shotguns. The guns were very expensive with gnarled wood and carving on the receivers. One side-by-side shotgun had three barrels with a rifled barrel underneath that would fire a rare nine-millimeter rifle bullet. It was about a sixty thousand dollar German made gun with a detachable scope for the rifle. The least expensive shotgun was twenty-five thousand dollars. All of the shotguns were twelve gauge.

Nick moved quickly but quietly while he opened the aluminum cases holding the two dismantled over-under barreled shotguns. He expertly, and as quietly as possible, snapped the three parts of the two guns together and then picked up a box of shells and began to load them. The primers of the shotgun shells had various colors. No color meant a regular shell filled with shot that could be used for skeet and even small birds, and red primers meant small rockets that would penetrate and then explode just the other side of a wall or door. Green primers meant that thirty caliber rifle bullets with embedded sabots. Shot was drawn on the inside of the shells giving each the appearance of regular shotgun shells loaded with simple small shot. Blue primers were the most complicated; they were penetrating grenades that would blow into a fireball with a metal piercing titanium projectile toward the front that could destroy an engine block. All specialized shells were placed as every fifth shell in the shot shell boxes. For quick protection, the final yellow primers meant the shells were loaded with nine thirty caliber copper coated buck shot made specifically to kill any human intruder at close range. He loaded the top barrel of both over-under shotguns with the blue primer explosive rounds that would stop the engine or start a fire if the gas tank was targeted. The bottom barrels he loaded with the yellow primer copper coated lead buckshot. He propped both shotguns against the wall beside Candice quietly and walked to the door. "I hope your bites don't bother you too much. I'll go back down and get the other equipment." Candice looked worried as she looked Nick straight in the eyes and mouthed the silent words, "Be careful."

Nick went down the stairs and noticed the large luxury auto driving away. Candice had several pictures of the men from the window and was running them for identity on line. She was surprised when nothing came up. It was as if they did not exist. Nick appeared in the door of the suite again with a load of equipment. With an OK sign from Candice, he began to unload and dismantle the two shotguns and placing the shells back into their respective positions in their boxes. If the suite had been searched extensively, expensive hunting shotguns owned by a rich x-playboy would usually not cause suspicion.

Both continued to be conscious of their speech and got ready for bed. Sleep was sporadic due to both worrying about the two bugs in the apartment. At 6AM, Nick answered the phone. A man speaking English with a Spanish accent began by saying, "Hello Mr. Lippincott. My name is Juan Pablo Cortez. My employer asked me to invite you and your wife to dinner tonight at his home. Will this be a problem for you?"

Nick signaled Candice, and she closed her eyes briefly and nodded. Candice sat up on her side of the bed and immediately picked up her laptop, copied the phone number, and began to trace the call.

"Would you tell me what this is about? My wife is very busy with her studies, and we do not want anything to do with time shares."

"This is not about time shares Mr. Lippincott. All you need to know will be explained to you tonight. My employer is very prominent in this area. The dinner will be top rate, and the wine will be old and rare. A man of your tastes will find the wine and food wonderful. My employer has an excellent chef. But, the dinner could be only the beginning of good things. I know you are rich Mr. Lippincott but knowing my employer has many advantages."

"What are the advantages?"

"All that will be explained tonight if you agree to attend the dinner."

"I do not know you or your employer. I will have to decline, but I thank you for thinking of us."

"Would it be better if my employer met with you in say, a local restaurant?"

"I would feel better, but I still do not know you."

"Very well, would you give me your e-mail then? I wish to contact you with some proposals. There are still some things I can provide you on-line."

"No, I do not think that I would wish to do that."

"Very well then. I will inform my employer about your decision."

"Good bye," said Nick.

"Mr. Lippincott, before I say good bye, there is one final thought that I wish you to consider."

"OK, what is that?"

"It involves an incident, probably nothing, but it happened about six years ago. Things do happen, but intoxication can be a major problem when someone dies."

Nick signaled Candice that his semi-hidden dark but made up secret past had been found. Candice signaled back in agreement.

"Mr. Cortez, you have my attention. My wife and I can meet tonight at a local restaurant at 8PM."

"That is wonderful Mr. Lippincott. I will call you back with the restaurant's name and location after I speak with my employer about the change in plans. You will not be disappointed."

The restaurant looked old world inside, and the waiters were dressed in black suits and ties with clean white aprons. Candice and Nick were dressed well with Candice wearing a simple black dress while Nick was wearing a ten-thousand-dollar tailored suit with a white silk shirt but without a tie.

Candice noticed the man who was sitting alone at a big round table with white table cloth and red napkins was the same man who was sitting in the back of the red limousine near the hotel; the table had the only red napkins among all the other white napkins noted at the other tables in the restaurant. Also, there were no other customers in the restaurant. The man looked handsome and in shape but at least in his sixties. He wore a black expensive looking suit, white shirt, and red tie. The waiter moved the couple toward the table. As they walked, the two men that Candice had seen sitting in the front of the limousine at the hotel filed in on either side of the couple. They motioned for them to step into the hall where the restrooms were located and quickly frisked both for weapons and wires. After the two men were satisfied they had neither, they moved them to their seats sitting in front of the man.

"Good evening Mr. and Mrs. Lippincott. I hope your stay has been a good one."

Nick spoke first, "Do you wish to propose something to us? You also claim to know something very private about me. Do you wish a pay off or something like that?"

"Oh, the young are so direct," the man said and then took a sip of his red wine. "Mr. Lippincott, please try the wine. It is what you would like based on my assessment of you, and I do not wish a payoff. I wish to pay you. Your wife has some abilities that I could use in my business."

"We do not need money."

"Oh, everyone needs more money. Of course, being poor is not considered a sin, but it could be very unhandy. You see, I prefer to pay you rather than have your services given by other means."

Candice looked fearful and spoke as Nick acted annoyed. She asked, "you mean the incident from six years ago."

"I never want myself or any of my employees to speak of that incident again."

Candice swallowed hard and asked, "What are my qualities that you wish to purchase?"

"You seem to have some drones that I would like to purchase from you. I believe you use them in your bird studies. Also, I would like for you to educate us on their use."

"It would take me at least a month to get them replaced."

"What is a month to the young?"

"Is this all you want?" asked Nick.

"For now. But, I assure you, you will be well compensated. You like to hunt Nick, and by the way, those guns of yours look wonderful. I can place you on both good hunting and even good fishing if you are interested. You can stay with your wife all the time of her training us on how to use the drones. I assure you no harm will come to either of you. Of course, if you tell anyone about our meeting or about our agreements, I will have to eliminate any threat that might involve my business or myself."

"Understood. So, you were in my suite? What did you look at besides my guns?" asked Nick. Then Nick looked deep and without fear into the man's eyes and proclaimed, "Candice and I would like to know how long this will take."

Candice nodded in agreement with Nick.

"Oh, where are my manners?" The man then signaled for the waiter to come to the table.

Dinner was delicious and perfect in every way except for the company. Nick started to pay, but the man motioned that the expense was all his. He said, "It is my pleasure to treat you. I hope we can enjoy a dinner again such as this."

"The dinner was excellent," said Nick while looking annoyed. "I hope we can conclude our business with you as quickly as possible."

"It should not take long Mr. Lippincott, but it is best if you do not try to travel away from our area for a while. Of course you can still drive to and fro to spy on your birds."

Candice looked at the man and asked, "but without our drones? We attach cameras to them. Are the cameras included in the deal?"

"I expect delivery and training on the drones within the week. Here is a number to call with a convenient time for you. I do not believe we will need the camera equipment. We will be asking you to fit other equipment to the drones."

"You can get drones. It is no trouble for you to get a fleet of them."

"But, your drones have special abilities that I have not seen in others. They can fly around tree limbs, can hover for hours, can carry amazing payloads for their size and can be set upon a target like one of your birds which they seem to recognize and follow. They seem to sip fuel and are quiet for their power. There are other qualities also that have been observed or recorded by my staff. No, we want your drones."

"When did you spy on us?" asked Nick.

"Spying is such a bad word. We were interested in your protection."

Suddenly, Nick's face turned from confidence to real fear because he had not seen or heard anything around them while in the woods. This man had good people who knew what they were doing when it came to hiding and seeking. He said in a real choking voice, "We will call tomorrow." The man had gotten to Nick without knowing how because Nick thought his strong point was mastery of the terrain. Candice knew Nick well enough to surmise that he was not acting when he was displaying the fear.

"Excellent, my men will follow you home to ensure your safety. I do appreciate your understanding concerning our needing to purchase your equipment. You will be well compensated for any hardship."

Candice and Nick watched as the valet drove the collectable black German made classic convertible sports car to the entrance. The valet got out of the car and handed Nick the keys. Nick walked over and opened the door for Candice.

They acted worried and harassed driving home while being followed by a red limousine, yet this was the break they wanted. They were in, at least at some level, and the mission could now take on a new direction.

The suite was left intact, but it had been searched. Candice picked up her laptop and informed Nick that the hard drive had appeared to be crashed. Nick waited silently while she bypassed the fake crashing and awoke the computer. She began to scan the suite for bugs. "Nothing found," she proclaimed.

Nick knew the laptop and tablet hard drives could not be copied except for a few facts about birds, and at one point, all hard drives would appear to crash unless the right code was typed in. Candice had also set up the computers so that more tampering would end in a total erase and a real crash of the hard drive and systems.

They began to look for missing items and found that all the expensive items such as cameras and guns were still there. The two ten box cases of hand loaded shotgun ammunition containing twenty-five shells per box were still there and appeared to not have been assessed by the intruders. Clues left such as writings on the dissertation, books, and notes on birds of the Yucatan were left out in the open. The bugs were gone.

Candice began to assess the suite with a special laser scanner disguised as an ink pen that could pick up finger prints and transfer the data to the laptop. Yet, no unusual fingerprints appeared. The intruders used gloves.

Nick sat down on the sofa and looked toward Candice who was busy looking for any evidence or clue and asked, "Do you think they found what they wanted?"

"It depends. They are looking for evidence to ensure we are what we appear to be. Hopefully, they will not look outside the box."

"If they do, how difficult will it be for them to find out the truth about us?"

"Not too great. I have information layered. The information about you and the drunken driving incident was within one of my second layers. The more they struggle to find the information, the more it becomes real to them."

"Who do you think the man in the red tie is?"

"He could have been the leader, or he could have been an imposter. Identifying himself with a red tie and also red napkins could be a way to establish decoys. People would look at the red first instead of the facial and other features."

"I wonder what Charles would say the red means?"

Nick looked surprised as Candice answered the question, "He says that red usually means passion but can also mean anger or even a tremendous will to survive."

"Is he on line now?"

"No, this may be a rare occasion when he is asleep. I can contact him later after I have assessed the suite a bit more."

"A red tie really stands out with a black suit and white shirt. Actually, it looks sharp," said Nick.

"Yes, we are seeing red, but red may not be our main clue. As I said, the whole thing may only be a decoy. At any rate, at some level we are into the cartel."

Nick looked guilty and pronounced, "I guess I dropped the ball; I did not know anyone had us under surveillance when we were in the woods. I guess they followed us."

"Nick, I doubt it. I think they used sophisticated surveillance equipment watching us. It puzzles me too, how they knew where we would be. I do not understand, but I will figure it out."

"Candice, avoiding snipers is one of my strong points, that is, until today. I think someone was hiding and watching, and I did not detect them."

"How can someone escape the heat signature detector that I used?"

"Well for that matter, how could your electronic equipment not pick up equipment used to spy on us?"

"That's a good question, and now, I'm worried. Thank you very much Mr. Lippincott."

"Oh, you are very welcome Mrs. Lippincott. I think we should worry more tomorrow. Are you sure there are no bugs in here?"

"Nick, I cannot detect any bugs, and I am tired right now. I would work longer if I thought we were not safe. Besides, I think we are probably overlooking something simple. They could have even surmised the things they said about our whereabouts from our pictures and information about my bird studies."

"My dear wife, you are right about that. I really feel better. You are so smart."

"Yes. And, we are also sleepy with a long day ahead tomorrow."

Candice slipped out of her black dress as Nick watched. She had Nick's entire attention as she moved toward her pajamas in her underwear. She commented, "Did you like the show?"

"I love it when you throw off clothes like they are suffocating you," said Nick.

"I love it when you look. Do I need to sleep in the living room?" asked Candice.

"No, I can control myself."

"Nick, it gets difficult for me sometimes too but getting physical might be too much of a distraction. Besides, there will be a time when it is perfect if it is to happen."

"I understand. Now, lie down beside me and place your hand on my chest."

"Yes dear," Candice said sarcastically.

As she laid down on her right side and placed her small, strong left hand on Nick's chest she heard Nick whisper a sleepy, "Now, that's better."

The next morning Candice checked her last messages from Charles. She texted him prior to sleep about the restaurant meeting and especially about the man in the red tie. The reply came back at 2:17AM. She realized Charles is not sleeping again and probably staying up with his books.

The reply read that the man in the red tie was spiritually like a tall building at night with lighted windows that gave the building a tall appearance, but if the building could be seen in the daylight, it would be nothing but fake with only slender metal poles holding up the windows with dark scrim like materials draped along the sides.

She texted back, "So, the man is a fake. Hope you slept well last night."

"I slept an hour or two. Is he the leader?"

Candice wrote back, "maybe. But, he would need a second leader if he is as fake as you say. It needs to be someone he can trust who is also an organizer. Maybe the second leader is a family member."

"So, the cartel snake has two heads," wrote Charles.

"If he is the flamboyant leader, yes."

"I will pray and think more about this. Please take care. Thanks."

"No, thank you."

She noticed in the corner of her eye that Nick was getting out of bed. He stretched. Candice looked at him with slight tears in her eyes. She was beginning to see more to Nick than a good partner in this mission. She knew the dangers, but she thought that at one point she could no longer shield her heart. Charles would know this too, and knowing she could not speak to Nick freely about her feelings for him, she once again began to focus on her particular part of the mission since she was the top point on the tetrahedron presently. Her current parts of the mission were to set up communication between all four members and to gather digital information concerning the leadership hierarchy of the cartel. Her final mission would eventually be to digitally discover the branches with names of all involved of the cartel that would harvest the organs, distribute the organs, and collect payments to include the banks involved, the doctors and nurses scattered throughout the US, and all others involved as the organs were sent by black market into hospitals over the United States and to send all the information to the proper authorities. These were monumental tasks.

CHAPTER 12

Juan Visits the Garcia Home

THE SUN WAS beginning to show through the roof windows in the Garcia home. "Senor Garcia, there is a visitor in the living room," said the butler.

"Who is he?" asked Mr. Garcia as he seemed to enjoy the small imported coffee prior to his breakfast. He was dressed in silk pajamas with a silk robe and soft leather house shoes.

"Juan Cortez, sir."

"Please see him in now."

The butler said, "yes sir" and proceeded to escort Juan into the living room where Mr. Garcia sat in an overstuffed burgundy leather chair. Mr. Garcia motioned for Juan to have a seat on the sofa in front of him. Juan sat down but with back straight and hands resting in his lap. Juan spoke with Mr. Garcia in perfect Spanish.

"I am meeting with Mr. and Mrs. Lippincott today. My orders seem a little vague, so I want to check with you for clarity," said Juan.

"Did my brother confuse you?"

"No, I did not speak with your brother. The orders came down through the hidden connections. As I understand, we are to kill them if certain knowledge is gained."

Pasqual Garcia entered the room from the adjoining lavish dining room and said, "Juan, how are you?"

Juan looked at Pasqual and said, "slightly confused. How are you feeling today?"

"The chemotherapy is not treating me well. The food smell is making me nauseated. I am stepping outside for a few minutes." Pasqual moved through the front door and disappeared.

Juan watched him disappear and said, "Mr. Garcia, I wish your brother well. Would you tell me your orders concerning my meeting with the Lippincott family today?"

"It is simple Juan, you are to observe them and their equipment. Let me know what they have that is special. Also, let me know about their behaviors. Pasqual and his staff are busy reviewing their history. It seems the rich are very protected, but their histories can be uncovered."

"Yes sir. So, you do not want them harmed."

"Not yet. I might find them very useful. If it is needed, your assignation talents will be useful. Juan, are you hungry? I would enjoy your company at breakfast."

Juan knew of no instance where Mr. Garcia ever asked any help to dine with him. Fear came upon him, and he thought it better to decline but with a very good excuse. "Senor Garcia, I am grateful for the invitation, but the meeting will be soon with the Lippincott's. It is a good distance from here, and I need to leave to meet with them."

"I understand Juan, but the offer still stands. You are welcome in my home, and also, you are always welcome to ask me to clarify your orders. My brother is trying his best, but he is sometimes not available. His staff is good, but some of my other underlings are more thugs than organizers. You are bright, deadly, and deal in permanence. You never fail me."

"Thank you, sir. I will have secret cameras set up for your review of the meeting."

"Juan, send your information through Pasqual. He is still the best at computers and intelligence that we have. Now, be careful with the meeting. Remember, some men do not appear dangerous, but when afraid, some can do great things. Be very careful not to threaten Nick's wife; he might be more man than he appears."

"Understood, I will be careful not to push him too far."

Juan was surprised when Mr. Garcia stood up and walked through the door with him and said as he stood on the elaborate veranda, "I need to check on my brother. Would you walk with me for a few minutes?"

The two men walked together into the driveway while looking around to find Pasqual. Juan asked, "Concerning the judge, are there any changes in plans for her?"

"She is becoming a real problem with her religious convictions to her so-called goddess. We still need her for potential legal problems. Can you have explosives buried around her sacrificing area just in case she needs to disappear?"

Both men stepped from the drive and began to walk the grounds. Juan began to explain, "Some call it the killing hole. She is not sacrificing lately. I think that some of the police are having second thoughts about protecting her. Is by the end of this week soon enough to get the explosives secretly placed?"

"The end of this week is good. You are very efficient. In case you or someone else important to the cartel is there when the explosives are detonated, are there escape routes?"

"There are two escape routes already there as told to me by one of my spies. I will make sure they are left intact from the explosion. May I tell everyone involved that if they speak about this to anyone, I will personally kill them?"

"You may."

Near the flower garden to the right of the home stood Pasqual looking pale and sickly. Mr. Garcia moved over to him, placed his arms around his waist, and said, "Juan, I want to thank you for coming. I will take care of Pasqual."

Juan walked back to the black SUV, got in, and drove away.

Nick and Candice loaded their SUV, and Nick hid what weapons he thought would not be detected. Both felt vulnerable. The back roads were rural and bumpy as they drove to the secluded designated place to meet the man named Juan Cortez who had spoken with them earlier and sat up the restaurant meeting. Nick was driving the SUV as Candice confirmed the destination by satellite on her tablet using ten-digit grid coordinates.

The SUV made a grunting sound as Nick pulled into the corner of the field with the sun strategically at his back. Juan was getting out of a black SUV while two other American made four-wheel drive SUV's were parked across from them on the other side of the small field. Nick was looking for anyone carrying weapons and anyone hiding in the woods. He also noted a large hole at the end of the field; it appeared to be a cave or a sink hole.

A medium built man dressed in complete khakis to include the floppy jungle hat got out of one of the black SUV's and begin to walk toward Candice and

Nick. Nick noted that he had no weapons showing or hidden except possibly on his lower legs which could not be seen well in the ten-inch high grass.

Candice was the first to get out of their SUV as Nick kept the motor running and watched for any sign of danger; his plan was to crowd the man with the SUV while allowing Candice to jump back into the ride. She left her door open. The man approached her, stuck out his hand, and spoke in English with a Spanish accent. Candice recognized the voice as belonging to Juan from the previous phone conversation. "Tell your husband to get out. There will be no harm come to either of you."

She glanced back at Nick and motioned with her left hand. Nick got out of the automobile and began to make his way through the grass and stopped beside Candice.

"My name is Juan Pablo Cortez, and we spoke last night before you went to the restaurant. I am glad to meet both of you in person. Today as agreed, we will be testing the drones that my employer will be purchasing from you. Are you ready?"

Candice had already programmed the drones to another laptop that was totally dedicated to them. She looked at Juan with a disgusting face and pronounced, "We are ready."

"Excellent, I would like for you to have your drones fly into that sink hole ahead. You will notice, if there is a light source on your drones, that the water, after the thirty-foot drop, is blue and pristine. The water hole is about twenty-five feet wide. There is a cave also on the west side of the sink hole. I request you explore it. Please show me what your drones can do."

Nick pulled the two large drones from the back of the SUV and put them together to include placing the four propellers on each. He started the engines while Candice set up a small folding table for the laptop and three small folding chairs. With the drones ready, Candice sat at the table. Nick sat at her right hand and Juan at her left.

The lap top showed the forward areas of the two drones on a split screen. Constant twelve-digit grid coordinates ran across the bottom of each of the split screens. The correct code would also activate the built-in cameras on the front and back of the drones. Then, the top of each split screen on the laptop would be the two forward views, and the bottom section would show the back views from the crafts.

The drones dipped out of sight as they entered the sinkhole. The LED lights quickly came on and the water could be seen as blue and pristine as described. In an instant, both were in the cave sending back pictures and coordinates. Suddenly, oxygen sensor ratings came on the screen in large red numbers showing the cave did not have enough oxygen to sustain flight. She quickly recalled them, and they flew out of the sink hole back to the front of the table where they hovered for a few seconds and then landed.

"Mrs. Lippincott, that is incredible."

"What is? I could not explore the cave. The oxygen was too low."

"It is excellent that your drones alerted you to this and did not shut down. Tell me; can an external oxygen source be mixed with the fuel for such flights?"

"It would depend on the weight of the canister and the distance you intend to fly in an oxygen depleted environment."

"Could you work up some plans and numbers on both?"

"I can get you the numbers. I need to look for a compatible oxygen canister. I can work on the canisters. Another thing, I really need to keep the attached cameras. The man in the red tie at the restaurant said he did not want our video and still cameras."

"That is correct, and for the package of the drones and laptop, my employer wishes you to have this gift."

Juan motioned with his right hand and the two dark suited men with dark ties got out of the other SUV and proceeded to walk forward. The man on the left walked with an aluminum suitcase in his left hand. Nick knew this was their most vulnerable time, yet he knew they must appear vulnerable and also armatures. He also had no weapons near him except a small pocket knife that would expel a stream of a severe irritant if sprayed in the eyes. The blade had to be pulled half way open and then pulled back suddenly like a trigger. He decided to sacrifice himself for Candice if guns suddenly appeared from jackets.

Juan placed the case on the table, opened it, and pronounced, "The combination, Mr. and Mrs. Lippincott, is five six nine."

Candice and Nick were looking at an almost empty box except for two necklaces splendidly displayed against a red background with eight large perfect looking clear diamonds in each necklace. The smallest of the diamonds appeared to be about four carrots. One necklace had an arrangement of six large rubies and the other with six large emeralds arranged with the diamonds. Also, there was a small watch box. Juan opened the watch box which had a rare golden 1854-S American Double Eagle coin. It appeared original and in perfect condition. Candice seemed mesmerized by the necklaces and asked, "Are they real?"

Juan spoke, but his accent did not carry the words well, "Oh, what do you give the rich? They are all real and valuable too."

"I believe it," said Candice.

"They are yours, but I will need you to submit your plans for the oxygen canister and extended distance of the drones. Also, this is only the first payment. Other payments will come."

"The necklaces look magnificent," said Candice.

Nick looked upon the coin as something to add to a collection. He did not seem impressed.

Juan, noting the lack of enthusiasm in Nick asked, "Is the price too small?"

"No, but I want all this business to be finished when the drones have been delivered. Also, we want to give the drones for free if that would mean we are finished."

Juan looked at Nick and pronounced, "Your beautiful wife is to also train our personnel on the use of the drones."

Candice looked at Nick with girlish eyes and said, "But, Nick the jewels are so beautiful, and you do collect old coins. What is wrong? All I have to do is just fix the things, so they will fly in low oxygen. Anyway, that should not take long. We can order some other drones for my bird studies. I don't mind staying here a little longer."

Juan pronounced, "Excellent, you have my number. Call me with the plans."

"Oh, we will call," said Candice looking like she would enjoy the prospect of more gifts.

After Nick had packed the two drones into their cases and the laptop in its case, the men who accompanied Juan took them, got into their SUV, and drove away. Juan said, "I am awaiting your leaving. I assure you that no one will come after you or be waiting for you later down the road."

"Juan, are you sure that the drones are all your employer wants?" asked Nick.

Juan looked at Nick and answered, "You are rich, but my employer is very rich. It is better if you do not ask too many questions at this time."

Nick looked angry and proclaimed, "I want this finished; tell your employer that."

"Mr. Lippincott, you are to leave now. We will be in touch with you. All your questions will be answered soon."

Candice looked concerned and said to Nick, "Honey, let's go. We can continue this later."

Candice and Nick appeared nervous and fearful as they got into the SUV while looking in all directions and drove away with their gift case in the back seat.

Candice scanned the SUV again, due to the cartel people being around their ride, for safe measure and pronounced, "no mosquito bites this time."

"Good. Candice, you know that if we have those things when this is over, they go to the government."

"Oh yes, they may be perfect jewels, but they do look gaudy. I am not much of an expensive jewel person."

"Anyway, that information you let them discover about my collecting old coins was pretty good also. I told you that I collected coins, but I did not tell you that it was a few wheat pennies and some mercury dimes. Did you know that it is really not the god Mercury but a winged helmeted Ms. Liberty on the mercury dimes? I couldn't afford anything else."

"Well, you do know some things about coins, but you need to really read up on them. Otherwise, that annoying look you gave Juan when you saw all the contents within the case was incredible. You played that so well. You should have won an Oscar. You looked like a spoiled rich boy looking at some petty gifts."

"I pretend the jewels and coin are fakes."

"Do you think they are?"

"No, I think they are real, and possibly real enough for the people running the show to want them back."

Candice contacted Charles via e-mail to give him the update on the recent happenings. Candice was constantly keeping in touch with him and Dr. Calhoun via secure e-mails and texts, and they were always trying to share significant information to include pictures of roads and areas for clues and for possible escape routes. She saw that Charles had sent an attachment that contained pictures.

Nick was in charge of escape and evasion and needed all the information he could get for planning successful escape routes.

Charles was in charge of studying the people of the cartel that Candice and Nick met psychologically and even spiritually if possible. He was looking for the identification of that certain weak link that could be manipulated to work for them, and he had feelings that someone was very angry at the hierarchy of the cartel. Charles spent most of his time in the small stone church he was renovating. Currently, he was depending entirely on the communications by Candice and Nick and their descriptions of the cartel's personnel that they had met. Charles only knew that today Candice would give her two customized drones over to someone at the cartel. He would await the descriptions of the cartel people involved. However, something seemed odd about Candice's earlier description of Juan's phone call to Candice and Nick for the restaurant date. Charles saw in his mind's eye a lot of red with some yellow. He interrupted this as a lot of anger mixed with some fear, yet he did not know the reasons for the emotions.

Candice continued to explain to Charles about the cartel personnel that participated in the handing off of the drones. She described their meeting with Juan and also described him physically to include his dress in khakis. She explained his mannerisms and any parts of the conversation she could quote while asking Nick who was driving for confirmation on each part of the conversation. Then she e-mailed a question, "What do you think about the cave exploration?"

"It may be a distraction or a test. I doubt if they want to do much in a cave with poor quality air."

"Should we start looking in caves and exploring them for clues?"

"I think that would be what they want. Then, they would know you are not what you appear to be. No, my advice is to stay low like you are doing and let them continue to pursue you. You are appearing to them to be scared amateurs that want to get away from them as quickly as possible with the exception, of course, that you are charmed by the jewels."

"You should have seen him Charles; Nick acted so well. He appeared to be the perfect rich snob."

"Good. I want you to know that Dr. Calhoun shoots e-mails to me at least daily but is very busy, and we use the private e-mails you set up for us.He reported yesterday that he is doing at least two surgeries per day in addition to seeing patients during clinic hours about every ten to fifteen minutes. He says that he sent a message to Intercontinental Missions and Health Services that a dentist is badly needed."

"Please, both of you be careful and stay in touch. Nick and I will continue," reported Candice.

"Good-bye."

Candice informed Nick about the e-mail conversation with Charles and assessed all the happenings of the day.

Nick was busy updating possible plans of escape using the pictures of the terrain that Charles had provided for evasion plans on his laptop. He updated the five planned different escape routes that would take them close to the caches, all to the north side of the Yucatan. Helicopter or boat to ship would be the final ways off the peninsula.

After they arrived to the hotel suite, put away their equipment, and fulfilled other necessary duties, Candice and Nick decided to try to sleep early due to the stressful events of the day.

CHAPTER 13

The Police Visit

DR. CALHOUN FINISHED removing a skin cancer from the left lower jaw of a fifty-two-year-old man. He placed the specimen into a bottle of fluid and asked the nurse assisting him to make sure it got to the pathologist. Earlier, he sent photos via e-mail to the nearest dermatologist who was located in Cancun. The suspicion was melanoma. Although the cancer was very dangerous, it may have been caught in time. The scar would be huge due to Dr. Calhoun making sure he had pristine edges. All the cancer appeared removed, and the sutures were intact. Antonio was interpreting Dr. Calhoun's orders written in English to the Spanish speaking patient for the wound care, follow-up, and keeping his head and face covered from the sun. The patient was nodding in agreement and ended by handing the patient a small bottle of sunscreen.

Noticing it was close to lunchtime, Dr. Calhoun walked to the small three bed recovery ward in the clinic and asked Joyce Jamison, the nurse anesthetist, to join him for some fish with rice cooked by one of the volunteers at the clinic. She finished bandaging the surgical wound that had bled through. She removed her gloves, washed her hands, reported to the recovery room nurse, and proceeded to follow him to the small kitchen and dining area attached to the clinic.

Joyce was in her late forties and had slightly graying dark brown hair. Her eyes seemed to change colors with what she wore, and today, they were green due to her blue-green surgical scrubs. Yesterday, her scrubs were a light blue, and her eyes looked blue. They were really a greenish blue with brown surrounding the pupil that grew more brown the more the light. Dr. Calhoun was mesmerized by them due to only seeing her eyes during surgery due to her mask and hat. She looked beautiful to him, and often, he wished that he was only a practicing surgeon due to her.

Joyce was very dedicated to her work and had volunteered for a month. Often, she would give her vacation time to the Intercontinental Mission and Health Services to help others in need, and for the past five years, she had volunteered for the Yucatan. Her five foot ten slender frame slumped in her chair while her long graying dark brown hair was pulled up and held loosely on her head by a big brown clasp. Fussing about, Dr. Calhoun took a few seconds and looked longingly on her face as it pointed straight forward with her eyes closed. Dr. Calhoun made himself look away and filled the plates for both of them. Then, he poured two glasses of cold ice tea and placed a little bit of lime and a tablespoon of sugar in Joyce's glass which was just the way he had observed how she fixed her tea before in the break room.

Dr. Calhoun sat down and noticed Joyce still had her eyes closed. He pronounced, "You are tired. Why don't you take the rest of the day off and rest?"

"Dr. Calhoun, you were up most of the night too."

"Would you call me by my first name?"

"I can't see you as a Filbert. I am sorry, but I don't like that name."

"How about Phil then?"

"Ok Phil, I'm too tired to argue. I know you would like to see my eyes right now, but I'm too tired to open them."

"What do you mean?"

"I know you like my eyes. Also, I know you like me."

"What is this?"

"Well, you did ask me to lunch. When are you going to get around to making a pass at me?"

Dr. Calhoun swallowed hard and stumbled with his words, "I am afraid, and besides, I don't even know if you are married."

"Well, I am not married. My husband is dead. He died about ten years ago of cancer; it is all in his family. I am not interested in men right now with the exception of the one having lunch with me. Are you married?"

"No. Sorry to hear about your husband."

"You know, we are so busy that I haven't had a chance to speak with you much, but I keep noticing you always looking at my eyes."

"They change colors."

"They are hazel like. They do that." Joyce remained seated with her eyes closed but continued to speak, "Phil, are there other things you like about me?"

"Only about a million so far."

Joyce smiled, but kept her eyes closed. She asked Dr. Calhoun where he lived when not volunteering for the mission service.

"Right now, I'm between homes, but I would like to live in Texas. I'm surprised that as much as we have worked together that we never asked each other about our homes."

"I live in Ohio in a small house on a small lot near Cleveland."

"Do you have any children?"

"No, couldn't have them, and you?"

"No, but I wish I had."

"Me too."

The fish and rice tasted home cooked and exceptional, but the break was ended by Antonio showing up wide eyed by the table and pronouncing in a loud voice, "The police are here!"

Dr. Calhoun looked at Joyce and said, "Excuse me, I will cover for you for the next couple of hours. Why don't you just sit here and rest? Also, I would like to speak with you some more about the ideas you have, especially that passing thing."

Joyce smiled and said as she closed her eyes, "thank you. That would be good. Maybe, we can have dinner together tonight."

"I would like that very much. Now, I guess I'll go and see what the police want."

"See you soon."

The dark haired slender woman police officer looked in good running shape and was in a simple gray dress with a light jacket and a white blouse with an area of ruffles that followed the v of the jacket. Her weapon was worn on a simple belt with her badge on her holster. The man was dressed in a dark gray suit with a white shirt and an oddly patterned multicolored tie with his badge on the left side of his belt opposite his automatic pistol.

Dr. Calhoun met with the police in his small clinic office that was crammed with x-rays and paper charts. They seated themselves in front of the desk as Dr. Calhoun sat down. The police woman spoke first.

"Dr. Calhoun, I am Inspector Vega and my partner is Inspector Mendoza. We came to ask you about a recent patient named Nickolas Lippincott. Do you remember him?"

"Just a minute, and I will pull his file." Dr. Calhoun got up and moved to the filing cabinet and pulled open the third drawer. "Oh yes," he said as he read the file, "He was here during the recent storm. They seemed to be having trouble getting to the clinic in the city. He had a malaria flare according to my notes. I see a lot of people, but I guess I connected them with the storm."

"Did you know that he is rich?"

"Antonio, my orderly, mentioned that. I guess because of the luxury SUV. I remember being very busy due to an emergency appendectomy that I had to perform. I remember seeing him and his wife while the surgery patient was being prepped. I was in a hurry at the time."

"Did they speak about anything other than the malaria to you?"

"I really do not remember, but I do not think they did. What is it about them that concerns you?" Dr. Calhoun knew they would never answer that question, but he would get a chance to read their expressions.

Inspector Vega looked worried as Inspector Mendoza spoke while appearing annoyed, "We are not at liberty to say," said Inspector Mendoza. "We need a copy of the file, and we will return if we have more questions."

Antonio made a copy of the file while watched by Inspector Vega. Then, Dr. Calhoun walked with them through the crowded waiting area and said "goodbye" as they left the clinic. Dr. Calhoun excused himself to his office where he reported the two inspector's names, physical make-up, and mannerisms to the other three tetrahedron members via e-mail. He also informed them that Joyce Jamison, his nurse anesthetist, had wanted to spend time with him. He reported she had volunteered for the Yucatan, giving up her vacation time each year, for the past five years.

Dr. Calhoun received the unanimous agreement from the other members of the tetrahedron that he should start a relationship with Joyce mainly because she was hiding something according to Charles. Charles knew that Dr. Calhoun could override his feelings and stay on mission; his only concern was that she could be hurt due to his fear that she could be innocent. Candice was to immediately start researching her history. Dr. Calhoun also knew that he would have to keep his feelings in check even though he was strongly attracted to her.

It was late evening when Dr. Calhoun arrived at the small cabin near the clinic where Joyce slept. He knocked on the door, and she answered dressed in a light blue dress with her hair fixed. She looked beautiful to him. She turned toward the small kitchen and said, "I hope you like what I made. I didn't have much time."

Dr. Calhoun did not speak but stuck out his huge right arm, turned her around, pressed her body against his, and kissed her passionately. Joyce was startled for a few seconds and then kissed Dr. Calhoun back.

"Why Phil, you do have a way with conversation."

"I have been wanting to do that since I first saw you."

"I'm glad you finally got around to acting on your feelings. I know you are aggressive, but I like it that you are sometimes spontaneous."

Dr. Calhoun took a deep breath for control and released his hug. Joyce hugged him back just as hard and asked, "Are we eating dinner tonight or doing other things?"

"We are eating. I will behave now."

"I hope you will not behave too much."

"It's just that I wanted to hold you and kiss you."

"I like it. Now, if we are about to eat, let's eat. We may get interrupted, and I look forward to being alone with you." They had dinner with a crisp and cold bottle of Chardonnay wine and then sat down on the sofa.

Joyce awakened fully clothed on the sofa. They were both exhausted from the day before, and due to the fatigue, a good meal, and white wine, they fell asleep before anything could happen.

She said, "Phil, you look so much more gentle when you sleep."

"I'm not asleep. I'm just paralyzed. What time is it? Are we late for the clinic?"

"It's Sunday Phil."

"Oh, are you busy today?"

"Only if Dr. Calhoun needs me in surgery."

"I'll try to prevent him from needing you today," said Dr. Calhoun.

"Now, I wish to ask another question. Do you think Phil might need me today?"

"Oh, I think he will," and with that they held each other and passionately kissed. Suddenly, both cell phones went off at once with the automatic alerting system that they were needed in the hospital. Both stood up from the sofa, looked at each other, and both pushed the numbers into their cell phones that they received the message.

"Phil, it was a good try, and at least you know how I feel about you."

"I feel the same. It is good to know you find me attractive. Most people think I am about as sexy as a cement block."

"Oh, that is really not true. You are handsome to me and some of the other women who help in the hospital."

"What are their names?"

"That is a good question. Let's go Phil, or we'll be late."

Chapter 14

The Yucatan Commander
of Police

Commander Morales sat at his desk with the large wooden ceiling fan spinning over his head. Sitting in front of him were Inspectors Vega and Mendoza. It was early morning, and he was on his fourth cup of strong coffee that he brewed at a small station behind his desk. Often, he drank coffee to counteract his arthritis pain medication that he took six to seven times per day. His six-foot body with protruding abdomen was sitting with a right slant in his tall, overstuffed desk chair. He expected more information than what he was receiving and began to get agitated at the two detectives. He took another drink of his strong but smooth coffee, and while noticing it too cold for his taste, he got up and walked to the pot again topping off his cup.

Inspector Vega reported, "I give you my word that we found in Nick Lippincott's chart that he has a history of malaria resulting in a flare. The roads are in bad repair even now after the storm. That is the reason they stopped at the free clinic."

Looking at Inspector Vega, Commander Morales asked, "Do you think they planned the visit using the storm as an excuse?"

Inspector Mendoza answered the question, "It may be, but the witnesses that we questioned after they left the clinic that day say he really had symptoms."

"OK Inspectors, I want you to look up everything you can on the good doctor. And, look up everything again you can find on the Lippincott's. I want to know why they are being contacted by the cartel. I am still trying to determine if it is some kind of blackmail or if the Lippincott's are trying to make more money."

"Yes sir," said the two inspectors almost in unison. They began to arise from their chairs when the Chief said, "Wait a minute."

Both stood up and waited. The chief continued, "What about the militia forming around here?"

The inspectors both looked agitated, and Inspector Vega said, "I do not believe they are very big or powerful."

"Good, I want nobody taking the law into their own hands. You two do what I said. Let me see, this is Thursday, so I will expect some news by Monday. Feel free to work the weekend."

The Inspectors looked disappointed as they left the room.

As Commander Morales walked from his office near the young officer's desk near his door he said, "I need to eat lunch. I will be back later. Call me on my cell if you need me."

CHAPTER 15

Charles and the Children

CHARLES WAS SECLUDED at the stone church most of the time. His personal history stated that he was a PhD in theology and that he spoke fluent Spanish. Reverend Dorgan, according to his new history, had graduated from a protestant seminary but later changed many of his ways to reflect more of what he thought the Bible really said. He kept records of the roads disguised as where those who came to his church lived. Also, he tried to assess people he could trust if problems arose.

At first, the older women and a few children would show at the doors of the old stone church to beg for money and food. Reverend Dorgan never gave money but did give out food and sometimes used but cleaned clothing to anyone in need.

Charles loved children and invited them with their parents often to the church where he fed them and played children's movies in Spanish on the ancient round tube TV that he would wheel out into the small auditorium of the church. Also, children would want to speak with him as he tried to work. Then it happened; the idea of a school for the children was proposed to him by a group of the parents. He reluctantly agreed and called the main office of the mission service in Dallas, Texas and asked if they knew of volunteer teachers in the area. A list was sent via e-mail with phone numbers and points of contact. Volunteer instructors began to show at the church. The children were divided into groups by age and were given whatever text books Charles could scrounge. The school was four to six hours per day with Charles teaching many of the classes for history, mathematics, and reading. Also, many of the parents requested English classes due to Charles being bilingual.

Charles would only allow the children to call him Mr. Dorgan and made them act well while someone was teaching. Otherwise, he would play games with them, especially soccer during breaks and after school. Outside, Charles was making progress with the local people, but inside, he was becoming more agitated by the day. He was all alone during the night, and he felt the loneliness like a profound isolation. The small amounts he was able to sleep was laced with nightmares. He also felt some presence around him like a mechanical evil. It felt like the same mechanical type evil he felt in Tennessee. Often, he would work nights by electric lights fixing up the old church, but the feelings kept getting worse. The feelings were like a paranoia or an anxiety encapsulated with anger that could not be fully defined or explored. He prayed each night for the tetrahedron members and anyone innocent that could be harmed during the mission.

The tetrahedron had been in country for over two months. Candice was submitting plans to the cartel for the update of the drones but were no closer to the inside than when they met the man in the red tie at the restaurant. However, Charles felt change was coming and felt it might be tonight.

The night seemed eerie with clouds overhead with the wind howling, and Charles thought voices were in the air that no one could understand. The darkness was without stars or moon. Blackness seemed to fill every void. Charles awoke suddenly by the knocking on the old thick wooden door of the stone church. He got up trying to fight the sleep from his eyes and noticed on his alarm clock that it was 2AM; he had only been asleep for a couple of hours. He put on his pants and bathrobe and walked to the door. A woman stood outside with a small girl that he guessed was about ten to twelve years old. They stood out against the dark background. He felt nothing dangerous around them, so he asked, "Would you like to come in?"

A Mayan woman, that he assessed was in her early thirties, walked with the girl through the door. Her eyes and face displayed tremendous fear as she began to speak to Charles in Spanish, "Will you help us? We are marked?"

Charles looked confused but asked back in Spanish, "How are you marked?"

Both the woman and the girl raised their left arms, and there was a small band aide in the crook of their arms. The woman pulled off her band aide displaying a small red dot right over a blue vein. It looked as if someone had drawn their blood. Charles looked at the small red dot on the woman and then asked if the band aide could be removed from the girl's arm. The girl also had a red dot over the vein that appeared blood was drawn. Charles was confused concerning someone drawing blood but continued to investigate the problem. "Please tell me about your being marked."

The woman looked directly into Charles' eyes with tears forming in hers. Charles sensed her fear and anger. "They came to us and told us they are taking care of us. They drew our blood, and then, we disappear."

"Disappear?" Charles asked back in Spanish.

"We will disappear, and nobody will see us again. Can we stay here tonight?"

"Of course, but I only have one bed. I can stay in my study, and both of you can have my bed."

"We would be very grateful."

Charles took them to the small attached bathroom. He asked them if they would like to wash themselves, and told them in Spanish to call him if they had any questions as he pointed down the small hallway to his study where he had a short sofa. He knew his tall frame would not fit well on the old couch and did not plan to sleep anyway. He immediately contacted Candice, Nick, and Dr. Calhoun about what had just happened.

Candice was asleep in her usual position on her right side with her left hand on Nick's chest and awakened when the whistle alarm informed her she had an e-mail on her tablet. She got up as gently as possible trying not to awaken Nick, but he informed her, "Don't be so careful. I'm awake and just had a bad dream."

"We'll get to your dream later," she said as she woke up the tablet.

"What's up?" asked Nick.

She said, "Charles sent us an e-mail. I can read it aloud."

Nick raised himself to a sitting position in bed with his hands resting in his lap and said, "That would be good. I'm listening."

Candice read the long e-mail to Nick, and both of them looked at each other with worry. Candice was first to speak, "Does Charles think the blood drawing is part of the way they pick organs for specific customers?"

"He didn't give an opinion, but I think he thinks that."

"What in the world will we do with the woman and the girl?" asked Candice.

"Get them out of here I suppose. This is a break, but it could be a costly break. We need to help Charles; he says that Dr. Calhoun is on his way to the church."

Dr. Calhoun drove himself in the clinic jeep to the church. He came through the door of the church's auditorium hurriedly while carrying a boxful of medical supplies. Charles asked the woman and the girl to come out of the room; he explained about Dr. Calhoun and that he would be examining both of them. The woman explained that her name was Rosa and that the little girl, Madeira, was her daughter to Charles as he interpreted to Dr. Calhoun. Dr. Calhoun examined the small spot on the small of their arms and began to ask quick questions to Charles to ask Rosa and her daughter. Charles also texted Candice about the progress of the examinations. The word marked began to take on a new meaning when Dr. Calhoun found a small scar on the back of their left hands with a small disc embedded under the skin.

Candice and Nick had gotten out of bed, had dressed, and were getting in the sports car when Candice received the message describing the embedded discs. Nick started the engine and began to drive toward the church. Candice, while also continuing to assess for electronic bugs, kept in contact and informed Nick about each new message that Charles texted. Upon reading about the small disc like objects in the back of their left hands, Candice immediately texted back to leave them alone due to the possibility of them alerting someone in the Cartel, or they might be booby trapped to deliver some kind of lethal dose of poison.

Dr. Calhoun would wait until Nick and Charles arrived to the church before he would chance an exam due to the embedded chips. When Charles met Candice and Nick at the big wooden doors to the auditorium, he ushered them in quickly and asked, "Are there any problems with flies? They are bad this time of year."

"None," said Candice.

Charles brought Candice and Nick to his study, closed the door, and reported, "They came to me for help. As I wrote you, they report they are marked."

Candice looked at Charles and began to explain, "You know if they are spies, they have us all together with quite possibly a chip embedded in them that will alert the cartel to where we are."

"It's not that Candice. They have real fear without deceit."

"That is good. Now, take me to them," said Candice.

Nick began to secure a weapon from one of Charles' hiding places in the old, rickety wood furniture of the study. He informed Candice he would be searching the perimeter and making sure no one followed them. Candice and Charles nodded in agreement.

Nick felt the warmth of the outside as he left the small air-conditioned study. The auditorium was air cooled with windows and screens but the small area in back of the church that held the study, bedroom, and bathroom had small air-conditioners each. He looked at the darkened leafless trees that spread their silhouettes against the sky. Blending into the woods, he stood motionless in the dark watching for any movement around him. Once he finished surveying the area, he moved again slowly in the shadows to ensure no one was trying to sneak to the church. He saw nothing unusual, and after a while, he went back inside.

Per Dr. Calhoun's request, Candice continued to stay in the room while Dr. Calhoun was doing the examination. Charles stood behind a rigged up sheet to allow privacy but allowed him to interpret their Spanish to Dr. Calhoun and to Candice.

"Dr. Calhoun, what do you think?" asked Charles.

"Healthy in every way, but that thing in the back of their hands bothers me."

"It bothers me too," said Candice. "I thought something like this may be up, so I brought a small scanner with me. I need to scan the chips into my laptop to analyze them. My problem is, the chips may alert someone that they are being scanned."

Charles asked, "Do we have a choice?"

"I can't think of one," said Candice.

Charles began to explain the equipment Candice was setting up to Rosa and Madeira. Then, Candice placed the scanner on the back of Rosa's left hand first.

Candice explained as she scanned the chip and then waited while Charles interrupted, "I recognize the chip; it is very similar to the ones placed in us but more primitive. It sends out ten-digit grid coordinates about every twenty minutes, and I can manipulate it to send out false coordinates. Only one problem, a smart operator can figure out it is being tampered with."

"We don't have much time. Is it booby trapped?" asked Dr. Calhoun.

"I can't tell. It may be, and that is why I am leaving it alone. Besides, deactivation would be too suspicious. I do have an idea though. Dr. Calhoun, can you draw their blood?" asked Candice.

"Yes, what are you thinking?"

"If their clothes were found near an area where I have seen a cougar, that might buy us some time. If done right, it might be a complete cover-up."

Charles said, "I think it's a good idea." He explained to Rosa and Madeira about the plan and instructed them to go to the used clothes and find something to wear. They looked afraid, and their faces showed emotions of having no other choice except to trust four strangers.

They dressed in the bedroom and passed their clothes out through the door. Candice, Charles, and Dr. Calhoun came into the bedroom, and Charles told the mother and daughter that they would need to draw their blood. He informed them in Spanish that their clothes would be found torn and bloody from their own blood where a cat was last seen. They agreed.

Dr. Calhoun had them both lie down on the bed and began to draw vial after vial of blood, first from Rosa and then from Madeira. Meanwhile, Charles was getting his SUV ready for transport. Candice contacted the closest thing to a headquarters which was the ship they had off the coast and asked for a friend with a small boat. Coordinates with a time came back within a few minutes. Charles informed the two that he would be driving them to a boat that would take them away for a while. Also, he told them that they would be treated well, but people would be asking them a great amount of questions. He informed them that their cooperation would save other lives. Candice sent the coordinates where Charles would meet the people from the boat. The friends would be on their way shortly.

Dr. Calhoun was to tear the clothes and place the blood on them at the location where the mother and daughter were to supposedly be attacked by a large cat. Candice, after she had made the chips send out false coordinates, would be traveling with Nick back to their suite and began to make arrangements to move into their rented home as if nothing had happened. Information from Rosa and Madeira would be sent back to the tetrahedron members during and after their interviews by protected communication. This whole process would save two lives and possibly make some headway into their mission; however, it could also spell doom if discovered that all four members of the tetrahedron were together in the same location. They knew you can always be seen by someone in some way.

CHAPTER 16

The Spiritual Side

CANDICE WAS COORDINATING text messages at 7AM from Charles and Dr. Calhoun. Both returned to their places after taking care of the marked mother and daughter and seemed to be doing well. Dr. Calhoun reported that he was tired but would begin his day as usual. Charles reported no one had visited the church today. Candice signed off and assisted Nick with loading the SUV for today's move to their new home. Both were loading their suit cases, the new drones, the computers, and other equipment when Candice's phone rang. She pulled it from its holster, swiped the lock, and placed in her key- a backward C- to answer.

Juan's voice sounded sarcastic, "Young married lovers taking an early morning ride in a sports car sounds very romantic."

"Is there a law against riding in a car with the top down?" asked Candice.

"It depends on where you go and what you do."

"As you said, it is romantic and especially when you can't sleep," said Candice angrily.

"Anyway, where you go is your business so long as it does not interfere with ours."

"You are right, Juan. May I ask why you are calling us this morning?"

"Oh, I have another proposition for you and your husband from my employer. He wants another meeting with you to explain. I think you will find the pay very good. Did you like the jewels and the coin? I know it is a Monday, and you may have other plans."

"I love the jewels, but I don't think Nick is all that impressed with the coin."

"The coin was the best I could do at short notice. I already had the jewels. Would you wear one of the necklaces tonight to the restaurant?"

"Yes, and I will tell Nick about your call. What time do we meet if we decide to come?"

"Seven PM. Coming will be very good for you, and not coming will be very bad for you. Remember, Nick is very vulnerable to the law."

"I remember."

"Then I hope my employer will be seeing you at 7PM."

"Juan, this is rather short notice. We had plans for moving to our home today. I will need to cancel."

"I will see you are properly rewarded for your inconvenience. Maybe, I can send over some people to assist with your moving?"

"Not necessary or wanted. I will tell Nick you called."

"Thank you, and if you do decide to attend, do not forget to wear one of your necklaces. Good-bye."

Candice texted Charles about Juan's phone call and asked that he brief Dr. Calhoun. A secured e-mail came informing Candice that Rosa and her daughter had arrived to the ship and were being transported to Texas with information as obtained from them to follow.

Charles asked via e-mail if Candice had a little time for conversation, and she replied, "yes."

"There is something spiritually evil about this mission. I thought of it as mechanical evil for lack of a better name when we were in Tennessee. I am not surprised that Juan knew you had left. Did you see or detect anyone or find any surveillance equipment with your scans?"

"No."

"Yet, they knew you had left, and I bet they knew your whereabouts a lot of the time."

"Why would you say that?"

"It goes by several names, but some call it soul travel. Also, witches and other people can use watchers or certain symbols that allow them to see."

"This all sounds strange to me. I don't really know what you are talking about."

"Just believe me," said Charles. "Can you still enter your old hotel suite?"

"Yes, we can even stay here tonight if we need to. I am in the suite and still packing. Nick is outside loading sensitive equipment."

"Then, look out your window for any type of unusual letter or symbol outside your suite."

Candice took the binoculars from her back pack and began to look around the outside from her window. There was a restaurant sign about a block down the street to the left with what seemed to be a funny looking A on the sign that was painted red. She took out her telescope and trained it on the letter. The A was in the circle with the cross bar extending to both sides of the circle directed in an upper right hand slant. She described it to Charles.

"That is one, and I would bet there may be others. It is called an anarchy sign, and being in red, it could have an even deeper meaning."

"So, what do we do? Do we blow up the sign? Oh, wait a minute, I am tired and didn't mean to sound sarcastic."

"Understood. Besides, you are moving to your new home. Just know it is there and what it can do. I need you to look for certain things around your new home, and I really wish I could come over and anoint your home and grounds. I sensed weird spiritual tactics before we came here, and that is why the church and its grounds are anointed. Also, I anointed Dr. Calhoun's clinic and hospital."

"Charles, do you mean they can see us through that sign?" Candice asked seriously.

"You have told me twice about their knowing your comings and goings, but your surveillance equipment did not give readings. So far, the signs are somewhat blocked by prayers, and they cannot get a good long look at what you are doing. But, they are watching you."

"Someone at the hotel could be watching. Even a staff member on the night shift could see us coming and going. All of us are in agreement that moving to a rental home would be safer due to the number of possible people who are watching us in the hotel. I hope Nick and I are doing the right thing by moving."

"I wish that were true about people watching you in the hotel. It would make it easier. However, I do not feel that to be the case. Watchers disguised as funny looking letters probably are somewhere past your hotel also and on different roads. Have you noticed graffiti on bridges, road signs, and such?"

"There seems to be a lot lately. It seems to grow as we travel," reported Candice.

"Don't take pictures of the signs or the graffiti; it might bring on suspicion. I will try to find an excuse to come and see them. Remember, this is spiritual and evil. You cannot detect these things with electronics."

"What would be some of the things to look for at our new home?"

"Anything that looks unusual as far as a symbol or letter. Also, look for two sticks placed on a path or corner making an X."

"So, what do I do if Nick or I find one?"

"Break the lines by removing the two sticks, and you can paint over the letters if it is on your walls or another place where it can watch you. I doubt it will bring on suspicion. Nobody likes graffiti or stray sticks on their property."

"Done," said Candice.

"I need to get to your home and anoint it and your grounds, or you can do it. Just place oil that you have prayed over around your doors and windows and each corner of your property. I know that Nick will probably think this is weird, but tell him not to interfere. Remember, this spiritual surveillance is more effective than electronic surveillance and cannot be detected by anything you have other than your spirit and heart. Please be careful and watch out for anger episodes and any unusual behavior from both of you. Pray for your protection. Good luck explaining this to Nick."

"He's having bad dreams lately."

"That is a sign of somebody breaking through the barriers. Let me know if someone you have met shows up in either of your dreams. Pray for your protection and call me with anything unusual you find. Whoever it is knows what they are doing, and this is very dangerous."

"Understood. I'll explain it to Nick. Please be careful, and thank you."

"You are welcome. Good-bye."

"Good-bye."

Candice explained the dangers that she and Charles discussed to Nick. He held a look of disbelief during their conversation, yet he knew that Charles knew what he was talking about. Nick said when Candice finished, "It is a bit hard to swallow, but they seem to know where we are without your equipment notifying us."

Candice looked thoughtfully at Nick and said, "I don't think it is the equipment, but there could be other explanations. People could be spying on us from different means."

"Except, there are not even heat signatures when we look around outside with our thermal imager, and you said Charles does not feel anyone working in the Hotel is working for the cartel. Also, we assess randomly the hotel's personnel and always find nothing. How can we not find anything?"

"Nick, Charles is never wrong- at least so far. I trust him, but I still do not know how people can see through a weird letter."

"I know. We are to trust him on this," declared Nick.

Candice looked at Nick with worry and a sense of loss of control over their environment and reluctantly pronounced, "Yes, we are."

It was set in the plans from Tennessee that Candice and Nick would move from the hotel to a rental home just outside the city. Nick advertised job offerings in the local newspaper for a good maid and a good cook. During his stay at the hotel, he ordered nothing but the best foods from room service and ate at the most expensive restaurants. He made sure the rental home had more than five thousand square feet of living space and had a three-car garage. Also, a great view was a must have. The monthly rent was more than most people's yearly salaries employed in the area. The move was painless due to only a small amount of luggage from Candice and Nick accompanied with cameras and the replaced drones, and all could be moved in the SUV. The rental furniture along with pictures, sculptures, and paintings were chosen and set in place perfectly by the best interior designer in that area. Nick gave cart blanch to the realtor and designer proclaiming that he did not have time to trouble himself with small details. In fact, he did not visit or approve the home by personally visiting the home. He decided on the home by pictures and verbal communications only.

Candice and Nick arrived to their new home and were both surprised by its long circular drive with large native flowering plants on both sides of the paved road. Also, the open drive went through the shaded porch covered by a metal curved roof. The front of the home was almost all windows on both the lower and upper story. It sat upon a hill with the front view overlooking a small forest ending with the crystal blue of the ocean. Two large adjoined wooden doors with carvings of animals opened to a large marble floored foyer with an elaborate staircase with the steps topped with white marble with gray veins.

The maid and cook were both waiting in the foyer dressed in casual clothes except both had on practical aprons. The maid had a pair of yellow plastic gloves in the right pocket of the apron. Candice and Nick were shown every room by the maid after introductions. The house was immaculately clean, and the designer had fitted every piece of furniture and every wall hanging perfectly. The maid explained that the gardener would come on Tuesdays and Thursdays and that she would be glad to introduce him.

The time was getting toward five PM after their personal house tour, so Candice and Nick dismissed themselves to the master bedroom where they began to unpack and get ready for their date at the restaurant with Juan's employer.

Nick drove the sport's car with the top up and the air conditioner on in order not to muss their hair or clothes. Candice dressed in a simple violet dress; however, the elaborate diamond and ruby necklace was stunning and matched the dress perfectly. Nick wore a simple dark blue suit but with a gold silk shirt with faint blue strips and matching primarily blue paisley tie. The cufflinks were large crystal diamonds. Candice could not help but stare at how handsome he looked. She thought that if she had just met him she would have thought him a rich playboy who was changed by a wonderful wife. She wondered if she was the best choice as someone who could tame someone like Nick portrayed. On the other hand, she was beginning to fall for him in every way and wondered if Nick felt the same for her. Nick pulled under the extended roof used for brief parking by the restaurant, and the valet dressed in a black coat with white shirt immediately opened Candice's car door. Candice stepped out like royalty and stopped a few feet from the car while Nick got out on his side of the car and gently tossed the keys to the valet who caught them with his free left hand. Nick was moving toward Candice's side while the valet closed the passenger car door just in time to receive the fifty-dollar tip in his right hand. The valet looked surprised as Candice took on her usual look of faked annoyance.

As they entered the restaurant, Candice closed her mind to her thoughts about Nick and began to watch the moves of everyone in the room. She and Nick were ushered into the private room in the restaurant by two large and well-muscled men. Candice immediately recognized weaknesses in both of the thugs if things came to self-defense. Nick noticed that both were carrying two concealed pistols, one in a left shoulder holster that had to be a high caliber and a small hidden 380 or nine-millimeter automatic pistol on the back right side of their belts. Nick felt naked because he had no weapon; however, they must look like amateurs. The thoughts of how to steal a weapon from them, if defensive actions were necessary, consumed his thoughts.

The round table was set in white again with red cloth napkins, and the same man sat opposing them again dressed in a black suit, white silk shirt, and a red silk tie. There were only two chairs at the table across from the man. The table was circular. The settings were elaborate with plates, crystal glasses, and fine ornate silver flatware. Nick reached for the chair to pull it back for Candice, but the two men pulled a seat back for each to sit.

Juan's employer spoke first, "It is very good to see you again. I took the liberty to order the wine. I trust you will like it."

The wine was brought in a bottle wrapped with a white cloth by a young man wearing a black waiter's suit with a white ruffled shirt. He poured the red liquid into the large, open topped crystal wine glasses. Juan's employer watched the wine being poured and asked if anyone would like to guess the type of wine.

Nick swirled the wine in the glass and then held it up to his nose and smelled the bouquet. He examined the legs against the light and then took a slow but small sip. Smelling one more time, he placed down the glass and then explained, "It is a fruity-especially black cherry bouquet but slightly dry Argentine red. It tastes as if it were placed in oak casts also."

"You are correct on every point. Would you care to guess the wine maker and the year?"

Candice looked on in amazement as Nick continued to speak, "If it is a 2003 De Antonio, it is a very rare and expensive bottle indeed."

The man signaled the waiter to remove the cloth which showed the label. Candice tried not to look surprised.

The man spoke again, "You are correct again. Only a rich x-playboy would be able to discern that. You have obviously had the wine before."

Nick looked at Candice first and then at the man and said, "A rich x-playboy does not like to speak about most of the things he has done in front of wife."

"Understood. Candice, how do you like the wine?" asked the man.

She took a small sip and proclaimed, "It tastes wonderful."

The man seemed to relax and said with a smile, "It is good to drink wine with those who appreciate it. My country does not grow good grapes, so few people drink wines. There are some liqueurs that are quite good made from such things as agave, and we have some good local beers. Anyway, I thought you might like some good wine before our meal."

Candice nodded yes as she took another sip of the wine.

Nick looked puzzled and asked, "Why do you want us here?"

"Americans seem to always be quick with business. I would like for us to enjoy the meal, and by the way, it is all Yucatan cuisine."

Nick looked again at the man and asked, "Again, why are we here?"

"Mr. Lippincott, you are here at my request to dine. I enjoy the company of people who enjoy the finer things in life. Also, you and your lovely wife are here to listen to a business proposition that I have for the two of you. I think it will be well worth your time."

"I do not eat well under certain circumstances," said Nick.

"Mr. Lippincott, you are here because you did some work for me to assist my deliverance of illegal drugs. If I add that to your past and some other interesting items that my staff dug up on your family, you are either to assist me in my endeavors or face certain consequences in the United States."

Nick looked at Candice sternly, and she said, "I am sorry" and unclasped the necklace to lay it on the table.

The man saw her removing the necklace and said, "You may as well keep it Mrs. Lippincott. We have lots of pictures and videos showing you wearing the necklace and also my sending it to you. Our story is to be mailed to the US government unless you cooperate. Do you think your story is believable?"

Candice showed fear as she picked up the necklace holding it as if it were a poisonous snake in her hands. The man noted her fear and explained, "Now Mrs. Lippincott, it is not that bad. I am just asking for you to come to our place where we make things like drones and teach us about how to place certain items in them. You seem to do well with such things.We talked about your helping us before, and Nick, we have a certain job for you."

"What is that?"

"We want you to be a, shall I say, front for us. You appear legitimate."

"A front man?" asked Nick.

"Exactly, you seem to have a way with you. A conformed playboy who is dedicated to his wife. Also, we know that you gave money to the free clinic that you went to while having a flare from your malaria. Might I add, it was a very rich donation."

"How do you know that?" asked Nick.

"I know many things Mr. Lippincott. Your past is buried but not well enough. Your wife must love you to stand beside you."

Candice looked guilty as she said, "Nick, this is my fault. We should have never come to this country."

The man looked at Candice with one eyebrow raised and said, "Your bird studies are disastrous for you unless you are willing to work with us. Just think about how a rich family that does not need money is difficult to convince."

Nick looked at the man and asked, "You keep saying 'we'. Who are the 'we'."

"My brother and I. Candice will meet my brother when she comes to work for us. He is a brain when it comes to computers and business."

"I want to know how long this will take and when we can leave this country," declared Nick.

"You can leave when we say you can leave. Also Mr. Lippincott, you are employing the best chef and maid in the country."

"Do they work for you?" asked Nick.

"No, they work for an agency on the island. I am a busy man, and I do not have time to employ maids and cooks in a business format. One of my spies told me."

"So, you are watching us?"

"Yes Mr. Lippincott, in more ways than you know. And Mrs. Lippincott, do not try to place us under surveillance or even block our surveillance. You are good, but we would know if you tried. Also, we have certain ways of watching that are far advanced."

Candice asked, "far advanced?"

"Now, do not worry about that. Just do not try to check in on us. We would know. Our IT department is very good."

"Understood," said Candice with anger in her voice.

Nick whispered to Candice who nodded yes and then looked at the man and the two thugs that had escorted them in and asked, "Is it imperative that we stay for dinner? My wife and I would like to leave."

"I suppose you have lost your appetite. Yes, you may leave the restaurant but not the country. I want to make that clear. Juan is responsible to call you tomorrow to inform you of the time for Candice to visit our facility. I know you will come also Mr. Lippincott. We will drive you there, and by the way Candice, you will be blindfolded during the trip."

The man signaled, and the two muscular men came to the table. Nick and Candice were escorted from the restaurant as the valet brought the sports car to the front. Nick opened the door for Candice and then walked around the front to enter. One of the thugs followed him and stood beside him as he opened the door. Nick seated himself without saying a word, started the car, and drove away.

Candice, when out of sight of the restaurant, took out her cell phone from her purse and sent a guarded message to both Charles and Dr. Calhoun that read, "We're definitely in."

Candice turned to Nick who was concentrating on driving and said, "There are no bugs tonight. Can we place the top down?"

Nick stopped and turned off the engine, and Candice reported, "I do not want the top down. I do not detect any bugs. I absolutely have to know. How in the world did you know about the wine? According to your history, your parents did not allow alcohol in the home. I hope that you do not mind my asking you about your personal life. I might be breaking protocol here."

"I do not mind answering. I am a kind of a lay expert on wines," proclaimed Nick.

"How could you be? To know stuff like you rattled off just does not come overnight."

"Well, I have always been fascinated by wines, but my parents wouldn't hear of me trying them. So, I read about them and imagined their tastes. If a wine said it had the taste of black cherries, I tasted black cherries. If it had a hint of tobacco, I tasted tobacco. I really did not like the taste of tobacco. If it had a faint fruity flavor, I mixed slight fruit in watered down vinegar and tasted it. The tar flavor was interesting; I actually tasted part of the road in front of our home. I got the flavors from wine review magazines and books mostly from the town library."

"So, you did it by tasting what you read was the flavor of the wines?"

"Yes."

"So, your ordering expensive wines is not an act?"

"No, it is a passion of mine, and I could not really afford some of the best wines until I got this job. I had to drink what wines I could afford and wish about the others."

"But, you don't even finish a full glass."

"It is the flavor. I am happy just to taste a small amount. It is about the wine."

"OK, I guess you cannot learn everything from a computerized history."

"That is true. Wine is serious with me, but I did not enjoy the wine tonight because of the company. Now, with you only, it would have been perfect."

With that Candice reached over, hugged Nick, and kissed him passionately. Nick was shocked at first and then kissed and held her back. They had kissed before in public for the mission's sake, but this time it was while they were alone in a parked car.

Candice lost herself for an instant and then backed off quickly. She looked at Nick with surrendering eyes, took a deep breath, and began to explain, "Nick, I want you so much. I fight it every night now, but I am afraid of what it will do to us and to the mission."

Nick ran his right hand up and down her back and said, "It is the most difficult thing that I can do, just sleeping beside you. But, your left hand on my chest is so important to me. I really don't think I could sleep anymore without it there."

Candice looked as if she was straining to pull her head back and to release her arms. She loved his touch. She looked into Nick's eyes and began to explain, "I do not want this to end. I mean our time together. Sometimes, I wish we were somewhere else dating and talking about our future. Promise me you will come to see me, no matter what, when this is over."

"You want me to promise you."

"Yes, is that a problem?" Candice asked not trying to hide her annoyance.

"No, it is what I want. Maybe we can begin again in a normal setting," said Nick.

"I would like that. Now, get the car started and let's get home. We have a long day tomorrow."

Nick cranked the car, turned on the lights of the sports car and pulled back on the road and asked, "Can we talk about wine again sometime?"

Candice looked at Nick and smirked, "So, you like what it got you this time?"

"Yes, I like it very much."

"No, that subject is off limits along with some others I will come up with tomorrow. You are certainly more than meets the eye and what meets the eye is a hunk to die for."

Nick looked vulnerable and then asked, "Would you care for me if my body was different? I mean if I got wounded or something. What if I lost a leg or something like that?"

"I might have to think about that. Oh, I know the answer, and it is yes, you chowder head! Do you think me that shallow not to love you however you look? Don't ask me that kind of stupid question again."

Nick looked at her while taking his eyes off the road too long for Candice's comfort. She said, "Watch the road."

"I would rather watch you."

"OK, you can't say that anymore either. I just added that to the list, and don't worry, I'll finish the list tomorrow when I'm not this tired."

Chapter 17

The New Home

DR. CALHOUN AND Charles planned a visit to the Lippincott's new home. The excuse was they were coming to ask for more money for the mission service to be used for upkeep of the small clinic and hospital and also the church. Candice, in preparation, had detected four bugs in the home and left them alone as planned if any were found. The bugs did not surprise her due to the fact that she had simply not locked the door while everyone was away from the home. It was a set-up for the cartel. The bugs were sound only, and none were cameras which made them perfect for this specific tetrahedron use. No bugs were detected on the grounds outside the home.

Dr. Calhoun and Charles arrived at midday and were welcomed into the home by the maid. Candice and Nick appeared from the back and offered the doctor and Charles some wine and snacks, escorted them into the large home, and asked them to sit in the large front room just to the right of the large marble tiled foyer. The wine was an expensive red, and Dr. Calhoun complained the wine was a little too dry for him. The maid immediately brought him a sweeter chilled white wine.The Lippincott's and their guests sat down after greetings.

Charles spoke first, "I work for the Intercontinental Mission and Health Services and been in country for about two and a half months. The stone church where I work needs several items. It is always unpleasant to ask for money, but I need to upgrade the old benches and some of the other furniture in the church. I can give you and our mission administration a list of the items needed. All money must go through the Intercontinental Mission and Health Services."

Nick spoke as rehearsed in reply to Charles, "You can give me a list, and I will see what I can do." Nick turned his eyes to Dr. Calhoun and began to speak but was interrupted by Charles.

"I need to excuse myself to your restroom," said Charles.

Candice nodded and said, "It is upstairs and to the left."

Charles said, "thank you" and left the room.

Nick continued the conversation thanking Dr. Calhoun for his care during his last malaria flare.

Dr. Calhoun spoke, "I want to thank you for the recent large donation to the mission. In this case, the administration sent all the money to us for repairs and upkeep of our clinic and hospital. There are some other needs. You are very generous. It is a great payment for the little care you received."

Candice said, "We are so glad you would see us."

Nick replied, "I appreciate your services and help with the poor in this area. Does the money need to be separate and designated specifically for the hospital or the church?"

"It is best that they be separate payments, but both need funds."

Charles found the bathroom at the top of the stairs. Quickly, he placed the olive oil that he had prayed over onto a clean, white cotton cloth. The small container was like a metal capsule about two inches in length with a protected oil filled small glass container inside. About half was poured over the cloth leaving the rest to be used for drops on certain areas. Charles appeared back in the downstairs sitting room where the three were gathered. Looking around the perfectly decorated room, he asked, "May I have a tour of your home? From what I have seen so far, it is very beautiful."

Candice got up and said, "sure."

Candice timed the tour perfectly with the maid being on break and the cook working in the kitchen preparing lunch. As the four went from room to room, Charles prayed over each window and door silently while completely encircling them with the cloth. For a coverage of any possible strange sounds, the other three made small talk about the rooms and furnishings. Charles noted that the maid was top rate due to very little dust accumulation on the cloth.

When the four approached the dining room, Candice said, "I took the liberty to have lunch served for us. I hope you can stay." The cook had placed four small but perfect lunches on the table with fresh cold water with lemon.

They finished the tour in the perfectly cleaned kitchen while the cook and maid were on break and then sat down to lunch. The small piece of roasted fish was perfect and had a small topping of avocado. The soup was brownish clear with small pieces of fish and two slices of lime placed perfectly in each bowl. The small avocado salad was resting on top of a freshly sliced tomato and was covered with an avocado dressing.

Charles asked, "What kind of fish is this? It is wonderful."

Candice replied, "It is freshly caught guianan snook. Being a biology student, I like to study about creatures around me. Also, every meal seems to be different with our chef. She likes to serve local fresh foods and is quite remarkable."

They finished their lunch just in time for the maid and cook to finish their breaks. The two appeared suddenly like clockwork and took the dishes to the kitchen.

The four tetrahedron members went outside and planned on continuing the meeting while musing around the SUV that Charles and Dr. Calhoun had driven to the home. Candice checked her phone and discovered that no bugs were in the immediate area of the automobile. She signaled to the other members of the tetrahedron that it was a safe zone.

Charles seemed disturbed and pronounced to Candice, "There is still something here, maybe more than one thing. Please remind me again about the gifts you received from the cartel man?"

Candice replied, "I got two necklaces, and Nick got a gold coin when we demonstrated our drones."

"Yes, I remember you informing us," said Charles. "But, I feel something eerie about them. I think they are cursed someway."

Candice's face looked doubtful and fearful at the same time. She got up, went into the house, and retrieved the two necklaces and the gold coin. Charles looked at the coin first, took it out of its box, drizzled the anointing oil on it, bowed his head, and prayed. He proclaimed, "The coin is harmless now, but the necklaces are a different story."

Candice asked, "What do you mean?"

"The coin was cursed with a spirit. This may be why Nick was having the bad dreams. It is not uncommon to hear about spirits in objects. In Japan, priests blessed the ore for a samurai sword causing a spirit to enter the oar. The spirit of the sword then found the man who was worthy enough to own it. I know of one person who bought an authentic samurai sword who had bad dreams and eventually cut himself very badly with it. The sword was cursed from its conception."

"What did he do about the sword?" asked Nick.

"I cannot tell you where it is, but I am certain the sea water has deteriorated it by now. It may not even exist anymore. You see Candice, these necklaces are cursed from their conception. The demonic powers cannot be anointed from them. The diamonds, rubies, and emeralds are OK and can be anointed with good results since they were fashioned by the earth, but the metals were cursed before their being formed into the necklace. One thing that can be done is to remove the precious stones, melt down the metals, anoint and pray over them, and then reform them. Or, you can just simply place the jewels into other settings that are not cursed."

Candice looked at Charles and asked, "I guess we need to get rid of them. Why not just sink them in the ocean like you did the sword?"

"Because, the cartel will want to know that you have them. It is a controlling factor with them. I think I have a better solution."

Charles walked to the SUV and picked up one of his many Bibles that he brought on the mission. He opened the book to Revelation and crowded the necklaces between the covers of the book as best he could. Then, he asked Candice, "Do you have some tape on hand?"

"There is some in the bathroom. I'll get it for you."

When Candice returned, Charles took the white bandage tape and wrapped it around the Bible several times. "I know it does not look very good, but I feel the attached critters are bound up now. Is this new territory for you?"

Candice looked at Nick who appeared to be fighting his disbelief and drifted her eyes toward Charles and asked, "Can they see us through the necklaces or even the coin before it was anointed?"

"No, these critters are like marauders. They depress, cause nightmares, confuse people, and stress relationships to mention a few things. They can even turn deadly by causing people to commit murder or suicide. Even the people who curse objects with them do not want the marauders to return in any way because they are dangerous to everyone. Those who cursed the objects will probably not know the thugs have been bound up or even cast out in the case of the coin."

"What about the maid and chef?" asked Nick.

Charles answered, "They do not feel bad to me. I think they are independent and OK. Candice, have you done a real back-ground check on them?"

"Yes, I found nothing really to worry about."

"Good," said Charles. "I know this spiritual side is probably new for all of you, but it may be why others who came here to do something about the cartel

120

failed. Candice, do not take these necklaces out of the Bible and find some excuse to not wear them. Nick, I did not see a safe in the home, but if there is not one there, I sincerely advise you to get one and lock these necklaces up."

Candice looked at Nick and said, "The cartel people think that I am disgusted by them because they got you in trouble."

Charles said, "Find whatever excuse that works, but do not wear them. Give them back immediately if by an outside chance they ask for them. Beyond that, be very careful about accepting any more gifts."

Candice and Nick almost spoke together, "understood."

The tour continued with a walk around the property at which time Charles dropped a few drops of anointing oil on each corner of the property and again prayed silently. The tour ended, good-byes were said, and Dr. Calhoun and Charles drove away.

The house felt lighter, and Candice had a way of closing down the bugs without causing suspicion. She caused the bugs to go into a static mode much like a TV giving bad reception. The bugs would be assessed as dying for some unknown interference, and it would also copy a surge of energy caused by a phenomenon beyond anyone's control.

When evening came, Candice and Nick went to bed early. After a night of peaceful slumber, Nick awakened normally and turned his head to look at Candice who still had her eyes closed and said, "I know you. You're not asleep."

"Just lying here noticing that you are not groaning and twitching like you usually do before you wake up."

"I did not have a bad dream."

"OK. Since Charles is not here, I will ask the psychiatric questions. Did you dream?" asked Candice.

"Yes."

"Was there a house in your dreams?"

"Yes, how did you know?"

"I thought so, and never mind that; I'm on a roll."

"Did the house have a motor on it like a motor boat?"

"No."

"I thought not," and Candice began to snicker under her breath while she raised up on her right elbow and made a goofy face at Nick.

"You heard me say the word house in my sleep didn't you," declared Nick.

Candice batted her eyes and with a sarcastic smile said, "Well, if you must know."

"You know, sometimes I want to kiss you, and sometimes, I want to..."

Candice interrupted, "You better stop there because what you say next I just might enjoy too."

Nick grabbed Candice and kissed her passionately. Candice kissed back and then both broke the embrace. Nick looked Candice in the eyes and said, "See what you made me do."

"You blame me for your hormones now."

"I blame you for making me love you."

"OK, that's another phrase on the list of things you cannot say. Let's get up before we do something I might enjoy and feel guilty about later."

"You can't just turn me off like that," said Nick.

"What about me? You have to turn yourself off. I'm too busy turning off myself." With that last statement she jumped out of bed and disappeared into her bathroom.

Nick got up slower and yelled through the closed door, "Is the chef here? I'm very hungry."

"What time is it?"

"Eight-thirty-five. We overslept," said Nick.

"Oversleeping is good sometimes. It depends on who you oversleep with."

"I agree. Dear, did you at least check to see if the house needs an exterminator. I don't want any more bites for either of us."

"I can call one if I see the need.You know I sprayed last night, but I want to make sure none came back," said Candice.

"Nick picked up her tablet and keyed in the correct sequence that she had shown him. The bug in the upper corner of the screen was on its back and not moving. He said loudly through the bathroom door, "There does not seem to be any alive. By the way, what do you think about the price of eggs in China?"

Candice's voice changed to a command, "You don't have to search for something to talk about. You can tell me you love me and want to ravish my body if you wish. Otherwise, I'll be in the shower trying to get my mind off you and back on the mission."

"OK, I love you and that other thing too. Have you noticed we are playing again?"

"I noticed that. I feel free," said Candice.

"I do too. Maybe we should have Charles and Dr. Calhoun over more often for dinner or something."

"Maybe. But now, I am just about to turn on the shower. Please watch for bad people while I enjoy my total body cleansing."

"What if I watch you?" asked Nick.

"Then bad people may come and get us both. No, you watch for bad people first, and then I'll watch for you."

"Maybe you do not know what you are missing."

"Believe me. I know, and that is another line you cannot say again," came Candice's watery voice from behind the door.

Nick waited until Candice was finished and then took his shower while Candice dressed. Both went downstairs to breakfast together which was soft scrambled eggs and native sausages made with chicken and turkey that were spicy hot. A cold bowl of sweetsop fruit mixed with fresh milk accompanied the sausage to help put out the fire. The breakfast was served with strong coffee with cream and sugar. The orange juice was fresh squeezed. Every part of the meal was both simple and perfect.

Candice loved the new home and spent most of the day setting up her observation equipment and cameras outside the home under the guise that it was for her studies. The maid went about her work and asked no questions when instructed that Candice would be unpacking the rest of their personal things. Nick went out back and explored his personal shooting range which was designed for skeet and pistol. He cleaned his expensive shotguns outside on the wooden bench at the back of the range. The gardener had picked up all the skeet fragments and empty shell casings, so every inch of the range looked pristine. All twenty-six acres of the house grounds were immaculate.

Nick was well pleased that he had no bad dreams the night after the anointing. Candice lost all eerie feelings and did not realize the impact they had chronically on her. Both were enjoying the day and felt isolated and safe in their new home, but both were also alert to problems that might occur.

Candice had more energy than usual, so she came outside and asked Nick if he would like to do some bird watching on the property. They used the newly set-up surveillance equipment and took pictures of birds to make more believable the excuse of the equipment set-up. Several bird species seemed to congregate toward the front where the flowers and exotic fruit trees were in higher concentration.

CHAPTER 18

The Priestess Judge

"WHERE ARE YOU Juan?" asked Judge Baez over her cell phone as she waited in the small secluded diner.

Juan's voice sounded strained as he replied, "I may not be able to make our meeting. The cartel is watching you closely, and you are not considered a friend anymore but a dangerous asset."

"We lost a girl and her mother for sacrifice. Also, somebody is spiritually feeling what we are doing and is blocking us. The watchers painted on the signs and near the buildings are not working. We lost much of our spiritual sight. There is somebody who is spiritually strong."

"My greatest suspect is Reverend Dorgan. He may be better than I originally thought. I will personally watch him."

"I never let the cartel into the sacrificial area, but I plan to take care of you handsomely. I really need the sacrifice of a strong person for my goddess."

"Reverend Dorgan would be a good candidate for that. He seems to have spiritual strength. The cartel is watching him also," said Juan.

"I know you do not know much about spiritual things; that is why I like to work with you. You are just a pure killer sold out to the highest bidder."

"That is why you are planning to care for me so well when you get your priests in place for the takeover. Let me know who I need to take out, but I warn you that too many sacrifices now would bring a lot of problems. Commander Morales is becoming a problem also."

"Why is the cartel trying to court the Lippincott's?" asked Judge Baez.

"That seems simple; I think it is about the control of money and power," replied Juan.

"Juan, I want you to let me know what happens with them."

"I will keep you informed. Thank you and good-bye."

"Good-bye Juan, the money will be hidden in the usual place. I will let you know when someone needs to be delivered for sacrifice, but I will back off for now."

"Good-bye," repeated Juan.

Juan pulled the ear phone with the wire microphone from his face and placed it on the table in front of him. Mr. Garcia who was facing Juan from the other side of the well-polished mahogany table also pulled off his ear phones and also laid them on the table in front of him.

"Juan, do you think she suspects anything about your false betrayal of the cartel?"

"Mr. Garcia, she suspects nothing. You did not want it in the past, but do you want the money she is paying me?"

"No, please keep that with my blessing and stay close to her. There is no love between us, but we may need her soon. She does not understand that the police and also Reverend Dorgan may be serious threats."

"Mr. Garcia, do you believe the things she is saying about sign watchers and such?"

"I do not know how she does it, but she is coming up with some good information that we cannot seem to collect. I know she is some kind of an evil witch, and I fear that she will turn on us," said Mr. Garcia in a worried voice.

"In that case, I will simply kill her," said Juan. "She can do nothing if she is dead."

"You are correct, but I need you to watch her closely. Also, I have a question. How do you know she is not watching us now with some of that spiritual stuff that she does?"

"It is very simple; she is being blocked by Reverend Dorgan or maybe someone else. If I thought you in danger, I would not have asked you to listen to this conversation. Also, I usually use the money she gives me to bribe one of her so-called priests who really hates her. We may make money off the bodies from her sacrifice, but to her, the cartel is just a well-paid body disposal system. Besides, your brother tells me we are making more money off the drugs now since the organ trade has stopped."

"Thank you for your loyalty Juan. When you bribe someone, let me know. I will replace the funds to you."

"Thank you. I will continue to watch the Lippincott's. Now, I need to get to the money before someone else finds it."

"Goodbye Juan but keep me informed if you need anything or if anything changes."

"Yes sir," Juan replied. He got up from the table, and walked out the nearly hidden side door of Mr. Garcia's elaborate home.

CHAPTER 19

The Local Law

JUDGE BAEZ LOOKED down her hawkish nose at Angel Carrillo who was standing beside his lawyer just under her bench. As Angel's lawyer continued to speak, the judge seemed uninterested, and one time, she yawned. Angel, who had a recent history of dating some of the best-looking women in the area found it difficult to look into the judge's leathery, wrinkled face. Angel's lawyer was older than Angel and had bluish gray hair with a handsome, honest face. He knew once Angel left this courtroom, his life would be in danger, but he also knew that Commander Morales would need all the details he could collect. He continued to observe as he spoke about Angel until the judge lifted her gavel and interrupted by angrily saying, "Counsellor finish your argument."

"I am interested in my client's welfare once he leaves this court," said the defense lawyer.

The judge held the gavel high with her right hand as she brushed back some of her brown hair with two inch gray roots from her wrinkled brow.

"Your client is arraigned for theft and is to be taken to jail where he will await trail. His bail is three hundred thousand pesos." With her last statement, she hit the gavel down hard and called for a ten-minute recess before her next case. She left her bench, pulled her phone from her robe, and called the jail. Once answered, she asked one short question, "Are you ready for him?"

"Yes," came the voice back on the phone.

"Good, you will find the reward in the usual place."

"Thank you, good bye."

"Good bye."

Police Commander Eutropio Morales, the head of all the police forces in the Yucatan, awakened to his cell phone alarm. It was a few minutes after midnight. He moved his swollen, aching arms to pick it up from his night table as his wife groaned in her sleep. He felt like his sixty-two years on this earth only gave him worsening arthritis. Groaning while looking at the phone, he pronounced under his breath, "My angel is in trouble."

He began to put on his clothes as his wife began to speak while lying on her right side toward him and not opening her eyes, "Will you ever retire? Your groans are getting worse, so your arthritis is getting worse. How many more times will you be getting up in the middle of the night to save someone from the jail?"

"This time it is my angel."

"That code name again. He must be really special."

"There is no braver man. Unfortunately, he is also too good looking for his own welfare. The jail is one thing, but the women he dates are another. Anyway, I am leaving as soon as I can get ready. He is in jail courtesy of that woman judge."

"Did he date her?"

Commander Morales laughed and proclaimed, "not this woman. She is too ugly on the inside even for him. Also, she is out to get anybody who stands against her. That means me also."

"How does she even continue on the bench?"

He was putting on his pants while rapidly shuffling his feet for his shoes as he answered her, "Because, she has high friends."

"I hope someday somebody kills her and all her friends," said Mrs. Morales in a less sleepy but angry voice.

The Commander was putting on his shirt, and his feet were in his shoes while his knees continued to crack. He began to walk toward the bedroom door. He grabbed the tie and coat with his right hand that he wore to the office the day before and scooped up his 38 snub nose pistol still in his shoulder holster from his dresser top with his left hand. He wanted his tie and coat to look as professional as possible at the jail.

The road to the jail was uneventful as he drove his personal squad car complete with caged in back seat. He pulled in the small parking area in the rear.

There was starless darkness as he got out of his car and placed on his shoulder holster, then his tie, and then his coat. He quickly ran his pocket comb through his graying straight black hair. His dark blue dress coat fit a little tight around his large abdomen when he tried to button it, so he left it open.

He swiped his card at the back door receptacle and then entered into the well-polished gray plastic tiled hallway. An officer immediately appeared at the end of the hallway and said, "welcome Commander. What brings you out at this time of night?"

"You are holding a person important to me. He may be a criminal, but he is also to be a major witness in a case. I need him released to me."

"Who is he.?"

"Angel Carrillo," answered Commander Morales firmly.

Commander Morales walked to the end of the hall where the deputy stood. The deputy sat down at his desk and began to look on the computer. After the deputy keyed in the secret clearance and passwords for the information, a picture appeared that was identical to one of their prisoners, and the deputy stood up immediately and said, "Sir, I am sorry. What do you want me to do?"

"I want you to release him to me for transfer as it states in the plan on your computer if he is arrested. Now, print out the transfer orders, and I will sign them."

The deputy did as he was instructed. Then, he arose from his desk and moved toward the metal door where a guard could be seen, through the small opening, sitting behind a large metal desk looking down the hall of cells. The deputy declared, "We have transfer orders for Angel Carrillo."

The guard moved toward the door and took the papers from the rectangular metal reinforced hole in the door as the deputy handed them through. Without speaking, the guard walked to the large cell that held twelve men and was complete with chairs, beds, and showers, opened it, and brought the prisoner up to the front. Angel stood about six foot and weighed about 185 pounds, but tonight, he was slumped over holding his chest and abdomen. Commander Morales began to realize that he arrived just in time. The metal doors opened, and Angel walked out slowly and raised his eyes as he approached the Commander.

"Where are you taking me?"

"We need to leave. I am transferring you to another location. Turn around," said Commander Morales. Then, he placed the handcuffs on Angel. The handcuffs were to protect Angel due to the surveillance cameras constantly taking their pictures. He moved him while handcuffed to the back seat and put his hand over his head for protection as he lowered him into the vehicle. The drive was uneventful, and both men began to relax.

"Commander, I am hurt. I think I need a doctor."

"Going to one. You were holding your abdomen. Do you feel like talking?"

"Yes, the judge put me into a cell that housed some of my enemies. I should be dead right now except I kind of beat up a couple of them. The cell occupants are like other criminals. If they cannot get one hundred percent, they usually back off."

"How bad are the two men you hurt?"

"I think both are still breathing, but I might be mistaken. The guard is in on it since he did not try to stop it."

Commander Morales stopped in a driveway, pulled out his cell phone, and called the woman inside the home. Her sleepy voice came over the phone via the speaker, "Does your wife know you are here?"

"No, will you be telling her?"

"No, or else you will not come here anymore. You run out of your arthritis medicine again?"

"No, I need another special favor. Is it OK?"

Angel looked both frightened and confused. Chief Morales opened the back door of the car, helped Angel to his feet, walked to the front door, and took Angel inside while still handcuffed; he made sure the door was locked with both the door lock and the dead bolt. Dr. Maria Rosa looked at angel and blushed. She quickly turned her back to both men. Commander Morales looking on suddenly shouted, "Oh no, you did not do this!" as he removed the handcuffs. He pronounced, "I should leave these things on you. Evidentially, you cannot control yourself around beautiful young women doctors."

Angel began to speak but was interrupted by Dr. Rosa, "It is my fault. I did not mean to sleep with a felon."

"Angel, do you ever stop?" yelled Commander Morales in anger.

Dr. Rosa turned and said with even more anger, "What do you mean do you ever stop? Angel, what are you?"

Angel began to defend himself when Commander Morales spoke quickly, "He is my deputy who is under deep cover. Tell me he did not hurt you with his insensitivity."

"What do you mean insensitivity? I hope he loves me like he says he does. I wear his ring."

Commander Morales looked at Angel with disgust while Angel finally was allowed to explain, "Maria, I do love you, and I do want to marry you. I just could not tell you my real name. I do not date other women. I am true to you. Also, Chief Morales knows that I was a womanizer in the past, just like I told you, but all of that is done now."

"It is unreal that my deputy is engaged to the only doctor that I trust on the Yucatan Peninsula.Did you also know she is my wife's doctor?" His anger began to subside, and he said half-jokingly, "Well, I guess that I should give you both a toast or something. Anyway, how did you meet?"

Angel said nervously but quickly, "She is so beautiful when she dances. She is a Club Royale patron. We dance so well together."

While looking at Angel with disgust, Commander Morales said, "So, you both dance, and you just happened to be there and needed to ask her out."

Dr. Rosa suddenly realized that they had traveled to her home due to Angel being hurt. She quickly ran to him and hugged him while kissing him long and hard on the mouth. Then she said, "Come with me. I am so sorry. Let me examine you."

"I think I am going to be sick," said the Commander sarcastically.

"Oh be quiet, you wake me up in the middle of the night to take care of my man not knowing he is my man." She told Angel to take off his shirt and get up on her couch arm while she got her doctor's bag from her bedroom. She listened to his chest and ran her fingers over his ribs.She removed the makeshift chest bandage and examined the three inch in length by half inch deep cut on the left side of his rib cage. She said, "Someone tried to stab you, but it glanced off your ribs."

"I know. I think that I got the most of the bleeding stopped by holding a wad of paper towels over it before Commander Morales got me out of jail. I tore my bedsheet and made a bandage to keep it from bleeding."

"I can sew it up here if you do not want to chance going to the hospital. Also, you may have a couple of cracked ribs on the right. You want me to sew it up here?"

"Sure."

"Would you two like to be alone?" asked Commander Morales.

"No," said Angel. "I'm afraid to be alone with her right now."

"And well you should be," said Dr. Rosa as she began to clean the wound with sterile saline and then a brown iodine solution. However, she did not deaden the wound. She set up a wooden TV tray near the couch arm and opened a sterile paper towel she had in her bag to use it as a makeshift sterile field. She placed on her mask and put on her rubber gloves and then posed over the raw wound with the round needle in hand that held a long black suture and pronounced, "If you tell me your real name, I will deaden it. If you do not, good luck!"

Angel looked startled and cut his eyes to Commander Morales who said, "Oh, go ahead. All but one of the cats are out of the bag anyway. And another thing Angel, deep cover did not mean being under her covers."

Angel's voice sounded both scared and begging at the same time, "My name is Francisco Cervantes. My beautiful love, please deaden the wound."

Dr. Rosa put down the suture into her sterile field and then picked up a syringe and needle while asking, "I love your real name. Also, I am so proud that you are such a brave police officer, but if you lie to me again, the cut on your side will be deemed a pleasure to you compared to what I will do to you. I assure you; I can do much worse."

Commander Morales stood up with his handcuffs in his left hand and said, "Dr. Rosa, you will need to take a vacation from here as soon as possible. I will tell you when you can return through channels, and also, I will see that Angel gets to you. Are there relatives?"

"Believe it or not, some moved to Germany. I guess I can visit them."

"Good. After Francisco leaves you today, do not try to contact him, and if anyone should happen to ask, his name is Angel."

"Got it."

"Good, now I will leave you two love birds alone, but do not be alarmed if you see a police car pass by several times tonight," said Commander Morales as he exited the door.

Chapter 20

The Cartel Visit

JUAN CALLED CANDICE on her cell phone telling her that it was time for she and her husband to visit their factory.Candice and Nick made everything ready and clandestinely notified Charles and Dr. Calhoun about the meeting in the actual bowels of the beast. First, they would be very vulnerable because they could not carry weapons to the meeting. Both knew that if their lives were in danger, it would depend on how quickly they could take weapons from the guards.

Second, Charles and Dr. Calhoun would be standing by at a diner in the closest town where they would be having lunch. It was a risk worth taking, but everybody was on edge. Also, they were tracking Candice and Nick with their tablets via the chips inside their bodies while appearing to be conducting business at the diner's table. The result would be a possible rescue and also the location of the cartel's main building.

Candice and Nick arrived in his sports car to the small office building for the designated visit. There, they were herded into a red limousine where Juan met them and offered them silk blindfolds and were told they would be shot if they tried to remove them. The ride was long, seemed circular, and had several stops. When the limousine stopped and the motor shut off, Candice and Nick were led inside of a plain but large metal building, and their blindfolds were removed. The inside also looked plain with an inside glass wall whose entry was a large glass door blocking off the right corner showing an office with luxury looking, expensive furniture. Candice noticed the type and strength of the computers in the secluded area while Nick looked at the one way mirrors on the doors and walls. Also, Nick noted that from behind the two doors and the see through mirrors in the office area, it could be a perfect area for an ambush on a non-suspecting victim. A nicely dressed female secretary sat at the large desk and looked up when Juan escorted the Lippincott's into the office area. The secretary spoke good English with only a slight accent as she asked, "May I help you?"

Juan replied in English, "Please inform Mr. Garcia that the Lippincott's have arrived."

The lady behind the desk pushed one of two red buttons on her desk, and the phone rang back within seconds. She spoke a few words in Spanish and then hung up. Within a minute, a slim but pale man came through the glass door of the office area. He looked menacingly at Candice and Nick and said only "Follow me" in English as he turned to go back into the main part of the building. They walked by large groups of tall metal shelves holding what looked like packaged drugs. Also, there was one large group of shelves near the walls that held volumes of large self-cooling aluminum ice chests. Dry ice canisters were also in the back that looked like large open chests that must have held a minimum of a ton of the cold smoking substance. In the very back of the building, in a large designated area, were seven large drones with at least twelve-foot wing spans. Underneath the large body of the planes were types of sling loaders that could possibly carry at least one of the cooling canisters or possibly missiles or small bombs. Candice calculated quickly in her mind that the unmanned crafts could carry a maximum of two hundred and fifty pounds of payload.

Mr. Garcia stopped at a work area just short an area filled with large drones and said, "You met my brother, and he is interested in some aspects of your drones." He pointed his boney right index finger toward a large wooden table near the far wall where the two drones taken from Candice were taken apart; he said, "First, please tell us about the guidance system and how it works."

Candice asked if she could walk over to the two dissected drones that were previously hers. Mr. Garcia approved. She picked up a small round object and said, "This is strong and will even guide your large drones. I can show you how it works. Are you trying to incorporate parts of my drones into your large ones?"

"You are very astute," said Mr. Garcia. "The small drones can help us, but they are limited by their range and payloads. Also, we are concerned about their guidance systems if they are too far away from us. Your drones are different in that they burn fuel instead of using batteries, and they are almost as quiet as the small electric drones; they leave very little exhaust.

Their range is tremendously more than the regular drones of their size, and they are very fuel efficient. We can guide our large drones to a short distance. Also, we cannot get the quietness without sacrificing the power. There are some other things also about your drones that we need in our large drones," said Mr. Garcia who appeared also to be weakening.

"How much range?" asked Candice.

"I apologize. I need to take a break. I will write out all the details for you, and you can visit again," said Mr. Garcia as he began to make his way back to the glass office.

As Mr. Garcia disappeared into his office behind the glass wall, Juan signaled two guards who came forward and stood beside Candice and Nick. They were escorted to a small and dimly lighted break room that was made even darker by cheap wood paneling. They were given strong coffee and some form of sweet hard bread that was not poisonous but not edible either. After an hour of sitting and not speaking, Juan received a call on his cell and escorted them back to the drone work area again. Mr. Garcia looked a little less pale but still appeared weak. "You can ask me anything you like," said Mr. Garcia.

"What is the payload?"

"We are trying to achieve three hundred pounds."

Mr. Garcia walked to the nearest large drones and ordered the loosely fitted panels be removed on the sides of the body. Candice looked and pronounced, "Your engine is too small. May I see your wiring?"

Mr. Garcia said, "Yes."

Candice and Nick walked forward and examined every part they could see on the large drone. After twenty minutes Candice explained, "Your wiring is faulty and will not support the engine. Your guidance electronics are not up to speed. It will not work well as is. Also, a sling loader type of system is too primitive and will cause too much drag. If you need to fly it through trees, you are asking for trouble. How much am I allowed to redesign the drone?"

"Whatever you need," said Mr. Garcia.

"Then take me home where I can work in private. I can redesign your craft in two weeks."

Mr. Garcia looked annoyed and asked, "You are very astute on these matters. Why not sooner than two weeks?"

Candice looked back without expression and explained, "I can design anything within a day, but I cannot guarantee you can get the correct parts. The main research is finding the correct parts to make the drone work. For one thing, it is quite large, and the military may be the only ones who have parts for such a large drone. I assume you are bending the envelope yourself."

"That is correct."

"Can you stop the production of this contraption and go with several propellers? The wings will make landing and takeoff difficult in confined areas. You will always need someone there to make sure the landings and takeoffs do not damage the craft or the merchandise."

"But, we cannot get a large enough payload with propellers," said Mr. Garcia.

"I can guarantee you two hundred pounds with much greater mobility, and no one would need to be there to ensure smooth landings. It would be a much safer craft."

"I can check. We would need to repackage certain items, but two hundred pounds of payload may be better if it is safer for the craft and the load."

"Give me two weeks to learn what is available and what can be done. Otherwise, you may as well go with a full airplane with a living pilot. The drone you are working on will only take a slightly smaller runway than a small airplane," said Candice.

Mr. Garcia asked, "Why is two hundred pounds the maximum payload?"

Candice replied without emotion, "Two hundred pounds is even a stretch, but I really believe I can build it. However, if there is a way to get more weight, you would lose too much maneuverability. You want drones to be maneuverable above all, or else, you can just use an airplane or manned helicopter."

Nick continued to look around the building memorizing as many details as possible about the contents of the building and the terrain and vegetation that he could scarcely see outside the building's dirty windows. The guards stood away from the three but kept their eyes on both while they spoke with the Garcia brother who was second in command of the cartel. Candice continued to speak with Mr. Garcia about the plans and what she could do with the available technology. Finally, Mr. Garcia told them they could return to their homes and that Juan would contact them in two weeks to retrieve the plans for the new drone.

Juan suddenly walked into the area where the three were gathered with two guards following. Candice looked at Mr. Garcia just before she was blindfolded by the guards and proclaimed, "One other thing, I do not want to return to this building again. I do not like being blindfolded and getting car sick from your driver going in circles. Get me a place in a town close to where I live to build this thing."

Mr. Garcia looked at them both and replied, "I make no promises, but my brother and I will consider your request."

The ride back, to Candice's disgust, was like the trip to the building with a slowing, speeding, sudden stopping, and many sharp turns. Both Candice and Nick felt car sick and exhausted after the hour long ride. They were dropped off at their car and had to wait about a half hour to get over the ride before beginning the drive home.

Nick asked Candice, after she showed him the dead bug in the corner of her tablet, "Can you really build it?"

Candice replied, "I think so, but it will be difficult. However, the idea is not to build it but to slow them down. Their drone designs are not that bad. Maybe we can capitalize on Mr. Garcia's sickness."

"Candice, can you record what I am about to say?"

"Sure. Why?"

"I need to tell you everything I saw while you were speaking to the others about the new drone." Nick began to say every detail he remembered to include every box, canister, shelf, door, and even the terrain and vegetation he could make out outside the building's windows. She listened to each detail amazed at Nick's memory. Then, he began to list all the things that he saw inside the office area to include the see through mirrors in the doors and on the wall.

Candice recorded the entire conversation, encoded it, and sent it immediately to Charles and Dr. Calhoun.

Chapter 21

Prophetic Dreams

CHARLES AWOKE AGAIN from the same dream, looked at the clock that read 2:31AM, got up from bed, and prayed. The small air-conditioner was beginning to malfunction in his small bedroom, so he thought about sleeping on the uncomfortable couch in his office. Instead, he went to his office, turned on the air conditioner, and began to write the dream as he remembered again to see if any details had changed.

The dream was about a large lion that kept stalking him but could never catch him. In fact, the cat kept running into blind alleys and corners that became mazes. Yet, the cat persisted. Because the cat was stalking him and neglecting to hunt and eat, it was getting skinny with its hip bones sticking up from its body like two pins in the air. Its belly was slim. It had a mane, but when viewed from the back, it was definitely female.

He began to pray for an answer to the dream, and Nick's name suddenly appeared in his mind. Reaching for the tablet, he sent out a secured e-mail to both Candice and Nick asking for Nick to call him as soon as he awakened and got an immediate response from Candice. Nick had just awakened from a dream also and was telling the dream to Candice when the tablet signaled her.

Candice wrote back, "We need to talk with you also. Nick is having dreams, not nightmares, but dreams. They are confusing to us. They are mainly about houses: some big, some small, and some weird. Tonight, he dreamed about a cat that had a mane but was a female. The cat was stalking you Charles."

Charles wrote back, "It is the same dream that just awakened me."

"Why the same dream?"

"It is a message. I do not understand it yet."

"Where and when can we meet?"

"I will find a way. Meanwhile, be very careful. I feel the law has something to do with this, but it is just a feeling."

"The law? You mean like the police?"

"Maybe. But, I think it is higher up. Maybe it is the government. I do not know, but both of you be very careful."

"We will, but can I ask you one more thing?"

"Sure."

"Nick wants to know why him. He is saying that an atheist who does not believe in spiritual things and should not be having dreams like this."

"Is he afraid?"

"No, he just says he's confused."

"Tell him that the same dreams by two different people confirms the importance of the dream. Also, I need to get this message out to Dr. Calhoun. The reason why the other attempts did not work concerning the take down of this cartel by both the US and Mexican governments is because of the spiritual aspects of this mission. Someone knows what they are doing but is held back on their knowledge. The mazes and blind corners mean whatever authority that is stalking me runs into dead ends, but it knows I am out here somewhere and keeps searching."

Candice wrote back, "Nick may not be frightened right now, but I am. How do you fight something you can't see?"

"You do not fight it; God fights it. If the starving lion represents the judge, I surmise there are not enough human sacrifices to accomplish what she is trying to do. However, I do not know how the sacrifices are being blocked. We need to pray a lot about this."

"I pray Charles, but I do not know how to fight this," said Candice.

"This is why I am here. I am here, even though I am not the best according to some for the job due to my wife being killed by the cartel."

"Are you on top of the tetrahedron right now," asked Candice.

"No, God is, but Nick and I share some of the load. Anyway, I need to speak with Nick in person, and if possible, I need to speak with you and Dr. Calhoun also. This is very important. Now, try to get some sleep but be very careful."

"Done. Good night Charles."

"Good night Candice."

The morning came sunny, dry, and hot when Nick awoke noting Candice was reading her tablet while sitting up in bed. She leaned over to Nick and said, "Hello, how are you this morning?"

"Rather sleepy. The dreams keep coming, and I seem to have no control over them."

"Was it a house dream again?" she asked with a serious voice.

"No, it is the continued dream, just like the one before, about the lioness with the mane."

"The message must be very important."

"If it is a message. Are you sure the dreams were the same?"

"Well, Charles knew about the mazes and blind corners the cat kept running into, and we didn't say anything about it to him. I'd say it's the same dream. Anyway, Charles has a way for us to meet and help some people at the same time."

"What's Charles' plan, and what time is it?" asked Nick.

"Almost eight-thirty. I let you sleep a little later than usual thinking you needed the rest. The plan is to get some patients seen by a specialist at the hospital in Valladolid. I'm, uh we're, expecting a phone call any time. It will be bugged."

"Ok, what do I do?"

"Pay for their surgeries."

The phone rang and Candice answered, "hello." The silent alarm on the tablet showed a crawling insect.

Charles' voice sounded on the other end, "Hello, this is Charles Dorgan; I hope you are well."

"Dr. Dorgan, it is pleasant that you should call. What can we do for you?"

"I am not calling for myself, but I do have a request if you have the time this morning to speak with me."

"I am always glad to hear from you. We need to get together for dinner."

"I would like that, but I come begging today. There are seven people who need surgery by an ear, nose, and throat specialist. There is a specialist in

Valladolid, but he needs to be paid. You are more than generous to our mission service, but could you find it in the goodness of your heart to help?"

"Let me ask Nick. He's right here." The phone fell silent for a minute and she came back on. "Nick says he will pay all the expenses."

"Great," said Charles. "Dr. Calhoun is a general surgeon, but he does not feel comfortable with ENT surgeries. He is very concerned about one man who has tonsils that are touching each other. This is known as kissing tonsils, and the man is in a lot of pain. Dr. Calhoun would like to get him seen today if that is possible."

"Why don't we meet you. Nick and I plan to be near Valladolid today. I am sure Nick will not mind stopping by the hospital. Ask Dr. Calhoun if he can have the man there, and we can at least get him signed up."

Charles replied, "Dr. Calhoun is usually very busy, but I can call him and see. Do you mind if I bring the man if Dr. Calhoun cannot make the trip? Either way, I can get a consult from Dr. Calhoun."

"We do not mind at all. We can work around our plans."

"Thank you very much. You are wonderful for this, and I am sure the people will be very thankful."

"Nick always asks that the people he helps will not know."

"Either way, I thank you, and I am sure Dr. Calhoun is very thankful also."

"You are very welcome."

"Good-bye Mrs. Lippincott."

"Good-bye."

Candice and Nick, who had already guaranteed the payment for the surgery via telephone, walked into the hospital's main waiting area where Charles, who had picked up the patient with the bad tonsils from his home met with him and explained that Dr. Calhoun had signed the consult earlier but was busy. Charles reported that Dr. Calhoun wanted to meet with them later at his clinic. The patient was a short, stocky man who appeared in his late fifties or early sixties. Also, the patient insisted that he meet Candice and Nick prior to his examination in order to thank them for their charity. Candice and Nick appeared embarrassed, but both stood to meet the patient.

Charles began by introducing the patient, "Mr. and Mrs. Lippincott, this is Senior Arturo Fuentes, and he asks that I translate for him presently. He wishes to thank you personally." Charles turned to Senor Fuentes and did the introduction in Spanish. Arturo smiled and nodded his head to Candice and Nick and began to speak in Spanish. Charles translated, "He says that he is in pain and is very thankful for your help."

Candice and Nick looked at the patient and reported that he was very welcome. A man in a dark blue suit, white shirt, and light blue tie came into the waiting area and asked if everyone could come to his office. The four followed the man down the well-polished light blue tile floor hall. The hallway smelled strongly of alcohol and disinfectant. Hospital personnel in scrubs walked by speaking in Spanish. When they entered the office, Nick noted that it was plain and had a well-polished desk and well-polished woodened chairs. The man introduced himself in English and thanked Nick, Candice, and Charles for their time. The patient looked as if he felt out of place in the office. A young man brought in a manila folder and an ink pen. He handed the papers to Arturo and began to speak with him about the surgical paperwork in Spanish. Then, Arturo passed the papers to Charles. Charles read each page carefully out loud and in Spanish, and Arturo shook his head in approval and signed and initialed each sheet as designated. When the paperwork was finished, Arturo asked how much would be the cost, and Charles informed him in Spanish.

Arturo appeared rattled by the amount and looked at Nick with tears in his eyes and said in Spanish, "If there is ever anything I can do for you, please just ask me. From this day, you and your family will forever be in our prayers."

Charles translated, and both Candice and Nick were moved by the heartfelt thank you. Nick managed to squeeze out a "You are welcome" in broken Spanish while Candice had tears streaming down her face. With the closure of the business, Arturo stood up and grabbed Charles' right hand with both hands and shook it vigorously. Then, he moved to Nick and Candice and shook their hands.

The hospital administrator moved to the door and politely gestured while asking if anyone had any other questions in English and then repeated the question in Spanish. Then, he asked if anyone would like a coffee, water, or other refreshment before leaving. Everyone declined.

The four walked from the administrator's office through the main lobby and to the outside. Charles reported he would take Arturo home and would then drive to the clinic to meet with Candice, Nick, and Dr. Calhoun. Nick asked about transportation to pre-op on the day of surgery, and Charles assured everybody that he planned to bring both the patient and his family to the hospital and would stay with them that day. Nick thanked Charles again and all drove away.

The next morning Nick awoke again from a dream; the clock read 3:16AM, and Candice appeared asleep but restless. She began to stir and then flattened her left hand on Nick's chest and used pressure to push herself upward while bringing her knees up under her chest. Nick looked up at her sleepy eyes and said, "I am sorry that I woke you up."

Candice said, "That's OK. You are talking in your sleep again. Are the bad dreams back?"

"No, this dream is about Arturo. You know, he's the guy with the kissing tonsils. I keep seeing his face, but he is not speaking. He is overseeing a large valley that is full of trees, crops, and animals like cattle, sheep, chickens, and other food animals. The whole valley looks fertile and lush with a stream of crystal clear water flowing through it. But, right in front of Arturo is a large boat with the decks covered with blood. He is looking past the boat into the valley.

"Nick, did you see how strong he looked?"

"Pretty good for a man his age. Also, he must have been in the military. If he were in the US Army, I would guess he was at least a top sergeant."

"I agree Nick. I wonder what the valley and the boat with decks covered with blood mean."

"Don't know. It is good we have Charles."

Candice had a sleepy but curious look on her face as she looked down at Nick. She wanted to lean down and kiss him, but she fought back the urge. Instead she asked, "Nick, you don't believe in God, but these dreams seem to be pretty spiritual. What is giving you the dreams?"

Nick looked back at Candice with a quirky smile and began to speak as if he was giving a lecture, "There is a great force that surrounds us all, and if you look sideways out of your eyes as hard as you can for several minutes, sometimes you can see the edges of the force. You need to push your eyes as hard as you can toward the right and never the left unless you are left handed. Soon, you will begin to see colors and get a slight headache. Do not be afraid of the headache; it is signaling you about the other dimension of force."

Candice crossed her eyes and held her mouth wide open for a few seconds. She moved her face down toward Nick's face making it painful for him to focus. She asked, "Does it hurt to look at me? Do your eyes feel funny? I am demonstrating the force that says you are full of it. I wanted to kiss you, and now, I want to beat you up."

"I'll take either."

With that, Candice settled back down beside Nick and laid her left hand back on his chest. She snuggled and began to speak in a sleepy voice, "I never want to hear you try to explain anything spiritual again. You know I can both fight and shoot."

"Whatever, my beautiful wife."

Candice began to snuggle again against Nick's side as he settled a little in bed and then said, "And another thing, that is another subject on my list that is off limits. You are never to remind me that I asked."

"Well, you did ask. Ouch!"

CHAPTER 22

Angel and Arturo

ANGEL MADE ARRANGEMENTS to drive Arturo to his surgery and to retrieve him after the recovery from the tonsil removal.Charles was notified the day before by the hospital and felt that he should not be there anyway but could not define the reason, so he contacted the others and alerted them that something else was happening that he did not understand.

Arturo, after the surgery, reported that his throat was very dry. Angel had cold water handy, but it seemed to irritate more than it seemed to wet the back of Arturo's throat.Also, Arturo could speak but not well and mostly in whispers. The car was cool inside from the air conditioner that Angel kept turned to a little higher temperature than was normal coldness for him. Overall, Arturo seemed very pleased with his friend.

Arturo looked at Angel's face and his slow deliberate movements and asked, "Why are you guarding yourself, and where did those bruises and cuts come from on your face?"

Angel showed no expression on his face as he answered, "The prisoners in our illustrious jail are not very friendly."

"Are you out on bail?"

"No, I am free for now or at least until they make up some other bogus charges."

"Was anything said about our militia?" asked Arturo.

"No, it is another matter. My past is not good. Sometimes, they try to link me to other things. I am very careful not to speak about our militia." Arturo looked uncomfortable but trusted Angel, so he decided to leave the topic for now. Angel continued, "This is a good time to tell you; I may be arrested again. There is a past that I cannot talk about now. Also, my fiancé and I are separating for a while for her safety. If it happens again, do not try to get me out of jail. So far, I am able to get out by myself."

"I suppose your past is something you will tell me about someday."

Angel, taking his eyes off the road for a few seconds, looked at Arturo eye to eye and said, "Please trust me. I want only the best for you and our militia."

"Some militia. I will say this to you only. We are nineteen men strong counting you and myself."

"So, you got a couple more?"

"Yes. Angel, a couple more is actually good. I should be happy that we have anybody."

"Arturo, how are we doing on weapons and supplies?"

"Good enough for one good attack. Talk about small."

"Are we still disguising ourselves as a gun club?"

"Yes, there is one other thing. The woman judge is sending new members to the gun clubs. It is getting more difficult to keep the militia separated from the other members. However, nobody is snitching on us." Angel passed Arturo's home causing him to look confused. Arturo was getting sick at his stomach from the surgery and the medications. He wanted to be home.

Angel sensing his alarm reached in his pocket taking out his cell phone and said, "Call your wife."

Arturo scrolled down on his phone and swiped to make the call. His wife's voice sounded great on the other end, "Arturo, I love you. Angel is bringing you to me at a hotel room. I feel vulnerable right now with you hurt. Are you upset with me?"

"No. But, why did Angel not tell me?"

"He wants to keep your whereabouts quiet the same as me. We are both afraid of bugs. He believes we are safe right now as long as we stay here."

Turning into the five story and five-star hotel, Angel said, "Arturo, we are here. Your wife is meeting us, and I am not coming in."

Arturo's wife met him in the under parking at the hotel just in front of the main door. Angel immediately got out of the car, walked around the front to the passenger door and opened it for Arturo. Arturo got out slowly but was able to hug his wife, and both disappeared arm and arm in the lobby.

Angel drove to the parking lot to the side of the hotel, paid for his parking, and sat in the car watching closely. Suddenly, two police officers pulled in front of his car with the sirens blaring and lights flashing. They got out of their squad car with guns drawn and quickly took Angel into custody. The handcuffs were too tight, and his arms began to hurt. Also, the police officers were very rough with Angel slamming his head against the side of the police car as he was pushed into the back seat. The blood began to drip down on his light blue shirt as he appeared to fight for consciousness. Arturo and his wife heard the sirens from the lobby and had stepped outside to witness Angel's arrest and looked on in horror feeling helpless as the police car drove away.

The police officer who placed Angel into the back seat suddenly looked around and said, "My hand hurts after I blocked the door facing with it. It is not a good cushion for your head. I guess the blood pellet is a bit much. Your blue shirt is ruined."

"It is, but I do thank you for keeping my head from that bump. Also, thank you for not hitting my right side. What is up?"

The policeman driving said, "Commander wants to meet with you in private."

"To get picked up by his very special officers is a real treat. How many of you does he trust?"

The driver said, "We do not know, but it must be only a few. Since you brought it up, I think he is planning a general sweep of all the criminals in our department."

"A sweep is good, but remember, a uniformed officer makes less than four hundred pesos per month. You cannot even live on that. One drug deal with the cartel can get an officer a year's wages in one hour."

"Believe me; he is a good man to work for, but those above him hate him," said the driver.

"Yes, I realize that," replied Angel.

The driver suddenly hit his brakes, took a sharp left, and ended up under a bridge. Angel began to get a little afraid until he saw Commander Morales walking toward the car. The Commander opened the back door, took Angel out of the back seat, and took the cuffs off him. Helping him to his personal car, Commander Morales said a loud "thank you" to the men who brought him Angel.

Angel looked surprised as Commander Morales got under the wheel and explained, "The following is for your ears only; our great judge is planning another sacrifice soon. For some reason, she is not as active as she used to be. I want her shut down, but she knows a lot of people above me. I do not know who I can trust. I need you to concentrate on the militia and their plans against the cartel."

"Commander, what are you thinking?"

"What I should not be thinking. I know you trust them. How well trained are the militia men?"

"Arturo is good on some things but lacks in others. Tactically, he is brilliant, but strategically, he is not so good. You know he was a top sergeant in the military, and I would want no one else leading me into combat."

"So, he is best when the enemy is close."

"Yes."

"How is he concerning his men's safety? The last thing in the world I need is a bunch of dead civilians on my hands."

"He stresses survival all the time while also concentrating on the mission. He is well balanced as a leader. Also, his men respect him, and I believe, they will follow him in the worse conditions."

"Angel, I am asking you to do something that is somewhat outside the circle of the law. If you refuse, I understand. There are no orders past this but just requests."

"Say the requests."

"I want you to utilize the militia if necessary to help defeat the cartel. I know the Garcia brothers are partners with the judge, and I will have my hands full trying to shut both the cartel and the judge down. At this time, I cannot pass up the potential of nineteen well trained men with weapons. Also, I believe they can be trusted."

"Understood," said Angel as he took in a deep breath and let it out slowly, "If I get caught, what happens?"

"Let me put it this way. Both our carcasses will be stuck to a wall somewhere in a Mayan pyramid with politicians making it a point to spit on us prior to each election."

"What do I get if we succeed?"

"Your usual low pay with a need to keep quiet about everything."

"Commander, you make it sound so tempting. With all the benefits you mentioned, I would have to say that I'm in. I want to ask another question though."

The Commander looked relieved but braced himself for Angel's next question and said, "ask."

"How is my fiancé?"

"On the plane to Germany. One of my men is on the plane also, but she does not know. He is there to protect her."

"Thanks. That is a load off my mind."

The Commander looked at Angel again and proclaimed, "I am taking you out for a couple of days, and then, you are to infiltrate back into the militia." With the last words, Commander Morales reached in his pocket and pulled out a black metal watch with a square face and said, "Take this."

"Oh, you bought me a watch. I did not know that you cared. Being black, it will go with everything I own."

"Well, I do care, and you do not act smart with me. That watch tells me where you are at all times with ten-digit grid coordinates, and it also has a microphone in it. When you push the top button three times, I can hear your conversations and things that are happening around you. Now, put it on and do not take it off, even to sleep."

"Thank you for the watch. I really mean that. Thank you."

"I am the only one keyed in on it. Do not tell anybody about it, and I mean nobody."

"Yes sir. I will not."

Pulling off the road and driving through trees on a dirt road, Commander Morales pulled in front of a small cabin that looked to have all the amenities of home. He stopped the car and said, "Angel, there is an SUV parked in the back. Here are the keys. Now, try and get some rest. Things will most likely get horrible soon enough. Remember, you can hardly trust anyone. Also, here are some other keys."

"What are these for," asked Angel.

"Airport locker keys with money, luggage, new credit cards in your name, and a set of tickets to somewhere safe. If anything happens to me, get there fast and get out of here."

"Is it that serious?"

"No, it is worse. Now, get out and stay here awhile. Weapons are hidden in a false wall in the back of the hall closet. Load them and keep them near. Also, a suture removal kit is on the first shelf of the kitchen cabinet nearest the left side of the refrigerator."

"Whose cabin is this, Commander?"

"Mine, now get out and be safe."

Angel got out of the car with both sets of keys. As he approached the house, he heard the Commander drive away quickly. He unlocked the door and stepped inside to a plain wooden structure with dust covers over all the furniture. He tried the light switch in the living area, and the light came on. He tried the hot water in the small bathroom sink, and the water came on and began to get warm. After he secured the AK 47 and the 9mm semi-automatic pistol from the hall closet, he wandered to every room checking for anything unusual. His last stop was the kitchen where he found recently cooked food in the refrigerator and an ample supply of dried and canned foods in the cabinets. His Commander had thought everything out well, and he was sure that the Commander's wife had made the food for him. He checked the grounds, came back into the cabin, locked the doors, and after removing the sheet acting as a dust cover for the bed, laid down and went to sleep.

Arturo awoke the next morning beside his wife who was beginning to stir after the sunlight hit her face through the window. She raised up in bed while looking back at Arturo and asked, "How are you this morning?"

Arturo swallowed hard and said in a low, raspy voice, "sore throat."

"Here, I will get you some ice water. Maybe the cold will help your throat."

"Thank you."

Arturo's wife disappeared out of the hotel room while in her nightgown for a short time and then reappeared with the ice bucket dripping from the condensation. She looked at her husband of twenty-nine years and said, "I know you have questions about how we could afford this. It is Angel's doing. He came up with the money."

"I knew we could not afford it. He is the best man I ever knew."

"Why did you not try to help him with the arrest yesterday?"

"He told me not to help. He said he could get out of trouble. It worried me when I saw his head bleeding. Also, I am in no shape right now to try and help anybody."

"Are you sure he will be well? He was bleeding as they left."

"I know, but he told me to do nothing. You know, he already had stitches in his side from a night in jail."

"No, I did not know that."

"He is my right-hand man in the militia. I am so worried about him."

"Well, Angel usually gets out of problems without your help, or at least, that is what you always tell me. I can contact the militia members for you and have them try to find out what is happening."

"No, it is too much of a chance that we will be exposed. I just need to trust him."

"Understood. Oh, I got a call while you were in the hospital. The rich man who paid for your surgery asked for me to call him today and tell him how you are doing. Do you mind if I call?"

"Not at all. Why would a rich man from America even worry about me? I can certainly not give him anything. But, you speak English, and I do not. I would like to invite him to our home when it is safer for dinner."

"Do you think he would come? He is certainly not used to what we could fix for him."

"But, he did so much for me. I would like to just meet with him again and speak with him. I owe him so much. Please ask him for me. Tell him we will call him later with the time."

"Will you feel bad if he says no?"

"No. But, at least we asked."

Chapter 23

Juan's Intrusion

THE AIR SEEMED heavy as if rain was coming while lightening showed in the distance as Candice and Nick pulled into their driveway after a short trip to the country for their bird studies. The home had only the outside lights left on. This was the usual way the maid and chef left when Candice and Nick did not come home before the end of their help's work days. Nick walked into the house after he hit the button on the control in his right hand that unlocked the electronic lock on the door and shut down the alarm and surveillance devices in the home. Candice followed Nick through the front door and flipped on the light for the living room. To their surprise, there sat Juan in the overstuffed leather recliner in the living room holding a pistol with an attached silencer in his right hand. He had stretched both arms the full extent of the chair arms and appeared totally relaxed. At each side of Juan was a large man, and each were dressed in a black suit, white shirt, and black tie holding 9mm fully automatic weapons. Neither Candice nor Nick had a readily available weapon.

Juan looked at both standing in front of him and spoke English in his heavy Hispanic accent, "I came by to see the progress on the drone plans and to let you know we are making a place for you to work on them. I will tell you more as I get information. Now, do not be alarmed, but I also want to bring you some news from my leader. It seems that Candice belongs to me if anything should happen to you Nick."

Candice said angrily, "I will send you my plans at the end of the two weeks. That is agreed upon by Mr. Garcia. Juan, if you ever try to touch me, you will not like what happens next."

Juan nodded and said, "Do not press your luck, but I can wait for the plans."

Nick looked angry and tried to figure how quickly he could move to take out the three men in front of him or at least equal the odds somewhat. It seemed the only thing to do was try to get back out the door and hope nobody was outside. To ensure he was the most accessible target, he would place Candice in front of him going out the door and then move in front of Candice once outside. Candice's voice broke his thought pattern when she said, "Are you only wanting to talk?"

Juan looked at Candice coldly and said a simple and expressionless, "yes."

Nick felt himself boiling inside and promised to Juan, "If you touch her, I'll kill you, and it will not be a good death."

Juan looked at Nick with all the disgust he could muster and proclaimed, "After the cartel gets through with you, you will not be able to hurt me or anyone else."

Candice felt the anger coming up from her chest which began to hurt as she said, "If you hurt Nick, I'll do all I can to tear you and the cartel apart."

Juan then said, "Maybe you would feel more comfortable if I sent my two men outside? They do not understand English anyway." Juan told the two men in Spanish to leave the room.

Juan waited until the front door was closed and said, "You know I can kill you anytime, but tonight is not the night."

Nick looked Juan in the eye and said, "The cartel can be made to regret trying to give you Candice."

"Oh Nick, I do not want Candice except for some travel by air where she will have to do everything she is told."

The words slipped from Candice before she thought it out completely, "Do you want misery?"

"Candice, the travel will be something you want to do, and you will like me or maybe even love me before the trip is over."

With anger increasing, Candice pronounced, "You are a conceited fool!"

Juan looked around the room with his eyes landing back on Candice. He appeared to look at every curve on her body and then smiled before he said, "Candice, I do not want to argue with you or Nick, but these things are not predictions; they are prophecies. You will really like me someday after I am through with you whether I am conceited or not. As for you Nick, I promise you will not be able to touch me for anything I do concerning you or Candice."

Nick said, "If I can only kill one person here, it will be you."

"Promises," said Juan. "Many are made, and few are kept." Then, Juan slowly unscrewed the silencer from the pistol and placed it in his inside coat pocket. He placed the pistol into his tan leather holster underneath his suit coat and then proclaimed, "Any attempt on your parts to stop me from leaving will get all four of you killed."

Candice was startled but asked, "the four of us?"

"Yes Candice, your maid and cook are tied and gagged in your bedroom upstairs. Do not worry. We did not rape or harm them this time but tell them this exactly as I say this to you. If they try to stop me and my men again, there will be two deaths in this house. He looked at Nick and told him to repeat it verbatim. Nick, for the sake of the others in the home and with an angry voice, repeated the sentence as said word for word. Juan stood up and moved by them toward the door passing at the side of Candice so close that she could feel and smell his breath. It smelled like soured coffee. He opened the door and began to walk outside but paused and said, "Remember and think about everything I told you." Juan looked at both while saying in a laughing voice, "I will see both of you later. Now, try to sleep if you can." Juan closed the door while laughing; the motor of a car was heard, and for a few seconds, it was drowned out by thunder. It had begun to rain outside, and Juan, the two men, and the car they were driving totally disappeared.

Nick quickly made his way to his pistol hidden downstairs and then covered Candice as she made her way to their bedroom where she found both the chef and maid lying across the bed with their faces down with their hands and feet tied. She turned over each one of the ladies carefully to ensure no booby traps and then pulled the gags and untied each one. Candice and Nick were not frightened but were very angry. Candice hugged the maid first and then the chef as they cried. She assured them that they would take them home tonight and that they would not need to return tomorrow. Both were frightened but reported they would call some special friends to come and get them. Also, both agreed that they would take tomorrow off but would be back to continue to work.

Candice reluctantly agreed but began to notice a much larger problem. Suddenly, Candice saw coldness in Nick's eyes that she had never witnessed before. He placed the pistol in his belt and began to make his way toward the closet safe in their bedroom where his shotguns were kept. She saw him begin to sort the ammunition into a carry bag with an efficient and non-feeling methodology. Candice looked on with some surprise, and then it hit her. She moved quickly to his side and spoke quickly, "Nick, you will jeopardize the whole mission. We are OK."

Nick did not answer and continued to pack his ammunition in a small back pack kept near the guns.

"Please Nick, talk to me. I am sending the help home. They are alright. We are alright. Don't do this."

Something seemed to snap in Nick, and he said with anger in his voice, "They threatened you."

"Juan threatened me. I can take care of myself. Now, calm down."

While Nick stood like a statue, Candice began to unpack the bag and placed the guns back into the closet safe. Then, she came back to Nick and hugged him from the back. "Nick, your anger is too cold. I do not want to see this again."

At first, Nick tried to pull away but then just settled into her arms as she continued to squeeze with all her might. Also, he heard her crying, and he began to break down. He managed to squeak out, "I don't want you hurt. I'll kill anybody who tries to hurt you."

"Nick, remember Charles spoke to you about this in the cabin in Tennessee. Your feelings will make you go cold if somebody you love is in trouble. I signed up for this. You can't always protect me. I don't want to die, but it is possible. If it happens, you will need to continue the mission and not endanger Charles or Dr. Calhoun."

"I know you are right, but the only thing that saved Juan's life tonight is that he had weapons and I didn't."

"I know. Also, it's my fault Nick. He should not have made it in here without my knowing."

Nick regained his sanity and began to speak like his usual self, "No, it's not your fault. Either the maid or the cook let them in. Can we trust them?"

"I think so. I think Juan found a way to override the system and came in. Did you see the lock on the door?"

"I did not notice."

"It is marked, and I bet his fingerprints are on it. I will check my alarms. I think Juan either has help, or he is more than a thug. He may be more dangerous than we think. Are you better now? I want to check my laptop for any information I can gather on the break-in."

"I am OK, but I really want to kiss and hold you right now."

Her mind went back to the help who had moved nervously outside when they saw how Nick was acting. They did not seem too alarmed and were awaiting silently within the light of the porch. Candice went to the door and said, "I am so sorry about what happened. Are both of you still OK?"

The maid looked at Candice and said, "We will not tell what happened tonight. We like working for you. Do not worry about us; we will be alright."

Car lights showed at the end of the driveway and slowly approached toward them. The chef proclaimed, "That is our ride. We will be back day after tomorrow."

"OK," said Candice. "Please be careful, and once again, I am so sorry about what happened tonight."

The car stopped, and two men immediately got out, and each opened a back door. The women got into the car, and it quickly sped away. Candice tried as best she could to memorize the men's faces and the tags on the car. Then, she went back inside and recorded her memories. Nick had also watched the help being picked up and discussed the things he had memorized with Candice. After they were satisfied that they had recorded all they could remember, Nick stood still feeling guilty while Candice went to her small room off the bedroom to her vanity and picked up the small step stool that she used to get to the top shelf in her closet. She returned downstairs and placed the stool at Nick's feet and then climbed up into his arms and stared at him face to face.

"I thought you left me," said Nick.

"I thought you might want to kiss me," she said as she looked into his eyes. Both closed their eyes and kissed several times while holding each other tightly. Then Candice took Nick's arms and moved them down to his side while saying, "If we don't stop, I may get pregnant."

Nick strained as he pulled himself away completely breaking their contact, "You are right."

"If you ask me Nick, I probably will, so don't ask me."

Nick walked over to the dresser and picked up her laptop and pronounced, "I believe you have work to do. I'm going outside to secure the grounds, work out, and run twenty-five miles after I do a thousand push-ups."

As Candice sat on the edge of the bed and began to use her laptop she said, "My poor Nick, I would love the fact that you are in so much pain, except I am wanting more myself. I may need to work out with you later. When will you be running the twenty-five miles?"

She continued to assess each part of the electronic system via her laptop that protected the home and signaled alerts for intruders. The system was overridden by some kind of device she could not immediately identify.She continued to speak with Nick as he was putting on running shorts and tennis shoes. She continued to push the lap top keys. Quickly, she reached for her tablet that lay on the bed and awakened it.

"Did you find it?" asked Nick.

"Got it narrowed to three devices. It may take a little while."

"He must be pretty good to make you work this hard."

"Got it. Juan used a magnet. I did not even think about it. He fried the electronic locks with what would seem a very powerful magnet. Seems there is a flaw in the system."

"Can it be fixed?"

"Of course, Nick. It's called a dead bolt."

"Oh, so much for technology."

"Anyway, no more kissing like we just did. Who taught you anyway?"

Nick looked at her while rapidly blinking his eyes, "Nobody taught me. With me, making love just comes naturally."

Candice looked up from her work at Nick and stared at him with that cute look Nick had come to know and surrender to and said, "Really? I don't believe you. I did not want you to answer, but I did not want you to lie either."

Nick looked at Candice sadly and said, "You know I kissed and loved my wife."

Candice sat for a few seconds knowing she had forgotten totally that Nick had a real past. She looked at Nick and replied with a deeply heartfelt, "I am so sorry. Please forgive me."

"It is OK.Everything is well between us, but I want you to know that whatever happens, I love you," said Nick.

"I love you too, but don't ask me to say it again anytime soon. You are much too dangerous with feelings. Are you taking lessons from Charles?"

"No, I am just speaking dangerously from my heart, and I am going outside to kill some feelings with physical pain. Now, get in your running gear; I will meet you outside. By the way, what if Juan and his thugs are out there?"

"Then," she said as she held up her small pistol in her right hand, "It's their problem. Besides, I'm beginning to get turned on while watching you. Now, go outside. We'll get a deadbolt tomorrow."

CHAPTER 24

Dinner with Arturo

NICK WAS WALKING through the home when he felt the vibration of his cell phone. He answered, and Arturo wife's voice was on the other end. She spoke in a heavy accent that sometimes Nick had problems understanding. She asked, "Mr. Lippincott, is this you?"

"Yes."

"Mr. Lippincott, this is Arturo's wife. We spoke the day after his surgery about your coming to dinner at our home." There was slight worry in her voice as she asked, "Do you still want to come?"

"Yes, we do. It would be an honor."

"Is there a certain food you would like?"

"I would really like to just have home cooked food like you usually fix for Arturo and yourself. I know it will be wonderful."

"Do you like beer? You probably prefer wine."

"I love beer. Please, just prepare foods like you would normally cook. It would be wonderful I am sure."

Candice and Nick arrived in the SUV to the small one-bedroom home in the middle of the village where Arturo lives. The house was immaculate on the outside with a rock garden for a yard and a large desert elm growing from the smoothed rocks in the front. The roof was metal. Arturo's wife came out the door first with Arturo trailing behind. They stopped on the sidewalk while Nick was opening Candice's door. Candice stood up noting that her small frame looked even smaller while standing in front of Arturo's tall muscular wife. Both could smell the aroma of peppers and spices coming from the kitchen. Nick looked at Arturo and asked, "How are you?"

Arturo looked to his wife who immediately translated for him. Then she interpreted back his reply to Nick who was trying to interpret the Spanish for himself but had little luck due to the rapid speaking. Arturo's wife turned back toward Nick and said, "He says that he is doing much better thanks to you. We both wish to thank you and welcome you to our home."

Nick looked at Candice and then to Arturo's wife, "Please call me Nick and my wife wishes to be called Candice. May I know and call you by your first name?"

Arturo's wife looked slightly embarrassed as she said, "Please call me Paloma."

Candice said, "That is a beautiful name. Does it mean dove?"

Paloma smiled and said, "Yes Candice, it means dove. Thank you for knowing that." Then, she motioned for all to go into the house.

When the front door was opened by Arturo, Nick pronounced, "The smells from the kitchen are wonderful."

Arturo motioned for them to sit down in their modest living room. He disappeared behind the dark blue cloth curtain separating the living room from the kitchen and then reappeared with a tray that held a light golden beer in four frosted glasses, a bowl of queso made with homemade cheese and fresh vegetables to include peppers, onions, and tomatoes. Paloma followed with a large bowl of home cooked corn tortilla chips that were hot and salty. They sat the food in front of Candice and Nick who sat side by side on the small couch. Paloma explained that the guests must take the first bite. Candice immediately picked up a chip and dragged it through the queso. She said a big, "umm" while looking at Paloma and declaring, "Oh, this is so good!"

Nick picked up a chip and did the same with much the same response. Then Nick took a beer from the tray, looked at it in the frosted glass, took a drink and asked, "Paloma, where did you get this? I would love to purchase a case of this-maybe two cases."

Arturo thought he knew what Nick had said from his expression and spoke some of the little English he knew, "I make it."

Nick began to brag on the taste and the body while Paloma warned, "If you are not used to drinking homemade beer, you leave some in the bottom of the bottle so you will not get the dregs. That is why we served it to you in a glass. I tell you this because we have plenty, and you can take some with you if you like it."

" Oh, I love it," proclaimed Nick.

Paloma disappeared through the curtain again, and her voice came from the kitchen declaring, "It is ready. Please come and eat. You can wash your hands in the bathroom sink in the hall." She said something in rapid Spanish, and Arturo stood up and pointed to the right-side door in the small adjoining hallway. Then, he disappeared behind the curtain to help with setting the meal on the table.

Candice and Nick sat down at the small bright green table in the kitchen and noted the chicken cooked in banana leaves with the smells permeating the room. The chicken was farm raised and had little fat but was succulent and spiced to perfection. Also, the beer was perfect with the meal.

Arturo sat at the head of the table and pushed food first to Candice and then to Nick. Paloma made sure that the chicken was unwrapped correctly. Side dishes included steamed carrots flavored with vanilla beans and delicious starchy and sticky tasting plantain fritters. Nick ate so much he began to get embarrassed and proclaimed, "Paloma, I cannot eat another bite. This is just delicious, and the beer is perfect with the meal." Candice nodded her head and appeared to be straining as she backed away from the goodness on the table.

Paloma looked at Candice first and then Nick and said, "I did not know, but I made a small dessert."

Nick looked pained, but he said, "I at least want to taste it." Candice agreed.

Paloma got up and pulled four small bowls from her ancient refrigerator freezer that contained some type of pumpkin cake half submerged in an orange colored pudding. She said, "I hope you like pumpkin. This is an old recipe from my grandmother. It is well loved in my family."

Candice and Nick both took simultaneous bites of the dessert, looked at each other, and then at Paloma and Arturo. Nick spoke first, "I am glad it is so small; otherwise, I would certainly eat too much. Paloma, this is the best food to include the dessert that I have eaten in the Yucatan. Everything is wonderful."

After the meal, all four went back into the living room where they talked into the night with Arturo telling stories about his days as a soldier in the

Mexican army while Paloma sometimes looked embarrassed but continued to interpret. Sometimes, Arturo would ask a few simple questions about how long Candice and Nick had been married and about their likes and dislikes, and then, he would go back to speaking about his experiences. Candice and Nick always gave short answers and then directed the conversation back to Arturo by asking him another loaded question.

It was 10:15, and Candice and Nick reported they needed to get back home and thanked them both for the evening. With the interpretation from Paloma, Arturo motioned for both of them to follow him. He took them to an old large working refrigerator on the back porch, opened it, and showed them it was full of amber bottles of beer. He pulled out an old wooden soft drink crate that held securely twenty-four bottles and filled every wooden square with a bottle of beer. Nick looked on in surprise as Arturo picked up the crate with its roughly grooved handles and began to carry it out to their SUV. Nick lifted the back remotely, and Arturo slid the crate of the golden liquid into the SUV. Candice and Nick both said a heartfelt "thank you," shook hands with both Paloma and Arturo, got into the SUV, and drove away.

Paloma and Arturo returned inside the home and began to clean the kitchen. Paloma felt relieved that she would not have to interpret from Spanish again and started the conversation by asking, "What did you learn?" Arturo was picking up the dirty dishes and walking toward the sink as he began to explain, "Nick may be rich, but there is much there that does not fit. To begin, he was not raised rich. He was raised in much more humble conditions. Second, he was a non-commissioned officer in the military."

"How do you know this?"

"You get to be an expert on people after leading others for a long time. Nick was in war and is a leader."

"If you were not always correct, I would not believe you. Should we be afraid of him?"

"No, we should be afraid for him."

"What do you mean?"

"I think he and Candice are here to do much the same things we are trying to accomplish with our militia. I do not even know if they are married, but I trust them both. They appear to be very strong, and both are honest and trustworthy."

"They may not be married, but they are certainly in love."

"My dove, why would you say that?"

"Because, they are like us. They belong together. There is no doubt about that. So, what is worrying you about them specifically?"

"The cartel is courting them, and that jerk Juan is really trying to turn up the heat on them."

"How do you know this?"

"From their maid. She reports things to Angel about them."

"Are you telling the other members of the militia?"

"I plan on only telling Angel right now. But, it may be soon that the militia will need to either help them or protect them. Also, I think Pastor Dorgan and Dr. Calhoun are connected to them. I know that is only a hunch with me that goes beyond their actions, but I feel something is between the four of them more than we know for sure."

"Arturo, do you think they really enjoyed the food and drink as much as they acted? You know, he only drank about half his second bottle of beer."

"What I know was how he enjoyed every drink of beer and every bite of food. Also, I know how he seemed to be in his element in this house. It is like he was taking a small vacation from whatever he is doing. I think he is acting like he is rich and that someone or something is backing him up."

"So, is he a liar?"

"No, he is an actor trying to help others. Candice is like him. Please, do not get me wrong; they are stellar people. They are like spies with a serious purpose to me."

"If you know this, do you think the cartel knows it too?"

"Not yet. Remember, the cartel is made up of thugs like Juan; if he gets too close, I will personally kill him."

"No more talk like that tonight. It scares me. I know you are correct, but still, it really scares me." Paloma continued to speak as she tried to overcome her fear in order to finish the conversation, "But, I guess I should ask you one more question; what are you going to do?"

"Tell Angel. Try to get more information and wait."

Nick was driving from Paloma's and Arturo's home while Candice was notifying Charles and Dr. Calhoun about the meeting. Charles was first to ask questions after Candice's update. He wrote, "Nick, do you think he made you?"

Candice read the question to Nick, and he said back as Candice typed, "Yes, he did. I only acted natural, tried to say as little as possible, but I am sure he recognized that I was only playing rich."

Charles wrote back, "I believe so too. Both of you are alike in many ways. Both of you were soldiers, and both of you have strong beliefs between right and wrong. Also, both of you are brave enough to do something about the wrong."

Candice wrote back, "Are we in trouble?"

"No, I do not think so," replied Charles.

Dr. Calhoun asked, "What did you two gleam from the dinner date?"

Candice read Dr. Calhoun's question to Nick who said, "Tell them we learned we can trust Arturo and his wife. Tell them also that Arturo may be an asset if he does what he is supposed to do, but a liability if he moves at the wrong time. But, I feel no malice in the man or his wife."

Charles wrote, "I agree with Nick totally. We need to find out more."

Nick said, "Ask Charles what he thinks about Juan."

Charles wrote back, "If I have him figured correctly, Juan is one of the most dangerous men I have ever known. He is an evil man that can hide his evil spiritually. Spiritually, he seems like the wonderful neighbor who may be a serial killer on the weekends."

"If we kill Juan, how good would it be," typed Dr. Calhoun.

"Horrible," wrote Charles. "It would bring the entire cartel down on us. Anyway, we need more information, and like it or not, Juan is currently our best contact with the cartel."

Candice replied, "Well, if we do decide to kill him, I volunteer."

Dr. Calhoun replied back, "The most I will let you do is flip for him. I do not like him threatening you and Nick. I hope you agree though that we should wait."

"Yes, I will wait," typed Candice."But in Texas, there is a saying that some people need killing. I think he needs killing."

Nick asked Candice to write, "Charles, what about the cartel leader?"

Charles replied, "Remember what I said before. He is like a large building seen at night with lights high up in the air with a feeling of a large building, but in the daylight, you see it is just a series of lights with no building present. He is like a waterless cloud and is spiritually dead, but do not sell him short, he is a powerful fake."

"Wow," replied Nick after Candice read Charles' answer. "Please tell Charles that I think he has a pretty low opinion of him."

"He is a criminal," wrote Charles. "And, he will run at the first sign of trouble. He needs to cover up his shallowness within and demonstrate his fake power without. He is a total liar and coward. Those are his two greatest weaknesses."

"What keeps him going?" wrote Candice.

"His brother who is actually the brains of the outfit. His brother is the organizer and protector, but he is dying. The brother you mostly see is merely the flamboyant leader keeping the politics intact. Both make a dynamic duo, but take away one, the other will fall."

Candice wrote back suddenly, "These stupid bugs are bugging me. I need to put the top up on the sports car. Nick and I need to go." Everybody got out of the chat room immediately while Candice began to block the bug hoping she had caught and killed it in time.

CHAPTER 25

Joyce Jamison

THE SURGICAL STAFF started the IV, finished prepping the patient, and were waiting on Joyce for the anesthesia assessment and for Dr. Calhoun who always insisted on being present at the signing of the consent form; he was a stickler for answering questions about the surgery to the patient and family prior to Joyce medicating the patient with Midazolam that would make the patient appear drunk and not caring about the procedure. The consent form was signed, and Joyce Jamison had reviewed the chart and asked pertinent questions about the patient's history. This patient probably had slow but potentially very dangerous internal bleeding due to his being in an automobile collision near the clinic. The EMT's thought it best to get the patient to the closest medical help. The patient was slow of speech but appeared oriented. After Joyce squirted the happy juice into the IV port, the male patient in his late forties was moved to the operation room where he was placed carefully onto the operating table and prepped for surgery. Joyce moved to the head of the table and began to set up her meds and equipment to place the patient in a deep sleep.

After a time out to check all things were correct, Dr. Calhoun went to the small room where he would get ready for the surgery. He went about his business of scrubbing and gowning efficiently while the patient was being prepped. The operating room looked uneventful with the small volunteer crew setting up sterile fields and instruments. While looking through the glass at the patient, he noticed the patient's heart rate was over a hundred and the blood pressure was high, but the heart rhythm did not appear irregular as seen on the monitor above and to the left of the patient. The oxygen saturation was very good at 99, but the patient looked nervous, his eyes were wide open, and he seemed to be trying to watch all that was happening in the room. He thought, Joyce must not have given him enough of the medication to relax him but thought that would be quickly remedied as soon as Joyce noticed.

Dr. Calhoun loved to look one last time into Joyce's eyes before each surgery, but when he looked, he saw hardness. He thought she might be having a headache. The patient was being cleaned and draped as he was trying to watch everything in the OR and was looking more agitated by the second. It was unusual for Joyce not to give enough tranquilizer to relieve the patient's anxiety.

Joyce pulled her red work cabinet of drawers closer to her side that held her medications, intubation tubes, and other equipment. The top of the cabinet was just below eye level while she was sitting. She continued her set-up while paying no attention to the patient. She pulled a medication into a syringe and set it on her tray. The circulating nurse and the scrub nurse were now watching Joyce. Something was wrong, and Dr. Calhoun stopped everything to watch Joyce push the prepared medication into the IV. Suddenly, the patient's breathing stopped. The heart rate began to decline along with the blood pressure. The blood oxygen saturation dropped into the 60's. The patient was paralyzed, awake, and dying of suffocation while being aware of the entire process. Dr. Calhoun looked at the scrub nurse who glared back with her dark eyes. Joyce was frozen in place while the circulating nurse grabbed a bag mask device and immediately began to breath the patient.

Dr. Calhoun quickly opened the door from the preparation room and said, "Put the breathing tube in now!"

When he saw that Joyce was not responding but looked past the patient and crew in a thousand-mile stare, he moved to the patient's head breaking the sterile field and picked up the Miller blade. He snapped on the handle, quickly checked the light, and placed the blade expertly down the patient's trachea. The balloon was inflated and the airway was perfect.He motioned to the circulating nurse that he would bag the patient now. The procedure took seconds, and he began to bag the patient giving him precious oxygen.

"Joyce, is it pancuronium!"

"Yes," she said while crying with tears flowing down wetting the top of her mask.

"Joyce, give him a tranquilizer now while I bag him!"

She held the bottle up to show Dr. Calhoun it was diazepam. She pulled the medication into the syringe and gave it to the patient through the IV.

Dr. Calhoun asked the nurse as mildly as he could if she would set up the sterile field again and prep the patient again. The ventilator was working with the oxygen saturation climbing past 90. The blood pressure, heart rate and rhythm, and all vital signs were normalizing. Bending his back toward Joyce, he placed his lips near Joyce's ear and said, "You have to finish this; the patient cannot wait. I can't get somebody right away."

"I know. I will do it right."

The surgery was completed without another problem, and the patient appeared to be doing well after the bleeder was found and stitched together. Dr. Calhoun had not met the patient before today, but he had read the all the chart and history available about him. The patient had nothing suspicious in his history. The male recovery room nurse immediately set up the patient for recovery and began to do vital signs every fifteen minutes and assessing the surgical wound for bleeding.

Dr. Calhoun grabbed Joyce by the left arm with his right hand and pulled her with him to the small doctor's lounge. His fingers were boring into Joyce's arm. The lounge had a table that took up most of the room with chairs around. There was scattered food where everyone's lunch was suddenly interrupted from the wreck and the emergency surgery.

Dr. Calhoun looked at Joyce with hard eyes and asked, "What did you mean? You gave pancuronium knocking out the patient's breathing without the patient having a breathing tube in place. Also, you did not give him anything for the anxiety. What did you put into his IV before surgery? Was is just saline? You not only wanted to smother him by paralyzing his diaphragm; you wanted him to know that he couldn't breathe and was dying. What is going on with you?"

"There are some things I didn't tell you."

"Well, tell me now. Those nurses out there are not stupid. They are good, and I respect them. They know what you just did and may be calling the police right now."

"I know!" she said while trying to hold back tears but not being very successful.

"Start explaining yourself right now!" Dr. Calhoun spoke forcefully through clinched teeth.

"That man is named Lucas Sanchez. My brother and his family were killed five years ago, like I told you. Actually, the authorities found some DNA in a hole in the ground. The DNA identified my brother's son. They said they would let me know more information. I couldn't let it go."

Dr. Calhoun began to regain his composure with Joyce. The reason was clear; she had lost it. The patient's name triggered something. He asked, "So, you have been coming back here for the past five years to investigate your brother's murder?"

"Yes."

"What have you found?"

"It's complicated, but I think there is someone selling patient's organs. Lucas Sanchez was one of the names I discovered. Later, I was able to get information on how he looked. I was doing OK until that stupid wreck near this clinic and him needing emergency surgery without time enough to move him somewhere else."

"Who have you shared your information with?"

Suddenly, Joyce looked suspicious. "Why do you want to know? Who are you really?"

"A friend. And, you will have to trust me."

"Trust you? Am I in a lot of trouble?"

"Yes, but not how you think. Now listen closely and believe every word I tell you. You are leaving the country today. Get what you need packed quickly. It's close to lunchtime, so nobody should get suspicious if you go home for lunch. I'll watch Mr. Sanchez until he awakens."

"What are you going to do?"

"Get you protection and once again, out of here. Now, get home and pack. If you have notes, even on computers or thumb drives, leave them with me. "

Joyce looked nervous but said, "OK". She left the clinic.

Dr. Calhoun called Candice on her secured cell phone and pronounced, "We are to act now. Joyce is not an enemy. She is vital to us for research."

"What is happening?"

"She is in trouble for attempted murder of one of the cartel people during surgery. I can give more details later. Right now, she needs transportation with protection to the US."

"Is commercial OK? I can arrange a flight today. Did the patient have anything to do with the disappearance of her brother and his family?"

"According to her, the answer is yes, and the earlier the flight the better. She is packing. I can get her to the airport and then rejoin you."

"Tickets are to be on-line within the next half hour."

"Candice, I need another favor. She needs to be sick with a head condition, a tumor. I will send the diagnosis to you. I need it placed in her chart, and she needs a two year plus history of it. Is there any chat about this incident going on right now?"

"To check now. I do not see anything."

"Good. I am getting ready to drive Joyce to the airport. Please ensure a local friend is ready, and the FBI is alerted for their pick-up in the US. She will need to be immediately transferred to a major hospital. There are five years of her investigation notes in my possession. I will get them to you as soon as possible."

"The on-line tickets are ready. Call me if you have trouble with them at the airport. Also, I am notifying the FBI. Now Dr. Calhoun, go do what you need to do but please be careful.Everything is well here for now, and I can continue to coordinate all things as needed. Also, I am texting Charles and Nick as we speak."

"Be careful Candice. I will inform you if other problems occur."

Dr. Calhoun left the clinic within a half hour of calling Candice. Charles was also notified by Candice and awaited further instructions. Mainly, he was to be a back-up plan if anything went wrong. Candice and Nick were keeping in touch and coordinating from their home. Charles was on standby at the church and was awaiting orders. Dr. Calhoun was on top of the tetrahedron for this venture.

Joyce was nervous as she sat in the passenger seat of the clinic's sedan. Dr. Calhoun was still trying to put together the best words to ask for more needed information, but Joyce began to speak first, "I must know. Are you part of the organ trade or even the drug trade? I don't think you are, but I don't know right now." Joyce began to cry but was able to squeak out the rest, "Tell me something; was that an act your kissing me and all that?"

Dr. Calhoun looked at Joyce out of the corner of his eyes as he was driving and began to explain, "No, it was not an act. I am very attracted to you, but that is not as important as your safety right now. If the man you attempted to kill is part of the cartel, you are in tremendous danger. We are getting you out of the country. I know it is difficult to take all this in, but you are to trust me. You are to get on a plane and follow instructions to the letter. Your life will depend on it."

"I guess I trust you, but what about your life?"

Dr. Calhoun fixed his eyes back on the road and said, "My life is good. You worry about yourself. But believe me, times could get difficult if you do not follow the instructions you are given to the letter. Now, your hair is up like it is when you are in surgery. I need you to put it down. Also, I need you to keep your face grimaced like you are having a migraine. You are to complain about any light near you, like a light on you in the plane. Try asking for something to cover your eyes and appear in pain when you ask."

"I can try."

"You are not to be charged with anything in the US; this I promise you, but you may be detained. You are not to worry; you are not to be sent back to Mexico for any trail."

"What is my alibi for the screw up I did with the patient?"

"Listen closely, you have a brain tumor. It is effecting you badly. You kept it secret for a long time, but now, it is suddenly worse. I recommend you be sent for treatment immediately. The paperwork is filled out for your transfer, and your elaborate brain tumor history is being written into your medical records as we speak. Other friendly doctors in the US will be reviewing all your history to ensure authenticity."

"So, where am I going?"

"To a hospital for treatment. Also, a pharmacy near the airport will be delivering medications to you to include blood pressure medications. You are to not take them but to destroy each dose as if taken. You can deposit them in the bathroom if necessary- just make sure it appears as if you took them."

Charles pulled the car into the airport, opened the trunk from the inside, got out and grabbed the luggage. A sky cap reported the luggage was expected and proceeded to get it ready for loading. Dr. Calhoun also met the delivery lady from the pharmacy awaiting just outside the terminal to deliver the medications. He signed for the drugs. The plane was ready to take off within an hour.

They walked into the terminal and were instantly met by a woman in a light blue jacket with a white shirt and gray tie. Her gray dress pants were pressed perfectly, and her posture was perfect. Her black hair was pulled back, and her make-up gave the look of a professional, no nonsense employee. Her name tag was small, gold, and with black letters. She faked looking worried and pronounced to Dr. Calhoun and Joyce, "We hear you are sick and need immediate, special attention. I am here to assist you. You are in first class and to be placed on the airplane first." She escorted them to a small private room and said, "An attendant is to meet you here in about fifteen minutes. The lights in the room are dimmed per Dr. Calhoun's written recommendations."

A slim and well-dressed male flight attendant appeared in the room right on time and escorted Joyce away from Dr. Calhoun. She looked in pain and shielded her eyes with her right hand as she walked with the attendant. Dr. Calhoun watched as she disappeared down the hall toward the airplane door. The woman who had placed them in the room suddenly appeared in front of Dr. Calhoun and reported, "She is OK. She is seated in first class, and she will be treated well. We realize that she will have special needs. We will do the best we can to keep her as comfortable as possible."

"Oh, I think you are great at what you do," explained Dr. Calhoun. "Please allow me to just watch as the plane takes off. I really hope she does OK."

"You can certainly stay until the plane takes off. Would you like a cup of coffee?"

"I would enjoy that."

The coffee arrived about the time the plane was beginning to taxi to the runway. Dr. Calhoun took the coffee from the attendant, took a drink, and watched the airplane take off in the distance. He stood like a statue for a few minutes holding the hot cup in his hand without flinching and then threw the nearly filled cup into the nearby garbage can. Sadness engulfed him as he made his way to the sedan and drove away. As he drove, he hit the button on his cell phone and instantly called Candice. After she did not answer, he left a voicemail as follows, "in the air. Everything appears well."

Three and a half hours later Joyce was met by two disguised FBI agents at the Dallas airport who represented themselves as hospital employees. She appeared freighted, but they assured her that her condition warranted they take her to the hospital. A car pulled around with hospital lettering on the side. The two men sat in the front seat while a female who seemed to suddenly appear out of nowhere moved into the back seat beside her.

The man who was not driving was tall and began to speak first, "Ms. Jamison, I am Agent Stone and this in Agent Rutherford. Agent Pruitt is in the backseat with you. We are FBI and expect full cooperation. You are not under arrest, but for your safety and for others safety also, you are detained and possibly for several months. You are not to leave your assigned areas, and you are considered very ill. Do you have any questions?"

"Am I in trouble?"

"Only if you fail to cooperate. I warn you, many lives are at stake and especially Dr. Calhoun's life."

"I don't want him hurt. I'll do anything you say."

"Thank you, Ms. Jamison. Now, we will take you where you can get some rest. Please ask for whatever you need."

"Thank you. Will I get my luggage?"

"Of course. Now, try to relax. You are not in trouble, and the more you cooperate with whatever you know from your personal investigation, the more lives will be saved."

"I will do the best I can."

"One other thing, you are not to be charged with any crime either here or in Mexico. If you are asked questions, your illness caused you to almost black out and make poor decisions. You are being talked-up as a hero for being able to override your symptoms and take care of the patient in surgery. You are never to say anything other than the incident was caused by a problem with your illness, even when you are released. Do you agree to this?"

"Yes, yes I do." The word 'released' made her relax and take a deep breath. She believed this was to be a lonely, secluded time, but she also knew it would end with her freedom. She looked at the female FBI agent beside her and smiled. Agent Pruitt smiled back and said, "Now, that is better. We mean you no harm, but you must help us any way you can."

"I might as well tell you now- woman to woman- I think I'm in love with Dr. Calhoun."

"Do you know that love might never work out?"

"I didn't till now. So, I am not to ask about him again."

"That would be wise. However, I can tell you this. If you two still want to meet each other much later, it may not be out of the question. It is not feasible now for you to communicate with each other, and you are to never tell anyone about him or anything that has happened to you concerning this case."

"Understood, I really don't want him hurt. I will not speak of him, and I thank you for listening."

The car arrived at the hospital where Joyce was escorted via the back stairs to an upper room that would be both her sanctuary and her prison.

Candice began to review Joyce's finger drives that were delivered by Dr. Calhoun to her. She began to see a pattern of listening to everything but asking very few questions concerning her brother's disappearance. Also, she began to see that Joyce was also very busy for the time that she volunteered each year.

It was basically a scanty, small amount of information, but some things began to emerge in the notes. The first item was that Joyce noticed that the police often harassed each volunteer doctor at the clinic. She also noted that Joyce was finding Dr. Calhoun very attractive and wanted to have a relationship with him, but the main thing was the list of names that she kept describing people connected with the cartel. These were acquired mainly through her visiting local bars and just listening to conversations. One name that kept coming up was an assassin called the sleeper. The sleeper seemed to kill at will and often infiltrated a work area and became well-liked by all. His code name was recorded in all five years of her investigation.

CHAPTER 26

Suspicions

THE SMALL VILLAGE lights were dimmed to save electricity, and it was a secluded area. Commander Morales waited in his private squad car until nearly midnight. He sighed to himself that he was getting sick and tired of staying up late and getting more sick and tired. He began to see the shadow of a young woman come toward him out of the darkness of the alley he was parked near. She paused and then quickly slipped into the seat beside him.

"Hello Inspector Vega," he said.

"Good night Commander. Why did you call me?"

"Tell me what you know about the clinic you and your partner are watching."

Inspector Vega looked at the Commander and asked, "Do you mind if I smoke? I am trying to quit, but I need one occasionally."

"Only if you have a good cigar with you and if you never tell my wife."

"She will know, but here." She handed him a Cuban cigar wrapped in a cellophane wrapper. He quickly opened the wrapper and pulled the cigar slowly beneath his nose as he took a deep breath.

"Is it good?" she asked as she took out a cigarette from her small purse and lit it. Then she asked, "Do you want me to light yours?"

"No, I will let it tempt me until it begins to get old. No, I just wanted to think about how it could be."

She saw impatience growing in his eyes and said, "But Commander, you wanted to know about the recent happenings at the clinic. It seems that Dr. Calhoun and Joyce Jamison were lovers, or at least, they were trying to be. Both are very busy, but there is a growing fondness reported between them as reported by certain staff, especially Antonio. Joyce is currently out of the country due to sudden problems with a brain tumor and needs immediate surgery. She almost botched a surgery, and they are blaming it on the tumor."

"What do you think is going on?"

"I am trying to get information on Ms. Jamison. The bottom line is that she tried to kill a top cartel man either intentionally or unintentionally. She comes to the clinic during her vacation time every year as a volunteer service. However, her brother disappeared about five years ago in this area, and this is about the time she began to volunteer her services for the clinic."

"So, she is tied to the cartel."

"Yes, and I believe they know it. That is why she needed taking out of the country so quickly."

Commander Morales looked at the cigar longingly, moved his eyes away, and asked Inspector Vega, "Did you try to contact the authorities in the US about her?"

"Dead end. Sir, she is hidden somewhere. I would guess a hospital in the US and heavily guarded. Brain tumor is about all the information I could get. Someone is shielding big time."

"What can you tell me about the good doctor?"

"He seems too good to be true. He is dedicated to his work, and despite his poor Spanish, he takes care of a lot of patients who dearly love him. His ability to get Ms. Jamison out of the country so quickly amazes me. He is connected to people who know what they are doing," proclaimed Inspector Vega.

Commander Morales looked deep in thought as he replied, "He concerns me too, but he is working with Antonio to get him into a BS program; it was reported that Dr. Calhoun said Antonio could even become a doctor. It seems only a good man would be so concerned about a local person. Also, Antonio called me for a reference for college."

"Yes, Antonio is well liked at the clinic. He is very dedicated to his work. Can we use him to spy on the clinic?"

"I told him to call me back about getting into the college. If he calls, I can just casually ask how things are going in the clinic while I praise Dr. Calhoun for doing such a wonderful job. I want to change the subject. What about the jerk that is badgering our fine young rich American couple?"

"Juan is still a jerk. Want me to take him out?" asked Inspector Vega.

"Yes, but you cannot do that. We are the police."

"What if I dispose of him really well?" she asked jokingly.

"Then I would need to spend all my money trying to get you to a secluded island where you would need to look over your shoulder all the time."

She took another draw and blew the smoke out the opened window. She turned to Commander Morales and asked, "How much money you got, and how far can you send me?"

Commander Morales continued the joke, "Not far enough. Get me more information and put that lazy partner of yours to work. Next time, I will meet with him and let you rest."

"Sounds good except for one thing. I do not trust my partner, but I do like my new watch. Are you sure it will tell you where I am if I get in trouble."

"If it does not, I will return it for a full refund. You are one of two people who have one. It is a sign that I trust you. Remember, push that button three times if something is urgent. But, you do not get off that easy. What is going on between you and your partner?"

"He is leaving me a lot to speak on his cell phone, and he will not tell me anything that is said. Also, he seems to dress better and has just bought a new car. It may just be family stuff, but I do not think so."

"Actually, I am watching him also. That is one reason you have the watch, and he does not. Do me a favor and continue to watch him. I already know that he is spending more than his meager salary would allow. I want to ask you this personally, and I never want to hear about it again."

Inspector Vega interrupted, "Yes, I can arrest him or even kill him if I need to."

"Good answer. I do not want to lose you because he took you out. Continue to watch him and do not hesitate to contact me if things get bad."

"I will not hesitate to call."

"Then Inspector Vega, I am assigning you another person to closely watch. Since you are having troubles with your partner, do not include him in this. Reverend Dorgan supposedly made some people disappear who I believe were marked by the judge for sacrifice. Angel reported Arturo sent them to the good Reverend's church as an effort to save them. Supposedly, Juan is responsible for marking them. You are to get all the information you can on him."

"Were there not rags found with their blood on them where a big cat is loose?"

"Yes. But, there was no body parts found. I am very suspicious about how those two just disappeared. Now, concerning the militia, everything might work out. Angel is good at his job. Does your partner know about Angel in deep cover with the militia?" asked Commander Morales.

"He knows nothing, at least, as far as I know."

"Keep it that way, and I am also cutting your partner out of all pertinent communication. Remember, do not tell anyone about the watch, not even your partner. I trust so few people, and I cannot afford to lose those I can trust. Also, you take care of yourself. I will always respect and trust you and never take you for granted. Now, get lost."

She opened the door and dropped the cigarette butt on the ground beside the car and stomped it while looking back and asking, "How can I with this watch?" She disappeared into the night. Commander Morales started his car and drove away.

Charles heard the squeaking hinges of the auditorium door, but it was not unusual for people to come into the church auditorium and sit. It was Friday, and he had finished dusting his office and was moving to the auditorium benches when he saw a woman, estimated about his age, with long black shiny hair sitting in the middle of his right hand's back row. Her look was confusing to Charles who thought he saw her actually enjoying seeing him work. He looked straight at her and said to her in Spanish, "Welcome to God's house."

She replied in English, "I know you are Pastor Charles Dorgan. I am Inspector Vega of the Yucatan Police Force. I work for Commander Morales. I am here to ask you some questions about the disappearance of a mother and her daughter. Their names are Rosa and Madeira." She thought as she was speaking, I am being too cold. She could not help but see he was handsome and tall with looks like a Swede, but it was his actions that mostly impressed her. He seemed real as he was getting ready for church with his cleaning and making sure everything to include the furniture, benches, and even his office desk were neat, polished, and also, it was obvious that he made the most of everything that he had.

She was looking at him with her mind drifting when Charles broke the silence, "I did see them. I believe they were killed by a cat after they left here according to the local news."

Inspector Vega was trying to compose herself, but she also noticed that Charles was slightly trembling. Also, his lower lip had a small quiver. She thought, whatever she had, he had it also. She got up from her seat and walked to the front of the pews, stuck out her right hand, and said, "I do not mean to be so cold. It is from years of dealing with criminals. I do not believe you are a criminal, but two people are missing."

Charles shook her hand and said, "I understand. You are doing your duty. Do you mind calling me Charles?"

"I usually do not call people I am investigating by their first names, but in this case, I will make an exception."

"Also, I want you to do something else that would make me more comfortable."

"Charles, I never give my first name, but for some reason, it seems OK. My name is Milagros."

"Milagros is a beautiful name, and thank you for sharing it with me. I know it means miracle, but that is not what would make me more comfortable."

Milagros looked confused and slightly angry and asked, "What would make you more comfortable?"

"Since the beginning of this conversation, you are speaking in English while I am speaking in Spanish. Can we just speak one language?"

Milagros' face looked as if it would crack as her smile showed perfect white teeth which progressed to a loud laugh. "Charles, I did not realize I was doing that. I honestly thought you would feel more comfortable speaking English."

"I thought you would feel more comfortable speaking Spanish. Which one would you like to speak?"

"Well, I like to be in control when I am investigating someone, so I pick English."

Charles smiled and said, "English it is. May I get you something to drink?"

"I just had a bout with some kind of intestinal thing. Do you have some bottled water?"

"Yes. I will get it for you."

They sat in the auditorium speaking at first about the case and then drifted on to why Milagros liked being an inspector and why Charles liked being a minister. The time flew by before they realized they had spoken for three hours non-stop. Inspector Vega showed guilt to Charles as she looked at her watch. "I am so sorry Charles. I need to leave."

Charles was usually in control of his emotions, but this time the words came out before he could stop them, "Are you allowed to date those you are investigating?"

Milagros was stunned by the question, but she was trying to control her emotions also. However, she decided to not answer directly, "You do not even know if I am married."

"That is stupid of me."

"No, I am not married. You are not convicted of a crime, but it is not wise for us to see each other. So, are you doing anything at 7PM tonight?"

Charles was stunned again but managed to override the feelings and said, "The church should be clean by then, and tomorrow's sermon is already written. Would you like dinner?"

"I will bring it. I want us to be here in the church. Do not take this the wrong way, but I will feel restricted here. As I understand it, tonight is the beginning of your holy day."

"It is."

"Do you like Chinese food?"

"I love Chinese food, but where do you get it here?"

"There are sources."

"Milagros, are we doing the right thing?"

"No, but I do not want to do otherwise. Unless I chicken out, I will be here at seven. Please, do not hate me if I fail to show," said Milagros.

"I will be here," said Charles. He walked with her to the large wooden doors, opened them for her, and said, "good-bye. I really hope to see you again."

Milagros looked vulnerable as she walked from the church to her automobile. She hesitantly waved good-bye after the car started and then disappeared on the road.

Charles went immediately to his office and alerted Candice who replied, "hello." He noticed the bug was dead and on its back and wrote, "You need to tell the gang, I am in trouble."

"Why?"

"I just met a woman police inspector. She asked me about Rosa and Madeira. I did something very foolish. She is meeting me at the church tonight for dinner at 7PM."

Candice replied, "Nick is here and signing on. I just alerted Dr. Calhoun, but he may be busy. Are you doing this to get more information."

"No, I am doing this because I feel like my hormones are kicking me."

Candice replied, "Is she that beautiful?"

"Yes, and unless she is the best actress in the world, she feels the same for me. We are dining at the church, so there will be some restrictions."

Nick replied, "Charles, we are human, but I am totally confident in you. I do not believe you will do anything wrong."

Dr. Calhoun signed on to the chat and wrote, "just out of surgery. If I stop suddenly, it is because somebody disturbed me. Charles, I have met her. Would you send me a picture for reference?"

Candice replied, "Keep this serious. Now, what are you most concerned about Charles?"

"I feel helpless and trapped. I really want to be with this woman. She is bringing out some buried things in me."

Nick replied, "She sounds vulnerable also."

"She is, and normally, I would capitalize on that. But this time, the feelings are too great. Should I call it off?"

Three no's showed on his screen. Candice replied for the three, "We trust you. Keep the date and contact us if we are needed. I can call you with an emergency if you will secretly alert me like I showed."

Inspector Vega pulled the car over to the side of the road about a mile from the church and called Commander Morales. She heard the phone answer and said, "Sir, I am requesting that I be taken off the investigation of Reverend Charles Dorgan."

Commander Morales said, "Do I not even get a hello anymore? It is OK, but do you realize you are speaking in English?"

"I just spoke in English with Charles, uh, Reverend Dorgan, and we, I, am not doing well right now."

"Are you alone?"

"Of course."

"Then take a deep breath and relax. Evidentially, you like large, tall religious men."

"I did not say that."

"Yes you did. I was wondering when a man would wake you up. How vulnerable are you?"

"What's the use. I am a kid in high school again."

"How is he?"

"I think he is the same. I am so sorry, but he calls me Milagros. Also, we are dating if I show up tonight at 7PM. So, I will not show."

There was a long silence on the other end as she expected to be tongue lashed and told she was taken off the case, but the answer surprised her, "Milagros, protect yourself tonight. We both know our two ladies are safe somewhere thanks to the good Reverend. There is much more about him than meets the eye but please try not to get too deep too soon and run him off. If he is helping us, that is good."

"So, I should see him?"

"With what you tell me, I do not think you can keep from seeing him."

"I hate this feeling."

"What? You hate that vulnerable, sinking feeling that makes us mere mortals. It is called love. You cannot continue to run from life even if you are my miracle. Now, he seems to be a good man. Think of him as an actor trying to achieve a higher purpose and not a liar."

"What if I fall in love with him? What if he leaves, disappears, and never comes back?"

"Oh my dear, you are smitten. Would you send me a picture of you right now? I would love to see the sudden changes in your face."

"Commander Morales quit joking. What do you want me to do tonight?"

"Everything but business. Try just enjoying the evening but protect yourself. You still got the watch?"

"Keep it on all the time."

"Alert me if you need me, but be a woman on a date tonight."

"It is just Chinese food in a church."

"And the Mona Lisa is just paint on a canvas. No, it is much more than that. Enjoy yourself and call me if you need me."

"Yes sir, and thank you."

"No, thank you for all you do. Now, get lost."

CHAPTER 27

Angel's Fiancé

DR. ROSA SAT emotionless on the plane traveling from Germany to Florida. There would be a two-hour delay, and she would be on the joining flight to Cancun. She was looking forward to seeing Angel after being away for two weeks, but during the two weeks, she was very good and did not try to contact him.

The phone rang, and Angel could not believe who was calling him. It was Dr. Rosa. She sounded calm on the other end. Angel said, "Where are you? How are you Marie? I miss you so much."

"Angel, I am here in the Yucatan. I want to see you."

"Why did Commander Morales bring you back?" asked Angel.

"I am back due to him. He is giving us some time together before we are to meet him later. He says he will call us with the time and place. Meanwhile, we can be together if you want to see me."

"Of course, I want to see you. Where are you?"

"Just tell me where you want to meet, and I will be there," replied Dr. Rosa.

"Let's meet in a nice hotel in Cancun. I am fairly close to the city. How long will it take for you to get there?"

"About an hour. I really want to see you. I love you."

"I love you too."

The hotel looked like an oasis against the quiet and darkness of the night. There was music coming from the restaurant that adjoined the hotel lobby. Maria's dress was black and skimpy. Angel looked at her for a long time enamored by her beauty. She ran to him and kissed him on the mouth long and hard. She looked at Angel and then the restaurant and said, "I want to go upstairs. We can get room service. Also, there is a great bottle of red wine in the room."

Angel agreed and both went upstairs to Dr. Rosa's room where she quickly hugged Angel and kissed him again. She acted like she was having a difficult time pulling herself away but broke the hold slowly while looking Angel in the eyes, "I need to slow down. I never like to unwrap my presents too fast."

Appearing in shock from all that had just happened, Angel said, "Is there anything you want to do? I am so glad to even see you."

"Oh, I almost forgot. You have to taste this wine. She poured two glasses and took one to Angel. She took a drink from her glass and then swirled the red liquid rapidly. "She is showing some nice legs. I hope mine look as good to you."

Angel lifted the glass to his mouth and gently took a sip. He did not find the wine as good as Marie had said, and suddenly, it hit him. The wine was poisoned. He began to sink fast, and yet, he was able to find the main stem on the watch and push it three times. The vibratory alert pounded Commander Morales's skin. He quickly placed the dedicated blue tooth in his ear while turning up its sound. Then, he quickly copied the ten-digit grid coordinates that showed Angel's location. Quickly, he made a call to activate two uniformed policemen near that area and told them to move quickly. Then, he was totally surprised as he heard Dr. Rosa's voice as she talked to Angel, "You are feeling a little sick, but that will soon pass. You are a good man, and my goddess needs good men."

"Am I going to die?" asked Angel with a very weakened voice.

"Oh, not here. You are a sacrifice to my goddess."

"Why are you doing this?" asked Angel as he fought for consciousness.

"You and Commander Morales are the best men I know. You are both honest and moral. My goddess does not want the criminal but the people who fight evil. Do not worry, my goddess will take care of you. Of course, there will be pain but then paradise. You are a good man who needs to know the truth. When I pass, we will be together forever."

"I really love you, but I hope not," said Angel while he continued to speak hoping that Commander Morales was listening to the microphone in the watch. "What about the hotel? How are you going to get me outside? My head is getting cloudy. Are we in room 224?"

"Very good, you are still awake enough to be oriented to place. How about person and time?" she asked jokingly. "Do not worry about my lifting you by myself, I am alerting my help by my cell phone signal as we speak."

"Will I be awake when you cut out my heart with a flint knife?"

"I am not worthy enough to do the sacrifice. No, there will be a priest that will perform the ceremony."

"Will the judge be there?"

"You know the judge will be there. She brought me here to subdue you, and she is waiting with some specific others for your dedication."

"The dedication?" asked Angel as he began to slip into darkness. He could scarcely fight the drug anymore. He laid back his head and thought the end was near as he heard fading male and female voices and a door slamming. Darkness engulfed him, and Angel was unconscious.

Awakening in the arms of a large, strong man, he opened his eyes and saw Commander Morales' face peering at him less than six inches from his face. He could smell the Commander's breath mint.

"You are so beautiful," said Angel weakly while he was trying to focus his eyes and overcome his headache. "I really love my new watch."

Feeling both guilt and sadness, Commander Morales explained, "She is good at fooling people. I am so sorry."

Angel's eyes began to tear as he asked, "Where is she?"

"In the hospital along with one of the men who were guarding you. Even with the police here, they tried to take you to be sacrificed. She is wounded and may not live. One of the two men who tried to take you is dead. The other man will make it according to the doctors."

"Why? She is so beautiful. I do not just mean looks."

"Well, it turns out that she is a religious fanatic. She is a follower of the judge too. That is why they knew so much about you. I never suspected."

"How am I? Do you think there is permanent damage from the poison?"

"It is being analyzed; however, the doctors will determine if you are permanently hurt.I really hope you are doing alright. I am awaiting another ambulance to take you to the hospital. The first two had their hands full."

"Commander, I do not understand; she drank the wine too."

"The poison is dried in the glass first and becomes almost invisible to the naked eye. Her glass is clear of the poison."

"You know her glass?"

"That is an easy one. You do not wear lipstick."

"Well, I am still trying to get the clouds out of my head."

Commander Morales laid Angel's head on the cushion he had grabbed from the sofa and placed on the floor. The EMT people came through the door with a wheeled stretcher. They began to work with great efficiency rechecking vital signs and making sure the IV started earlier was still working well, and then moving him to the stretcher and strapping him down. Angel felt so weak he could not protest.

"I need to get back on the job," said Angel.

"There is still time. You concentrate on getting better."

There was a small pause as the two EMT personnel grabbed their bags, checked the IV's and the straps a final time, and then pushed the stretcher through the doorway.

Commander Morales looked at the female and male uniformed officers under his command and said a very heartfelt, "thank you."

The female officer said, "You are welcome sir."

CHAPTER 28

Charles' Date

MILAGROS KNOCKED ON the large wooden doors. Charles was waiting and had changed into a dark blue polo shirt and a pair of well ironed khakis. His brown belt and brown shoes matched perfectly. It was exactly 7PM as he opened the doors to see a simply dressed woman whose long black hair was down to the small of her back. She held a plastic bag of food in her left hand and a bottle of sweet red wine in her left. He stared a little too long at the nicotine patch on her right arm and she said, "trying to quit."

Charles replied, "It is not easy, and it took me awhile."

"You smoked?"

"Yes. Please come in."

Candice entered the church auditorium, and the aroma of Chinese food entered with her. She asked, "Where would you like to eat?"

"I cleaned off my desk and set up a couple of TV trays in my office. Do you mind eating there?"

"I don't mind."

They placed the food on the desk and ate off the wooden trays. They drank wine from the two coffee cups that usually hang on the wall behind the pot, and it went perfectly with the food. Charles began to feel a little tipsy realizing he drank about half the bottle. Milagros was looking around the room when he asked, "Is police work really important to you?"

"It is all I ever wanted to be. How about the ministry to you?"

"I do not think I could be anything else."

"How long did you volunteer for this job?"

"I am between homes right now. When I decide to return basically."

"Charles, can I confide something personal to you? I am not trying to take advantage of you."

"Sure."

"I do not know where this is going, and right now, I am just happy sitting here and sharing a meal with you. But, I know there is more to you than meets the eye. What if we go too far, and I do not see you again?"

"I go back to my faith. If God wants us together, we will be together."

"Charles, I might as well be honest. I feel stupid and vulnerable right now. I trust you, but I want to ask. Your files said you are not married, but are you seeing someone like a girlfriend or something like that?"

"Since we are being honest, I feel vulnerable too. There is nobody else."

"You do not understand about my relations with men. Men say I am pure stone."

"I do not believe that. Pardon me for saying, but you are so beautiful. With your looks, you could get any man you want if you tried."

"Yes, but I do not try. Charles, I want a real man."

"A real man? An alpha male with giant muscles?"

"No, I get hit on by that kind. No, I want a man who is real. When I watch you clean the church, I see a person who is real. There is no pretense. There is no acting. God help me, but I want to be with you. That does not happen with me."

"When I saw you sitting there on that back pew, my mind went east while my reason went west; they cannot meet again. Should we be confiding this to each other this early?"

"Yes, that is what I want. I want honesty and sincerity. I hate feeling this vulnerable, but I cannot just walk away either."

"So my beautiful miracle, where do we go from here?"

"To your bedroom."

"What!"

"Charles, I want to lie down with you and have you hold me. I figure in the church, and it being the beginning of a holy day with you, both of us are safe."

"Milagros, you do not know me very well. Are you sure you want to take that chance?"

"Very sure. If it involves both God and me, I am secure."

They walked to the small bedroom in back of the church, and both laid down fully clothed. She kissed Charles once on the mouth while holding his head gently between her palms. "You are precious," she said.

"Milagros, I am many things, but are you sure I am precious?"

"I am very sure. Now, be quiet and hold me."

Charles awakened in the darkness fully dressed. He reached over and felt an empty pillow. It was 4:17AM by the small clock, and he was alone. Reaching, he found the lamp switch and began to look around the room. He saw a small piece of paper on the night table with a phone number and some writing. He read, "I really want to see you again. Please call me."

He folded the note and placed it into his billfold also lying on the bed side table. Then, he got up and began his day feeling both light and worried at the same time.

CHAPTER 29

Another Month?

THE FOUR MEMBERS began the virtual meeting with each on their laptops. If the lady bug signal in the upper left hand corner of the screen turned over from its back and began to crawl, the meeting was to be cancelled immediately, and all were to sign off.

It was 2:00AM, and the night was clear and quiet without even a breeze outside. The stars showed bright. Candice and Nick sat opposing each other at their kitchen table. Charles was in his small church office, and Dr. Calhoun was sitting in his small apartment in back of the clinic.

Candice began the meeting first by writing the progress of she and Nick infiltrating the cartel. She mentioned names and where apparent weaknesses could be among the personnel.

Also, she wrote the monitoring on the local police forces was giving good information about who could be trusted. She began her report by saying, "The Police Commander Morales may be an honest man. He is having a great deal of problems with the people, with some of the judges, and almost all the politicians, but the chatter about him by those he leads is almost all favorable."

Charles began to speak about his current information concerning the female judge that seemed to be over human sacrifice, "I am sorry, it is difficult to get any concrete information on the woman judge who is supposedly doing human sacrifice in the area and her relations with the cartel. She is very protected from what I understand, and no locals will speak about what is happening for more than a few seconds."

Dr. Calhoun asked, "Are they that afraid?"

"They are, and it is getting worse. These people are fearful for their lives," replied Charles.

Nick then spoke into the small microphone as his face showed on the laptop screens, "We did not receive a gold mine of evidence from the two we sneaked out, Rosa and Madeira. It seems they know very little about the actual operation but did mention something about a 'killing hole'. They are vague about what happens there and where it is located."

Dr. Calhoun said as his face filled the lap top screens, "I am very sorry. My patients are taking all my time. I am trying to get Antonio to college and eventually to nursing or medical school. He is working out very well, and I trust him."

Candice then spoke, "Not unlike Juan Cortez. I tell you, he is getting to me. I hate the way that he speaks about his employer. He seems to be neck deep in the cartel."

Charles replied, "He continues to be a puzzle to me, but I do not feel evil from him. Yet, his actions tell me he is very evil. If he can do what I think he can in the spirit, he is evil that I have not known before. He can actually fake something like a spiritual good."

Nick said, "He seems to be the front man. I do not know how much he is involved with the day to day cartel operations."

"He is obviously there to observe you, but be careful if he tries to goad you into a fight. If you take the bait, it can be over for all of us," said Charles.

"Understood. So, what are the changes or improvements to our overall mission plans?" asked Nick.

Candice spoke up, "I propose no plan changes or improvements until we get more information, maybe another month. Information about people here is very difficult to obtain. It is set up with no one person knowing the whole truth. How do you feel about another month?"

All agreed.

"Oh, I almost forgot," said Candice. "Remember Arturo, the man who had the kissing tonsils operation. He seems to be over some kind of para-military organization. I think it is some kind of a small militia. Anyway, I am not able to find much chatter from them on the internet, but they seem to be connected to a habitual criminal named Angel. I can try to find out more about this later, but all of you can keep your eyes open for any information about them. Otherwise, I love all of you and keep me posted."

Everyone agreed.

CHAPTER 30

Encounter with Juan

JUAN PABLO CORTEZ received his orders by the usual means, a man told another man who then told him. The secret words and hand motions were all correct. He was to kill Charles Dorgan and make sure even his DNA could not be discovered. He sat in his small home and plotted his next moves. Charles Dorgan was to be killed tonight. However, he wanted to confirm with the older Mr. Garcia. His call was welcomed, and he went straight to the point, "Sir, sorry to disturb you, but I need to confirm the assignation of Reverend Dorgan."

"Yes Juan, I ordered him killed tonight. He is to disappear without a trace."

"My plans are to kill him before morning. May I use the hidden ship?"

"Yes, but be careful not to be seen. Juan, you are invited to lunch tomorrow. I want you to assume more responsibility within the workings of the cartel. Also, this time you will not be standing but will be dining with me."

"That is an honor sir."

"Yes, and my brother likes you too. His cancer is getting worse, and he wants you to be higher in the cartel for my protection."

A few seconds of silence came over the phone with Juan finally saying, "I am honored that you want me as your personal body guard."

"No, you misunderstand me. He wants you in the very top echelon of decision making for the cartel. He says you are intelligent and dedicated."

"Mr. Garcia, I am very honored. I can be back by 10AM. I know you are busy. Would you rather have a brunch?"

"Juan, you are very efficient, but I do not feel Reverend Dorgan is as helpless as he seems. You know our spies say he stays up all night sometimes. He is also a big man."

"But, he does things in patterns and cycles. Some nights he is asleep by midnight. I believe this to be the night. Anyway, there are other ways to kill him if he is not asleep. He will be killed and disposed of possibly by as early as 8 AM."

"Again Juan, I am ordering you to take him very seriously and be careful. My brother and I are making good plans for you. I expect to see you at lunch tomorrow by noon. "

"I promise to be careful."

"Oh, I almost forgot. I am still contemplating killing Dr. Calhoun. I may assign our person that is near him to take him out. What do you think?"

"Ms. Jamison did disappear very quickly. I am sure our person can handle it. Can we talk about it more over lunch tomorrow?" asked Juan.

"Yes, and I want your opinion on why the sacrifices have stopped. We can discuss that over lunch also. There are still questions I have about the judge. Remember, lunch is tomorrow at noon."

"Yes sir. Good bye and thank you."

Juan drove within five miles from the Charles's Church, parked and got out of the black SUV, and hiked the road the rest of the way. He arrived at midnight and thought nothing righteous can happen after midnight. Juan watched as Charles finally turned the light off in his small bedroom in the back of the church and waited forty-five minutes to allow time for Charles to get to sleep. Quietly, Juan began to walk in felt soled shoes specially made for him. He stopped at the front doors and picked the ancient lock. After easing the right-hand door open slightly, he paused with a tube attached to a syringe of oil. After carefully placing the tube on top of each of the three large hinges, he oiled each one slightly with the penetrating lubricant and waited two minutes for the oil to take effect. Then, he took his universal remote in his pocket and cancelled the alarm using the correct frequency. Juan was dressed in camouflage knowing that black really stands out at night while European style camouflage really blends in with outside surroundings in the dark. The slightest push on the door, and he was in the small auditorium moving silently along the tiles. The felt shoes made no sound.

In his right hand, he held a small 9mm automatic pistol with a long silencer attached. He wore an expensive brown tooled leather shoulder holster hidden underneath his light jacket sandwiched on top of his tee shirt. All his clothing was camouflaged. Eventually, he made his way to the bedroom door where he paused for a moment before turning the knob slowly. He opened the door quickly and with quick coordinated movements had the muzzle of the silencer on the back of Charles head.

Charles woke up but did not move; his mouth was immediately dry, but he was able to speak a few words while trying to remain as calm as possible. "Whoever you are, you seem to have me at a great disadvantage."

Juan spoke perfect English like a Midwesterner and without his usual accent, "My name is Juan, and you are not at all disadvantaged."

"I would really like to speak with you concerning the immediate alternative, but I really do feel uncomfortable with whatever you have sticking in the back of my scalp," said Charles trying to cover for his nervousness and dry mouth.

"Oh, it is the least of your worries right now Charles. Would you like to get up, and then, we can talk?"

"As I said, considering what could happen, I look forward to speaking with you." Charles was assessing his alternatives but saw no clear advantage presently.

Juan turned on a small flashlight with a red lens in order to not decrease their night vision. He moved over to the front of the closet and motioned with the light for Charles to get up. Charles stood with his white boxers showing pink in the red light and moved slowly toward his robe at the foot of the bed and said, "I hope you want me to put something on."

"That is correct Reverend Dorgan, and I want to follow you to the study where we can be alone and talk."

Charles put on his dark blue robe and moved his feet until he found his cloth slip on house shoes at the side of the bed. Then, he moved into the narrow hallway that connected his bedroom and study in back of the auditorium. When they moved into Charles' office, Juan instructed him to sit but keep his hands in his lap. Charles complied, and once he was settled in the chair, Juan turned on the light, walked over to Charles and laid the pistol in Charles lap.

Charles jumped as if a snake was placed on him. He quickly picked up the pistol, hesitated, and nervously asked, "Juan, are you well?"

"Actually, I was hoping to speak with you after this mission about my job anxiety. By the way, I received my orders today to kill you."

"Yet, you give me your weapon? And, when I learn how to cope with my job anxiety, I will be able to better assist you. You are really a prize!" Charles said sarcastically but with some fear in his voice.

"That prize thing is what my mother said and surprisingly in the same tone. The weapon should help you feel in control."

Charles picked up the pistol from his lap and pulled open the slide; the chamber was empty. He pushed the release button on the left side with his thumb, and the magazine fell into his left hand and was also empty. Charles, fighting shock, looked confused at Juan and asked, "What does this mean?"

"It means that I need you to trust me."

Charles feared his next question but thought the advantages of asking outweighed the disadvantages, "Are orders issued to kill others?"

"No other orders are issued as far as I know, but it does appear that someone else is to die. Listen closely, we do not have much time. Candice and Nick are in no immediate danger, but Dr. Calhoun may be. The head of the cartel is getting nervous about the sudden disappearance of Ms. Jamison. My job is to kill you, but someone else may be assigned to kill Dr. Calhoun. There is a cartel assassin working with him, but I do not know if he is activated. I think I bought the doctor time until at least noon tomorrow."

"Before we really get started talking, may I ask who you are?" asked Charles.

"I am a double agent sent here long before you arrived to infiltrate the cartel. I am identified as a friend. You really know your stuff, but Joyce Jamison's disappearance is your Achilles heel. Her attempted murder of a cartel member is really shaking them. You may not know this, but the woman judge is your greatest enemy."

Charles was fighting off the shock and looked at Juan in the eyes and said, "You are very good at what you do. I did not hear you or even sense you coming in. There is something else; your spirit does not disturb me."

Juan looked Charles straight in his eyes and said while smiling, "That is a great compliment. It was my first attempt at being an assassin. How did I do?"

"I would have to say, you did very well for the first." Charles then caught himself and said quickly, "Wait a minute!"

"Charles, you are too easy, but all my fun aside, I need to brief you quickly and then you have to kill me, uh, fake kill me."

"But your spirit, like I said, does not disturb me."

Juan looked at Charles in the small light in the room and said, "That is because we are kindred spirits. You and I both see things we should not see and hear things we should not hear. There are at least three of us here: Nick, you, and myself."

"So, we both believe in God, in certain ways, except for Nick. He is still fighting it. Currently, he is a proclaimed atheist. Nick excluded for now, we have certain beliefs that sustain and protect us."

"Yes, and we both know that without our beliefs, we are all dead."

"OK, you are convincing me to trust you."

Juan held out his hand to Charles with an empty ten cc and a three-cc syringe and said, "Listen, I must really like you. There is a tarp outside to wrap me in just in case somebody sees us, and here are two syringes with needles."

Juan pulled a loaded magazine from his shirt pocket and handed it to Charles. He asked him to load the weapon. Charles complied and said, "So, we need both arterial and venous blood to put on the tarp."

"Now, you are getting the picture, but we need to get on with the briefing. First, the woman judge is very dangerous. I assume you know some things about her and that she is evil deluxe, but she really does not run any part of the cartel; the brothers do. She just informs them when she wants the sacrifices and keeps them out of legal problems. She is also some kind of a Mayan witch with really bizarre plans for bringing back the priestly kings, that according to her, will eventually rule all the Yucatan again. She protects the cartel, and they bring her victims. Currently, I am blocking the sacrifices, but they will certainly begin again after I leave. "

Charles was still fighting shock concerning the events of the night but knew that he needed to override all feelings and listen very closely. "So, she is trying to bring back the ancient Mayan religion with priests that are also local leaders?"

"More than that Charles, she believes that she is doing this through her secret rituals and also her sacrifices."

"Explain the sacrifices."

"OK, the sacrifices are mainly to one goddess called Chac Mool."

"The goddess with the well in her stomach?" asked Charles.

"Well, bowl, or basket- who knows? The bowl in the belly of the idol is about two foot across from what I hear. I am told the idol is about ten-foot-long and looks like a stone female half way doing a sit-up. I am not allowed at the sacrifices, but I do know where they are done. It is called by some of the folks around here the killing hole. That two-foot-wide basket in the old gal's stomach is what the judge ensures is filled with good human hearts every so often with the rest of the sacrificed bodies divided up and sold for their parts. Some people will pay millions for a needed kidney that matches perfectly. Other parts like corneas, lungs, and livers are sold immediately. There is a small airport in the jungle that delivers these items as quickly as possible, and some transplants are done locally. The sacrifices are the responsibility of the judge who believes she is a priestess from a line of Mayan royalty. The trade and disposal of the other remains are the responsibility of the two brothers who run the cartel once the remains are delivered to them. Candice and Nick dine with the flamboyant brother every so often."

"Yes, and you coordinate the meetings."

"Not any more. Orders are for me to get out. Thus, you are to fake murder me. My demise is figured out and approved. So far, I am able to block the sacrifices, but they may begin again after I am gone."

"During the sacrifices, does the judge cut out the hearts with a flint knife?"

"You are very informed. She gets down to every detail of the old sacrifices, but as I understand it, the so called priestly kings are mainly doing the sacrifices. The priestly kings may be someone around you. They could be business men in various towns who gave in to the religion. Anyway, I only know about her and know nothing except what I am told of these so-called kings. Some of the assistant personnel who clean and help with the parking and general maintenance of the hole can be bribed, and I learn from them also. I have to be very careful with those that I bribe for information due to the judge being very astute about potential traitors to her cause. Also, Cartel people are not allowed near the hole, and the heartless bodies are delivered to a place outside the area very quickly in refrigerated vans. I am only on the business end and not the religious end. The things I am telling you about the actual sacrifices are just what I could gleam for the conversations of others. "

Charles was feeling more comfortable with Juan and began to relax. Having a loaded weapon in his lap also made him feel calmer. He needed to know more but felt time was of the essence. "Juan, if that is your real name, I still need some more information. I know time is fleeting."

"Juan is my real name."

"It is? Wait a minute. Stop that. You do not do that to a man in shock."

"Again, how long you been in this business?" asked Juan jokingly.

"Long enough, but I did not think I would meet my equal tonight."

"Hey, that is quite a compliment. But, I need to tell you quickly what else I truly know. You probably noticed that I look Mayan. My people migrated about two generations ago from here to Michigan. I am a Michigan Mayan. I need to tell you that I can still be contacted after you fake kill me."

"I should really kill you. I almost died of a heart attack. I never knew you were even around me."

"Oh, that is great! I am always looking for people to take me seriously. When I tried to scare Candice and Nick by sneaking into their home and tying up their hired help, they just got angry, and it seems they thought more about killing me than being afraid. Thank you for telling me that I scared you. But, let's get back to the urgent stuff. The judge thinks she is the descendant of a survivor of a person thrown into the well for sacrifice at Chechen Itza. She believes the ancient ancestor not only survived the sixty or so foot fall to the water but actually floated to the top with all kinds of weights attached and bound hand and foot miraculously surviving the sacrificial attempt. Legend is that the person was a woman who was made a priestess, and the judge is in a direct line of that priestess. There is a secret religious society here, and they believe tremendously in her and our lady of the belly bowl."

"So, what happens with the bodies?"

"That I can tell you. They are cut up like animals and cannibalized for their parts. After the pagan ritual, it is all mechanical from there."

"Mechanical evil?" asked Charles.

"If you wish to call it that. I want this stopped and the rituals and organ harvesting stopped. Also, I want everyone involved brought to real justice, but one of us is to go tonight. You are doing good work here. None of the others made it as far as you, and it is because you are blocking the witch with your prayers and spiritual abilities."

"One last question before I draw your blood and dispose of you, do you know any weakness that can be exploited concerning the judge and the cartel?" asked Charles.

"The judge and the cartel members do not get alone. There is very little trust between them. The cartel leader is already looking for a way to exclude the judge, but he needs her for legal protection currently. One other thing, during the sacrifice there are usually no modern weapons allowed inside the sacrificial hole but beware of the primitive weapons like paddle swords with that sharpened glass looking stuff embedded in them. They can make an awful mess of a wound. Also, you need to know the hole is set to blow sky high. I do not have a trigger with me, but a good explosion inside the hole could also set it off. Be careful who you trust. I am not for sure, but I will bet that the so-called roster of the priests reads like a who's who of local government and business people."

"Juan, thank you. Now, let us get you bled and sacked."

"Would you be a little gentler about my demise? Please! You sound so cold speaking about it."

"What are you worried about? It is a fake death according to you."

Juan looked at the two syringes and frowned. "That small syringe is a blood gas needle. I hate getting my artery stuck in my wrist. I am certainly dreading it. It was done before several times in an intensive care when I got shot. Anyway, please remember their major weaknesses are the judge and her cohorts keep a lot of secrets from the cartel and vice versa. But, either snake is very poisonous and can certainly kill you. Both are extremely evil and powerful."

"Understood. Now, is it time for me to draw your blood and get you out of here?"

"I suppose, but be gentle. Why don't you let me hold the gun while you draw the blood?"

"Juan, how long you been in this business?" asked Charles finally smiling.

Juan held pressure on his wrist to prevent bleeding from the blood gas stick while Charles, to imitate a struggle, sprayed the inside of his office with seven shots from the silenced 9mm pistol. Then he went to the door, looked around, and spied the tarp meant for him lying near the stone walkway just outside the front door. He moved quickly back to his office and spread the tarp out on the cramped floor as best he could. He took the two syringes and sprayed the blood inside of the tarp making sure some got on the floor. Juan laid down and allowed himself to be rolled up with two window cords tied at each end.

Juan crooking his head looked down at the cords and pleaded, "not too tight. I want to get out quickly if there is trouble."

"Understood. Here are the ends of the cords; hold them in your hand and pull if there are problems. The knots will come loose, and you should be able to roll out."

"The more I know you Charles, the more I like you."

"You seem like a moral person Juan. It takes moral people to defeat evil."

While Charles was busy making sure the tarp would hold and ensuring that Juan could escape, Juan asked a question, "Charles, do you think you will survive this?"

Charles looked serious and sad at the same time while he answered his new friend, "I do not know for certain, but I do not believe I will survive this. That conflicts heavily with my sincere goal that I would never become a martyr."

Juan looked at him seriously and said, "I will be praying for you and your team."

"Thank you. Things are touch and go now."

"Charles, if you get a chance, kill the judge. She is that evil, and I do not think it would be vengeance with you. Really, she is that dangerous. Also, you know that you need to drag me outside without my help in case anyone sees us."

"I know that I need to drag you, and concerning the judge, I am depending on God for my actions if I see her. Anyway, lie still and let us get this over with."

"OK. I just hate to leave such good company."

"I know. Now, stop moving. I am about to drag you outside and place you in the back of the church SUV, and I really wish you could help."

As Charles heard Juan's muffled voice as he slung the canvas loosely over his face, "Oh, just pull me and start my journey out of this forsaken place."

Charles checked his phone and saw the bug was on its back and dead. He called Candice and a sleepy female voice answered on the other end, "Hello Reverend. I hope that you are doing well. The weather has seemed to stop the biting bugs here. Are your bites healing?"

"Yes, my bites are completely healed. Candice, I need to tell you about some recent happenings."

"Good, what do you need Charles?"

"I have Juan with me. He is doing well and sends his regards."

Candice sat up immediately in bed fully awake, "What is Juan doing with you? I hate that creep."

"Actually, he is a rather good assassin and a double agent being sent back tonight. He speaks good English and has no accent normally. Did you know that?"

"Charles, you better start explaining."

"No time right now. I am taking his live body to dump it where he says. I am calling to inform you that, according to Juan, Dr. Calhoun has an assassin assigned to him."

"Do you know who he is?"

"Juan says he is the orderly named Antonio."

"I will get word to Doc immediately. You be careful with what you are doing- whatever that is. You know I trust and love you a lot."

"The same to you, but right now, I need to get Juan to his final resting place."

"Tell Juan that I still think he's a creep, but I will keep an open mind."

"Actually, he did not kill me tonight and is giving us a lot of needed information. Also, he promises to help after he leaves here. I need to go. Wake Nick and tell him about the good doctor's potential assassin. Also, watch out for things yourselves."

"Waiting to hear the whole story. We will protect Doc. Let us know when you return and what is happening."

"Sure thing."

"Good bye and be careful."

"Good bye."

The road to the map coordinates given to Charles by Juan led to the ocean. Charles went as far as he could on the road and then dragged the tarp with Juan's live body to the lonely small sandy beach in front of his automobile lights. There he unwrapped Juan at his asking and quickly folded and buried the tarp in the sand with his bare hands. Suddenly, a large flat bottomed boat appeared and ran up into the shallow waters of the beach but was very careful to not touch the dry sand with their boat or their feet. Four men dressed in dark camouflage with automatic weapons suddenly appeared in knee deep water and instructed Charles to drag Juan into the water. Charles complied, and Juan stood up in the knee-deep water with the small waves lapping at his pants and got into the boat. The motor was quiet but powerful, and suddenly, Charles was alone on the beach with no sight of the boat, Juan, or the men. Charles turned around, walked back to the SUV, and paused for a moment looking out over the quiet beach and waters illuminated by the automobile lights and asked to himself in a low voice, "What in the world do we do now?"

CHAPTER 31

Antonio

DR. CALHOUN WATCHED as Antonio went to his locker in the clinic. The large electronic clock over Dr. Calhoun's head read 4:16AM in large red numbers against a black face, and Antonio was never known to be at the clinic this early. Antonio opened the locker and pulled something black and small from under some clothes and papers; it was a small caliber pistol. Dr. Calhoun watched as Antonio flung open the cylinder and made sure it was loaded. Dr. Calhoun surmised it was a 22 caliber six shot revolver. It was an assassin's gun.

By chance, after looking in on a patient staying overnight, he had seen Antonio come through the front door to the clinic on one of the video cameras that informs nurses of the goings on in the clinic and small hospital. Dr. Calhoun was informed several times that Antonio had been asking too many of the right questions to the wrong people after Joyce had disappeared by different people working in the clinic and small recovery hospital. Dr. Calhoun watched as Antonio paused a few moments in front of the opened locker. Then, he moved quickly sticking the needle attached to the syringe into Antonio's right shoulder with his right hand while grabbing the gun with his free left hand. Antonio struggled, and the gun fired accidently. Antonio grabbed his abdomen and began breathing hard as he began slumping down to the floor in front of his open locker. He became still when he accomplished a bent over position. His grunting became more frequent and louder from the increasing pain.

"Were you about to kill me Antonio?"

"Yes", Antonio said in a low groan. "What did you give me?"

"Something to place the odds in my favor. I will get you to surgery. Now, be still and let me check the wound."

"It's too late. You can never get the OR ready in time. I really did not want to kill you. I like you and thank you anyway for offering to get me to the OR." His voice weakened. "I almost didn't try to kill you."

Dr. Calhoun knowing that Antonio's time was short asked, "Who are you really Antonio?"

"I am known as the sleeper, but my real name is," and Antonio gasped once and then stopped breathing in mid-sentence. He was dead.

Dr. Calhoun laid him flat on his back on the floor and examined the wound. He surmised the bullet hit his spleen causing him to bleed to death rapidly. There was little time to try to save Antonio, and with the time it would take to get everything ready, the surgery probably would not have been successful anyway.

The phone in Dr. Calhoun's lab coat rang startling him. He answered, and Candice's panicked voice on the other end said, "Dr. Calhoun, the bugs are dead right now. I need to tell you that Antonio may try to kill you."

"He just did. He is dead."

"Are you OK?"

Dr. Calhoun sounded both worried and sorrowful at the same time, "Yes, but everything is falling apart here. We really need to make some new plans. I am so sorry. I know we needed at least another month. It all happened so fast."

"Oh, I need to tell you a lot also. Juan is gone now. He's a double agent who just saved Charles' life and alerted us about Antonio possibly attempting to kill you. Anyway, Charles is currently driving back from Antonio's departure point. Please be careful. Nick is up and planning escape routes for us. We really need to all meet and get out of here. "

"Agreed. Call me with the meeting place."

"Nick says our home is the best place for us to meet. Pack the things we decided on before in case we are need to get away."

"OK, did you say that Charles is driving to your home?"

"Yes, and he should be here within the next hour or so. Come quickly. We are waiting."

"One last thing, can we salvage the mission?" asked Dr. Calhoun.

"Charles says he believes we can. He did not say much. He reports Juan giving him some good information. That's all I know right now. Please, I love you and get on the road quickly."

Dr. Calhoun fought back tears because he had just killed a man and managed to get out an old enduring saying for Candice in his choking voice, "sure thang my jelly bean."

"Dr. Calhoun, you did what you had to do. Please get to us quickly as possible. We love you. Good bye and be careful you cement block."

"I am coming to you. Good bye, and you be careful too."

Mr. Garcia was sitting at breakfast at 9AM when his cell phone rang. He answered, and the voice on the other end quickly said, "Sir, Juan never showed with the reverend's body."

He replied, "I will contact him immediately. Stand by in case he got delayed."

"Yes sir."

Mr. Garcia hung up and tried to call Juan. There was no answer, and he could not leave a message. Then, he activated his people to set out to find Juan. Word came back later that the church had bullet holes with blood in the study. Mr. Garcia knew that this was too sloppy for Juan, so he told his people to get the blood analyzed for DNA and then to check all areas of beach they used for body disposal. The blood analysis would take days, but the bloody tarp was discovered by his men at a small beach with footprints much larger than Juan's in the sand. It was almost noon when Mr. Garcia called his brother and pronounced, "We are dealing with professionals. I need you to get to the airport and leave the country immediately. I will take care of business here. Take guards with you, and you do not need to pack well. Take money, and I will send you more as needed."

Pasqual replied, "I will be leaving. In my condition, I am not much good to you anyway."

"Take guards and get to the airport as quickly as possible."

"What about Juan?"

"It looks like he is dead and gone. It appears the reverend killed him."

"Juan is the best I know. If someone killed him, that someone is very good and very dangerous."

"Another thing, I cannot contact Antonio. It seems someone is moving on us quickly and knows our moves. I am retreating to the mansion in the forest until I can figure out what is happening. Now, get to the airport. Contact me later."

"Yes brother. I love you. Please be careful."

"You too. Good bye."

It was still morning when Charles and Dr. Calhoun arrived almost at the same time to the home place. The rain was beginning to fall while Nick was busy loading the SUV with needed supplies. Candice was monitoring for radio transmissions from the small airport that Juan had told Charles existed in the forest. Charles had spoken with Candice while driving over the cell phones to inform her in more detail concerning what Juan had said to him. The new emergency plans were being formulated to include capturing or maybe killing the two brothers who lead the cartel, shutting down the judge with her sacrificial rituals, and shutting down the small airport. Charles was to take on the judge; Candice to ensure communication and plan changes among all the members of the tetrahedron, to get into the cartel's mainframe, and send the information out to different communication points to include their ship off the coast; Dr. Calhoun was assigned to formulate a plan for capture or killing the two brothers, and Nick to shut down the jungle airport and find a route out to safety. The goals were monumental and hardly any member thought their chances for success on any one goal was any more than slim.

Charles began to speak optimistically, "There are advantages for us."

Nick quickly followed up, "I know. They believe two of their best assassins are dead. It looks like we know what we are doing and that we are attacking with good momentum. If they panic and pull back, we may win."

Charles began to back track some and said, "Win may be too strong a word, but we can at least have a chance. We hope these are more thugs than professionals."

Candice then asked, "If they panic, where would they go?"

Charles said,"They would try to get some of their key people out of the country. For instance, I am sure the leader would try to get his sick brother out, so he could continue his cancer treatment."

Nick said, "Their private airport would be the most logical place to start on land. Candice can notify the ship to watch for any suspicious boats leaving the area. Otherwise, we cannot cover the roads. Let's hope they panic and try to get to the airport or to the ocean. However, it does leave a big tactical problem."

"I think I can guess this one Nick," said Charles. "The best of the real fighters will stay behind."

"That is correct," stated Nick. "And, they are more or less ready for anything our small force can muster. I would still like to try though."

CHAPTER 32

The Best Laid Plans Lead to the Airport

THE FOUR STOOD together almost ready to get into the black SUV laden with supplies and with what weapons they had at their homes, clinic, and church. They looked at each other, and Charles was first to speak, "I totally agree we need to get to the airport first. I think we can find a good working computer with valuable data on it and maybe get a prisoner who might tell us some needed information."

Nick looked at Charles and smiled as if he was in his very element, "You sound so sure of yourself Charles."

Charles sounded sarcastic about himself, "I know I do. I am also thinking if they throw all our ashes in the same place, we would stay together. I hate to leave this group. Nick, you are the tactical one. Tell us more."

"I think what you said about the airport makes as much sense as anything else. I also think that staying here and doing nothing is the worst thing to do. We need to get moving. We can pick up more weapons, ammo, and supplies at our nearest cache. Let's go take an airport."

Candice looked at Nick with almost amazement, "Aren't you gung ho?"

"No," said Nick, "I just want to get moving. Standing still is not good right now. If they think we have momentum, we may cause them to make mistakes that we can capitalize on."

Doctor Calhoun got into the right back seat and said, "I need somebody to drive while I sit in fear."

"OK," said Charles as he got into the left back seat. "Nick, you drive. Candice, you sit in front of me and look pretty, and Doctor Calhoun can help me with my heart attack."

Candice looked back at Charles with fire in her eyes, "Don't you even say you are having a heart attack you grouch. I break ribs when I do CPR."

Nick while eerily smiling sang in a poor operatic voice, "We're going to take an airport, take an airport, take an airport."

"It's Nick's singing that will kill us," Dr. Calhoun said as his head was slung backward by Nick's quick take off.

The cache had not been touched and was shallow due to the limestone bed rock in that area. They quickly dug out the items and checked each one for rust or depletion. Everything was in good working order, and they returned to the SUV while loading weapons. Nick reported he would keep his three-barreled shotgun that had a rifle barrel underneath the two side-by-side shotgun barrels. They were on their way to the airport as given the coordinates by Juan. They parked the SUV off the road and hiked to the edge of the airfield.

Candice directed the drones from her laptop as they darted through the trees toward the airport's coordinates. From her cameras, she could see a metal building that stood near the runway with five planes and a helicopter at the open front. Five men worked in the metal building seemingly to get the twin engine airplane ready when they were disturbed by the two drones. Two men picked up AK's and began to fire at the drones, so Candice simply pulled them back into the forest. She landed them in a small, grassy clearing in the woods and began to get ready for the attack.

The four tetrahedron members began to make their way through the forest together careful to stay away from the entry road. The planes and helicopter were around the hanger that was hidden from level sight by the trees. The five men scattered as Nick approached and held his fire until he thought the right man was in his sights. By chance, it was the second highest man in the cartel who was the leader's brother, so he held his fire. Instead, he stood ready to shoot as Dr. Calhoun ran across the runway toward the hanger with his back bent and his face looking from side to side. Dr. Calhoun had his 9mm pistol ready to fire if necessary. The objective however was not to kill but to capture. Candice and Charles came in from the back side of the metal building, and as ordered by Nick, both stopped and scanned behind them before moving near the back of the building. Candice stopped at the right hand back side of the building, and Charles stopped at the left hand back side of the building.

Dr. Calhoun came to a sudden stop at the open front of the hanger and stood even with Nick. Charles asked on his two way as he watched the men disappear into the jungle, "Do we pursue?"

"Charles, it is best not to, and Dr. Calhoun, it would also be better if you got on the other side of me behind this wall. Never allow yourself to be seen from a tree line."

Dr. Calhoun said, "understood" and moved over behind the metal side while still looking out the open front.

Nick went to a left-hand side window and began to search the tree line for movement.No movement was seen. Dr. Calhoun placed his binoculars to his eyes and began to search the area. Candice and Charles quickly worked their way around the open front of the hanger, and Charles stayed at the open front behind the metal wall while Candice went to the far side wall. Both began scanning the area with binoculars to detect movement.

Nick, with his voice low as possible, spoke over the small two ways, "Keep alert; they will be careful not to shoot as long as we are in the hanger. They need this plane to get away."

Charles began to ask about the other planes and helicopter not in the building when he suddenly heard a bang. Nick had moved to the middle of the front of the building, and with the rifle on his three barrel, he had placed an explosive round in the helicopter that punctured the fuel tank. It began to burn. Then, Nick placed shots in the other planes and all began to burn. The only flyable airplane now was the twin engine in the hanger.

Charles spoke, "So, if they fire on us, they might kill their only ride?"

Nick spoke again, "They have only one choice, but be on guard, they can still pick us off. Look for anything that moves and shoot at it, but if possible, shoot low. Try to wound whenever possible, so we can get information from them."

Three voices answered, "understood."

Suddenly, Dr. Calhoun saw movement in the tree line and began to fire. Nick began to look from the back-side window and trained his scope on something moving and noticed a man beginning to run toward the hanger window that Nick was guarding. Nick placed the scope on the man's right thigh and pulled the trigger. The man collapsed in a heap and then began to unfold while screaming at the top of his lungs when a second shot took him out. The man had been shot from the opposite direction and was motionless.

Suddenly, there were other shots from beyond the tree line with lots of movement, firing, and screaming followed by an eerie silence. Candice looked at Nick and asked, "What was that?"

"Help. I think."

Suddenly, a man appeared across the field waving his arms and saying in Spanish, "We have a wounded man; we need help. Three enemy are dead." Charles interrupted on the two ways.

Dr. Calhoun looked at Nick and asked, "Is that who I think he is?"

"Yes. That is Arturo, and I believe that he brought the militia."

Dr. Calhoun did not think about anything but the wounded militia man and also did not notice that the cartel people running toward the tree line were picking their routes. Nick was busy watching the tree line when Dr. Calhoun ran past him going straight toward the man who was signaling for help.

Nick looked and yelled, "no!" when the mine went off shredding Dr. Calhoun's lower right leg and throwing him about three feet into the air.

Now, Dr. Calhoun was lying still on his back with his arms sticking straight up into the air with clinched fists; nausea came over him, but he had no pain.

Nick, who was startled by the explosion made himself regain his composure, and he brought his full attention to Dr. Calhoun; he barked out orders, "Dr. Calhoun, stay still; don't even lower your arms or roll over; I am coming!" Arturo suddenly disappeared behind the tree line.

Nick yelled at the top of his voice, "Doc is down! Cover me!"Candice moved to a position where she had a good view of Nick and leveled her M-16 toward the front tree line while Charles began to scan the area all around his view for any movement with his scoped rifle.

Nick saw a sturdy fiber glass rod used for who knows what from the nearby open tool box and an extension cord hanging on the wall. He estimated the extension cord to be about 10-foot-long; he placed it over his head and left neck, and it angled to the right side of his torso. He hated to use the wire due to the copper and its possible effect of mines, but he was in a hurry. The cord was all he could find at short notice. He laid down his three-barreled weapon and pulled off his watch due to the electronics possibly setting off a magnetic mine and laid both beside the hanger wall. Then, he picked up a stick laying near the building. He ran to the edge of the black top, and even though figuring the mines did not begin immediately due to airplanes possibly running off the runway, he would not take the chance. All dirt in that area was considered dangerous to him. Quickly, he began looking for the indentions in the grass for evidence of Dr. Calhoun's footprints and began to pick his way forward, first pushing the stick into the possible safe area while on his knees and then stopping every movement he made to scan the area for anyone who might fire on them. Nick brought a deck of playing cards in case of mines and placed a card at each clear and safe step. He was making his way toward Dr. Calhoun when he saw a figure raise in front of him and began to shout apologies in Spanish. Charles answered back consoling the man. Then, Charles asked in Spanish, "Did you say three are dead?"

The man answered back in Spanish, "Three are dead, even the big man's brother in the cartel."

Nick continued trying to make it to Dr. Calhoun to prevent him from bleeding to death from the blast. Nick knew Dr. Calhoun's right foot had been hit by the mine and that a tourniquet might be the only thing between life and death for his injured friend. However, Nick also knew that information had to be gathered as quickly as possible and yelled to Charles, "Keep asking questions Charles and translate to us as necessary."

Charles asked, "How many are there of you?"

"Twenty-one."

As Nick continued to approach Dr. Calhoun, he heard from the back of the building a single shot and then a three-round burst of fire from an M-16. Candice yelled at the top of her lungs, "I shot one. There were two. They fired on me and are dressed like the airport people are dressed. Charles, watch the woods to the side we came in on. Somebody is running back there."

Nick saw movement and then saw a figure running away from him but could not make out if friend of foe, and he knew that chaos could erupt with friendly fire between them and their militia friends. He yelled, "Charles, can you see your man? If not, do not shoot. We will let these men go after him. Charles, ask them if they have anybody back there."

Charles said, "I did not see anybody until after Candice shot. My target ran off. I could not get a clear shot at him." He raised his voice as high as he could and yelled in Spanish, "Do any of you see any cartel people in the trees?"

Gunfire erupted again, but this time from the back of the building. A voice sounded in Spanish, "He is dead."

Nick fearing that other enemy could be in the jungle around them said to Candice and Charles, "Both of you watch your flanks. I am trying to get to Dr. Calhoun, and when I do, I will not be able to watch for the enemy or protect myself. Watch your areas well. Charles, ask the men who are helping us if they will show themselves to us while taking care not to endanger themselves. Also, show yourselves to them very briefly. Tell them to look for you to come out quickly and go back. We don't want to kill each other. They seem to be all the way on our side."

The jungle suddenly gave up twenty figures that were dressed in various camouflage and plain clothing. Then all disappeared within seconds. Charles stood outside the hanger wall first and then as quickly as possible disappeared while Candice showed herself for a few seconds.

"Done," came two voices almost in unison.

Nick made his way to the last bent grass and ruffled dirt. He bent over placing the longer stick on the ground and took a pencil from his pocket and begin to poke the ground in one inch intervals until he determined that the area had no mines on the right side of Dr. Calhoun. Then, he took the cord from his torso and began to wrap it just below the calf of the injured leg and said, "Alright, you can rest your right arm now on the ground but don't move anything on your left side."

Dr. Calhoun said, "I'm sorry. I suckered myself into a minefield."

"You did not mean to do it. Are you in pain?"

"No. But, I think I am going into shock. How is the foot?"

"It is ruined. I am tying a tourniquet."

Dr. Calhoun's voice was beginning to weaken, "Aren't you supposed to say something like- you are going to be OK. Maybe say, you are alright. Anyway, did it bleed much?"

"You are a doctor. You would know better about the condition of your foot and leg. But, it only bled a little."

"Sometimes, that's the thing about traumatic wounds. Sometimes, they don't bleed much."

Nick placed the fiberglass rod in the knotted cord circling the leg and began to twist. Dr. Calhoun did not grimace, so Nick knew the leg had no feeling. The boot, foot, and some of the lower leg was missing. What was left of the lower leg was intact enough to tie off the tourniquet and stop any bleeding. Nick cut off a generous piece of cord and tied it loosely above the calf and with it tied the long end of the fiber glass rod in place.

"You're pretty good at this. You done this before? I may not finish with you Nick. I'm afraid I might pass before you can get me out of here."

"Yes, I did this before, and awake or asleep, you're going with me. And, I am not about to let you pass as you say."

"What was that thing anyway?"

"Unfortunately, it was an American made M-14 antipersonnel mine."

"A toe popper?"

Nick continued to work feverishly as he said, "That's the common name for it. Try and take your mind off what is happening. Tell me something, why am I not to ask you about blowing your own trumpet?"

Dr. Calhoun's voice was trembling as he uttered his last sentences in a weakening voice, "Because, I would grab you from behind and squeeze your abdomen until you made a sound like a trumpet. I wish I could do that to you now. Nick, if somebody else squeezes you like that, it could cause damage. I am a doctor, so I can get away with it." His voice was weakening as he said, "I can pass out now because you are here and all that can be done will be done. I trust you that much Nick." With those words, Dr. Calhoun's left hand fell, but no mine was set off.

Tears formed in Nick's eyes, but he fought back the emotion and begun to work his way around Dr. Calhoun's left side attempting to ensure enough safe area to pick up Dr. Calhoun and carry him to safety. Meanwhile, Candice and Charles were looking with all their might to ensure that nobody from the cartel was hiding in the woods. They knew Nick and Dr. Calhoun were sitting ducks.

Two men from the tree line began to move into the field using sticks to find mines. Nick looked ahead and thought they were very good using sticks and wearing no watches knowing that metal and batteries can set off certain mines.

They were clearing a way for Dr. Calhoun and himself. Two other men appeared suddenly with a stretcher made from two long freshly cut poles with their shirt sleeves down each end of the poles leaving the buttoned bodies of the two shirts for Dr. Calhoun to lie on. Nick was beginning to have a real affection for these men.

Nick thought about his next move and yelled, "Candice, call in the helicopter from the ship. You and Charles make sure a landing zone is secured. Charles, ask the men if they will make sure nobody is around us and tell them our plans. Notify the pilots to not be alarmed by our new-found friend's movements and certainly not to open fire unless very certain of their targets. Our people can secure the grounds. I'm taking Doc to the twin engine in the hanger. It's the safest place because if someone unfriendly is still out there, they will not be firing near it. It's intact and their only way out."

"Done," came Candice's voice. She notified the helicopter as Charles began to scan the area for a landing zone near the hanger. Candice held her M-16 at the ready in her right hand with the butt stock against her right hip while holding her auto focusing binoculars to her face with her left hand. She was hiding behind a midsized rolling tool box but continued to look over the top with just her forehead and eyes exposed.

Candice nor Charles noted any movement. The proposed landing zone appeared clear thanks to their friends in the jungle. The militia men had made it to Dr. Calhoun, had placed him on the stretcher, and while two men poked the ground, two men carried the stretcher slowly toward the hanger. All the while, Nick expected to feel a shot- you never hear the one that got you- from someone lurking in the distance, but when the grass ended into the blacktop of the runway leading to the hanger, it gave him new hope for survival. Finally, they were clear. Nick picked up his three-barreled weapon and watch near the hanger wall. He quickly put his watch on his left wrist and then slung the three barrel over his right shoulder as he moved as quickly as he could into the hanger. Nick ran with all his might toward the twin engine, stopped just short of the left wing, and instructed by hand gestures to bring Dr. Calhoun to the back of the plane as gently as possible. The men laid Dr. Calhoun gently on the six-foot-wide area between the twin engine's tail and the back wall. Nick found a bundle of clean red rags on a back table and placed them under Dr. Calhoun's head. Then, he placed his index and middle finger on Dr. Calhoun's neck and noted the pulse was rapid but strong. Dr. Calhoun remained unconsciousness.

The ship's civilian helicopter circled the hanger twice as the gunner watched over his thirty-caliber machine gun. Candice called with the purposed landing zone, and

Candice, Nick, and Charles were all scanning the area ready to fire, but no movement was noted from anyone that looked unfriendly as three men came from the chopper dressed in camouflaged flight suits with stethoscopes resting on their shoulders. Nick made the man in front out to be the doctor. One of the following medics was carrying a rolled-up stretcher and the other a medical kit. It took minutes, and Dr. Calhoun was on his way on a new stretcher to the open side of the landed helicopter. Candice was given the OK to go, ran to the helicopter, climbed in and sat where the crewman instructed her. Nick was standing near the hanger and was looking into Candice's eyes when he signaled for the helicopter to take off. Candice was to use the ships strong computers to track the enemy and to communicate variations in plans with Nick and Charles. Suddenly, she yelled "no" and quickly slid out of the seat, ran back, and stood beside Nick. She prayed below her voice for Dr. Calhoun to be OK. After Nick signaled another go, the helicopter took off and disappeared quickly over the trees.

Nick looked at her with confusion and asked, "Why didn't you leave?"

"Nick, there is a computer in there. It is in that small room. I bet it's got a lot of good information on it. Can you buy me time to hack it before you and Charles continue?"

Nick looked startled that he did not notice the computer in the small office when he scanned it for possible combatants. He managed to say, "Sure, that's a really good idea."

"Don't feel bad. You are just trying to ensure our survival. You are wonderful. No matter what happens, I really want you to know that."

She turned her head quickly to hide her tears about Dr. Calhoun and ran quickly to the little room in the back-left hand corner. There, she woke up the computer and began to hack into the hard drive. Suddenly, names and dates began to appear. Then, business transactions with more names and places and even phone numbers. She knew that she was somehow connecting a main frame somewhere, so she pulled her super tablet from her small backpack, pulled off the protective plastic and padding, and began to download as quickly as possible. The data was coming quickly, and all of it seemed valuable.

Meanwhile, Charles and Nick were speaking with the men who had helped them secure the airport. They had two vehicles and knew the whereabouts of the killing hole and also the main leader of the cartel. Charles and Nick decided to spilt the force and each go after the two main enemies.

In minutes, Candice reappeared with her tablet. She looked at Nick and pronounced, "I hacked in. It is a lot of stuff, clear up into the US. There are names of people, hospitals, even drug deals, and you would not believe all I got. I am calling in the helicopter again for pickup. I need to get this data sent out to everyone, but I need the ship's computers to make sure I get all the information, send it out, and then close down the cartel's computers."

Charles and Nick looked very pleased and knew this was valuable. They had all confidence that Candice could succeed. But, the two heads of the monster still needed to be neutralized.

Candice looked both anxious and sad knowing she needed to be on the ship making sure all the connections were done and the information went out correctly, yet she asked, "Will you two be OK? I hate to leave you alone, but I need to get to the ship. Am I doing right, leaving you like this? I almost forgot; I left my laptop in the little room. Use it to run the drones if you need them."

Nick looked said to her as Charles nodded, "I'll get the laptop, and I insist that you leave. You are great, but you need to be there and make sure all the information gets out right. Now, go close them down."Also, Nick felt relieved that she would not be in immediate danger.

Candice looked at Charles with tears in her eyes as she heard the chopper begin to circle. The civilian helicopter stayed just off the ground with its main blade running as the door gunner moved just enough to let her small frame go through. The pilot was taking no chances, and the helicopter disappeared quickly. Once settled in the aircraft, she took out her tablet and began to transmit to the ship.

Aboard the ship, the communications officer was called over suddenly into the communication room of the vessel. A petty officer briefed the communications officer that new data was coming in and being safely downloaded. The officer viewed the data, smiled and declared, "We got them. Download everything and save."

The petty officer looked at his sailor working quickly to get everything and proclaimed, "You did good work son. Now, get me all you can."

Charles approached Nick and asked to speak with him alone. Nick complied, and they went into the small room in the hanger where the computer and Candice's laptop were located. While the militia stood guard, Charles asked, "Nick, I need to be rigged with explosives."

Nick looked at Charles with anger in his eyes, "OK, I do not like where this is going."

"Nick, it might be our only hope of closing her down."

"OK, I can do it, but it is to be done a certain way."

"What do you mean?"

"It is to be a removable jacket with the explosives. There is a big man in the militia who I think is bigger than you. He is dressed in an old battle dress uniform top with jeans for pants."

"I know about him."

"Go out and ask him for his top now. Explain to him what it is for. Also, bring me Candice's and your backpacks. There is extra stuff in there to include grenades and some C-4 with triggers that we got from the cache."

Charles returned with the backpacks while Nick was outside the small room trying to get as many needed tools gathered as he needed. Charles brought the jacket to Nick who immediately began to place in explosives on the inside and in the pockets. He said with his head bowed and moving his hands quickly, "Charles, the only way I will do this is if you can pull this off and trigger it from a distance." Nick looked at Charles and asked, "Will you divide up the men and get them ready? We need to get information from them. I will try to take out the cartel leader if you will go after the witch judge. I will keep some explosives for the drones, but what I am fixing you will take out everyone in a big room. Just be careful and get cover as quickly as possible before you set it off."

The jacket was loaded with the improvised explosives and seemed heavy and hot to Charles as he moved toward a large pick-up loaded with weapons and men.

Nick was riding toward the hide out of the main cartel leader as told to him by Angel. Charles and Nick gave their SUV to the leader of the militia, so two militia men could drive the wounded man to a local doctor and nurse who would care for him secretly. The remaining eighteen militia men were divided equally between Nick and Charles. Arturo and Angel accompanied Nick who were traveling in a pickup. Arturo drove while another militia man rode shotgun. Angel and Nick rode in the truck bed with the rest of the men. Charles and his group were traveling in the opposite direction in another pick-up to what the men called the killing hole.

Candice arrived to the ship via the helicopter and was immediately greeted by Captain Perkins who was a rather small, wiry female with a very stern face. She took Candice by the hand after she cleared the perimeter of the helicopter blades and congratulated her on a job well done. A tall, muscular man who appeared in his early thirties arrived on the deck and said to Candice, "Hello Mrs. Lippincott, I am Lieutenant Cummings, and I am the communications officer. Will you accompany me to the communications center?"

"I would be glad to, but please, call me Candice."

Both went through the bridge to the small open room in the back that was packed with computers and screens of every size. To a novice or even an educated computer expert, the scene would have been confusing, but Candice sat down immediately and began to work. She turned to the communications officer and reported, "I think I can get into their mainframe. Can I get permission?"

"What are the consequences if something goes wrong?"

"I do not believe it will happen, but it will fry the ship's computers. How good is your protection?"

"The best. What are the gains?"

"We can get all the information off their systems and then fry them. "

"So, we can shut them down?"

"Yes."

Lieutenant Cummings immediately called the Captain and said, "I need permission to get into the enemy computers. Good chances of getting all they have and shutting them down with a small chance of killing the ship's computers. Candice is known for her skills with IT. I trust her to make it right. Also, we have back-ups if problems do occur."

The commander's voice came back on the phone, "It is worth the chance, but let me speak with Mrs. Lippincott."

Lt. Cummings took off his head phones with an attached microphone and handed it to Candice who held it up to her right ear with her right hand and said, "Captain, I am here."

"Mrs. Lippincott, I need you to take every precaution that none of the ship's information goes out, so you are to abort immediately if it looks like it is going bad."

"I will Captain. I do not want any secrets, especially aboard this ship, to get out. Also, I will get Lt. Cummings to check with me on every step."

"Good, now be careful."

"Yes Captain."

Candice handed the head piece back to Lt. Cummings who nodded to begin. Information began to stream freely, and the lieutenant said, "It looks like a one-way street, so far, directly to us. You are quite good at this Mrs. Lippincott."

"Let's keep it coming only to us and nothing going out. We are also blessed that the brother who knew so much about the cartel's computer is dead. Also, I feel that at least some of the cartel's staff are scattered."

Candice watched as the rapid download finished. She turned to Lt. Cummings and said, "The download is complete. I isolated it also and made sure no viruses or other critters are present. It should be good, clean data."

"Excellent."

"Now, let's fry these eggs."

"How are you going to do that?" asked Lt. Cummings.

"I discovered a worm used to infiltrate other computers that could be used to try and infiltrate them. Um, it is being fed back to them as we speak with just some little changes."

"Their computers are eating themselves?" asked the lieutenant.

Candice was busy concentrating and had not noticed the audience of the usual workers in that section. They were behind her wide eyed and gazing with amazement. She looked at the two young male faces staring and then moved her eyes to the lieutenant and said a definite, "Yes." Then she looked at the screen again and pronounced, "They are crashed."

Both men and the lieutenant erupted in applause that disrupted the main bridge. The Captain called Lt. Cummings immediately and said, "OK, I surmise that she did it, but you need to keep it down back there."

The lieutenant looking embarrassed but still smiling proclaimed, "We need to hold it down, but Candice, I want to grow up and be like you." Both sailors nodded quietly in agreement.

Candice felt good for only a few seconds, and then, her mind went back to Charles and Nick. She asked the Lt., "Can I have a corner where I can operate my tablet? I need to keep up with my two friend's vital signs and whereabouts."

"Sure," said Lt. Cummings, and he added, "You can sit here with us."

"Thanks."

Nick and the militia men were arriving at the place of the last known whereabouts of the cartel leader. Angel was there to interpret. Arturo began to slow down at the curve in the road and slowed even more before turning into a dirt road in the jungle.

Angel turned to Nick and said, "We walk from here."

Nick nodded in agreement.

The jungle was thick, but the trail was well worn, once found, from the men using the trail to spy on the cartel leader's home. Suddenly, the large white house appeared through the edge of the wood line about 200 meters from his position. It had arches on the long porches supported with long columns about twelve feet apart. The house was deep, wide, and a three story with elaborate windows on every level.

The roof was red tile and appeared very heavy, too heavy to be penetrated by their weapons. A large black limousine was parked in front on the tiled circular drive. The entire home was huge, beautiful, and had elaborate gardens of native flowers growing at the sides of the drive and within the grounds.

They had the two drones and Candice's laptop because Charles and Nick agreed they would be of no use to Charles at the killing hole. Yet, the small amount of explosive kept by Nick would not make a great difference with the choice of a blind explosion in any part of the house. It was also too far to raid another cache.

Nick had a 7.62 mm semi-automatic rifle on his right shoulder and carried the three barrel in his left hand. He held his powerful binoculars up to his eyes with his right hand and looked for any movement both without and within the house. The squad of men watched him as if they awaited orders. His interpreter said in broken English, "We are waiting on you sir. Arturo says that you are our leader now."

Nick looked at the interpreter and stated. "Alright, I'm in charge."

The interpreter looked back at the men, spoke in Spanish, and then nodded back to Nick. Nick felt responsible for each man here as if they were a part of the tetrahedron and motioned for all to hide or lie down. Everybody disappeared behind Nick while he continued to look at the home looking for weaknesses. He spied each window and each corner of the home for surveillance equipment. The house looked empty without lights on and showed no other signs of life.

Nick looked at the far wood lines beyond and in back of the house.

The wood lines at the right, left, and back of the home were all about 200 meters away from the house. Realizing that he needed to make a plan quickly but feeling that they were in danger of being exposed, Nick took one last quick look at the home and each wood line. He did not know if mines were around the home but surmised it would be too dangerous to family members. He asked the interrupter his name, and he replied, "Angel."

Nick looked a little shocked by the name which he remembered Charles telling him one time that Angel literally meant messenger. He quickly composed himself and said, "Does the family live here?"

"Yes."

"Are there children, and do they play in the yard?"

"Yes."

"When is the last time children were seen in the yard?"

"Yesterday."

"Good, I doubt we're in a mine field. I want two men at each side of the house to include some hidden in the front. Everybody is to keep hidden and alert. Shoot if necessary. Also, I need you and another man with me. I am attacking toward the front, and I need you two to cover me."

Angel crawled back from Nick toward the main concentration of the hidden men and began to brief them in Spanish. Nick saw two men come forward and noticed that Angel had brought Arturo with him. He heard Angel say, "Arturo will be with us."

Nick felt tremendous respect for Arturo and said, "Thank you for all you did for us."

Angel spoke to Arturo in Spanish and then reported that Arturo replied that he was very thankful for all Nick and his friends had done for them. Nick nodded and then motioned for them to cover him as he would run oblique to the house's front porch. He instructed both men to cover for him specifically. He was in the open and running when two men from inside the house suddenly showed on the porch with automatic weapons. Nick thought armatures and thugs and suddenly dived down into the lawn with shots coming rapidly from Angel and Arturo. The two men were cut to shreds by the rapid gunfire, and then, there was total quiet. Nick stood up and began to run again toward the home. He stopped on the porch beside the front window nearest him. He noticed Arturo was also coming toward the home knowing that Nick planned to enter the house alone. Arturo was not about to let Nick do that.

Moving his older body as quickly as possible in a bent over position, Arturo reached Nick's side without incident. Nick nodded and said, "thank you" and motioned for Arturo to cover while he went toward the door left open by the two dead men. Suddenly, gun fire erupted from the woods in back of the home. Arturo and Nick hit the porch falling as controlled as possible in the prone position while watching the doors and windows in front of them. The shooting stopped suddenly, and Nick realized somebody tried to run out the back trying to make a getaway. Angel yelled and heard the reply that Nick understood, "dos hombres." He assumed the two enemy were dead.

Also, Nick began to realize how Arturo had trained and embedded discipline into these men. They were excellent at picking and neutralizing targets. He began to wonder why Arturo turned over the leadership to him. Anyway, Arturo was wanting to be in the center of the action and not place his men over his own safety. Nick began to admire the man beside him even more and felt a bond as much as anyone with whom he had been in battle.

Nick began to work his way toward the door by quickly going under the windows and stopping on the right hand side of the door. Arturo knew that Nick was being careful not to shoot wild through the windows due to children might be in the home. Nick went through the door with Arturo quickly moving in the front of the door with his weapon ready to fire on anything that moved in the room. The room was empty, and the house was quiet. A stairwell was in the living room with an open foyer with large white and gray marble tile with the steps of the stairs each with one-piece matching marble. The shiny gold banisters gave the room an even richer glow. Expensive double stuffed red leather furniture was in the room.The home was quiet.

Nick and Arturo started going from room to room finding no people while watching the top of the stairs whenever possible. The upstairs also rendered nothing. The home appeared empty of people. Arturo and Nick left the home and ran toward the wood line where Angel was sitting. Nick looked at Angel and pronounced, "nothing in the house. Where to now?"

Arturo looked at Angel and pronounced in Spanish, "We must go to the next place; they must be really afraid. I can lead us there."

Angel interpreted to Nick who nodded to Arturo in agreement.

Charles traveled to a place deep into the forests to a place where automobiles were hidden by brush. It was a quiet place with a deep hole in the ground around the deposits of limestone dug from the earth. Water stood in a vast pool outside but hidden to the naked eye when looking from ground level. There was a single door leading underground. The land looked desolate otherwise.

Charles asked in Spanish to the man nearest him, "Is this the killing hole?"

The man answered back in Spanish, "yes." Everybody began to make their way toward the door when Charles motioned for the team to stay behind. They looked at each other confused but complied. Charles believed he had to go in alone.

Charles made his way to the door without incident. If there were guards, they were hidden very well. He opened the door and disappeared into the darkness of the enclosed hallway carved out of the limestone. The torch lights cut through the darkness, and he stopped and closed his eyes for thirty seconds as he counted and then began again to look around. His eyes had adjusted, and figures began to emerge in the darkened light.

Judge Baez's older female voice spoke in English in the distance of the manmade cavern. "We are few in this land. We could not have you until now. My goddess told me you would be here today. You are to be our ultimate sacrifice. There are many to sacrifice, but you are the true man of your God. It is time the world see that your God is nothing and that our gods are all powerful."

Charles could make out the darkened outline of the woman judge. Also, he smelled the petroleum stench of the torches and the smell of rotting blood; however, the thing that made him sick the most was the spiritual feelings of the horrors of the sacrifices done here. His eyes continued to adjust, and he made out the goddess with the bowl in her belly. Juan had never seen her and described as best he could from the reports of others. Charles was not prepared to see her large mother of pearl eyes glaring back at him in the torchlight. Suddenly, he knew they wanted his heart in that bowl while still beating.

Charles looked around as best he could and said, "Let us talk a little before the sacrifice begins. As I can see only slightly in this low light, I believe you are not alone."

"Although we are few in this land, there are many here, and the priest kings are awaiting to sacrifice you to our goddess. With the death of a great man of the Christian God, we will then have the required blessings to take back that which belongs to us. We are the new leaders, lawgivers, and priests."

Charles was stalling and trying to make out a passageway to somewhere else. He began to walk down the wall when he felt a hand grab his right arm. The pistol in Charles' left hand barked and the arm let go. He backed himself against the wall and then tried to take aim at the female figure, but she had disappeared in the darkness beyond the torch lights. Another movement of a shadow, and he fired again. He heard a thud as someone hit the floor. Then he remembered that no weapons except primitive knives and swords were in the room. He began to believe this is a ritual, and they really believed this piece of carved soft rock with a bowl in her belly could protect them. He wondered if the men outside could survive and take this cave when suddenly he heard the female's voice again, "I am the judge priestess. You have violated our sanctuary with the blood of a priest king. In the name of my goddess, I curse you!"

Charles counted at least seven men in some kind of special regalia and noticed a faint and large wall painting of the pyramid steps with the feathered serpent, Kukulkan, at the base enlarged and in caricature. He could see it through the smoking torch lights. He began to work his way down the wall again looking for an adjoining room or hallway. He had superior weapons but the slight light of the cave gave them an advantage. Suddenly, he heard Inspector Vega's voice and then a shot that was not directed toward him. He saw a shadowy figure fall and heard a thud on the carved limestone floor. Inspector Vega's voice sounded, "There are two guns other than yours in this room, and there are protectors that are armed with primitive weapons. I just killed my partner, Inspector Mendoza, who is a traitor. Whatever you need to do Charles, please do it!" With those words he heard the whack of a macahuitl board sword. He heard another whack and knew the sharp obsidian, glass like, blades had hit their mark. Inspector Vega's gasps were getting fainter, and he immediately began looking for her. With Milagros wounded and the priest kings closing in, Charles began to think no other plan would work. As rapidly as he could, he slipped out of the jacket with the pockets filled with C-4 and grenades from the cache. Also, Nick had pinned in certain areas of the jacket certain quantities of gunpowder, nails and even small wrenches. Charles hung the garment upon an overhanging rock in the cave. He set the timer and began to move toward what he thought was Milagros body lying on the floor. Kneeling, he scooped her into his arms and began to move toward a rock hallway knowing if the timer failed he could also detonate the explosives remotely. He felt the wet and hot stickiness of fresh blood from her right arm and shoulder. She was panting heavily through her mouth but managed to whisper, "I love you Charles. Please put me down and get out of here."

He looked down at her face showing faintly in the torchlight and said, "No, this time I make the decisions. You know that you brought out a part of me that I thought was dead. I had rather die with you than live without you." Charles continued to move toward what he thought might be a dark shadowy hallway but was also being slowed by Milagros' weight and the strain of trying to move quickly in faint light.

The time before the explosion was growing short. All the enemy had to die in the cave, and nothing could protect them in the way of their pagan deities. Charles took a deep breath and lunged toward a darkened hole that he thought was their only chance for survival while squeezing Milagros tightly.

The explosion rocked the entire forest as debris covered with a cloud of lime dust flew more than a hundred feet in the air. The men that accompanied Charles to the killing hole were knocked down from the percussion but got up quickly and began to run in any direction away from the blast. Giant rocks began to fall into the forest breaking the trees around them. The men were scurrying to hide under whatever cover they could find until the sounds of the falling rocks ceased. The dust began to clear displaying a giant light gray hole in the ground. Everything at ground zero of the explosion was vaporized. The surprised militia men were saying among each other that it must have been an underground munitions dump due to the size of the explosion. A few seconds earlier, Commander Mendoza received the emergency signal from Inspector Vega's watch. There was no time to react; he watched in horror as the signal died.

Candice sat watching her screen when Charles' chip that fed back his whereabouts and vital signs suddenly stopped. She began to tear up but could not quit what she was doing due to Nick still showing signs of life. Suddenly, she felt a strange hand on her shoulder. Juan leaned down near her ear and said, "I see that. Is Nick still going?"

"Yes," she said trying to disguise her disgusted voice. "Juan, what are you doing here?"

"Waiting to see what I can do to help. May I sit down?"

"I guess so. All I can think about you is that idiot that spoke in a Spanish accent and was in cahoots with the cartel."

"Candice, I am not that person. Anyway, let me sit here and help you monitor the goings on. We may be needed."

Nick and his group arrived at the new destination that was only a rock farmhouse with a barn located clear from all woods and shrubbery. Nick calculated quickly that the long fields that surrounded the home to be in the vicinity of about twelve hundred meters. There were windows in every direction within the home. The barn near the home had all the windows open. Solar panels stood toward the south on the top of the barn tall enough for someone to fit behind. The largest caliber rifles he and the militia had would not be effective across the openness of the field due to the maximum distance of accurately shooting with their best weapons was about eight hundred meters. Also, the land had a downward slope toward the house keeping any way of crawling or using any kind of stealth. The most that could be done for attack is to wait for nightfall hoping the guards were not disciplined enough to stay awake; he hoped the guards might doze off about 2:30AM. The drones rigged with explosives could only take out a small portion of the home or barn. Otherwise, it would be a four-pronged attack with only two men to a side with weapons that would be best for firing within five hundred meters provided these men had been trained to fire well at that distance. He did not suspect mines in the area except for those that could be triggered remotely; otherwise, the grounds could not be mowed so bare. Nick also knew that an air attack from a helicopter from the spy ship was strictly against the rules. Their helicopters could only be used for ship protection, search, rescue, and medical evacuations, and this was strictly enforced. However, if the helicopters were fired upon during their duties, they could defend themselves.

Nick was thinking; any way I go, this is suicide for all of us. He took the men to a safe distance from the house and told them about the problems of the attack. The men, including Arturo, wanted to end this once and for all even if it meant their lives. Nick made it very clear that any attack with their weapons, even if these people were not professionals, could end in disaster, but the men insisted. Nick agreed to attack with them knowing he might never see Candice again.

Nighttime came, and the men found places to sleep under trees where they could be hidden well. They passed around insect repellent to every person. There could be no fires. Each man slept for two hours and then was awakened for guard duty with at least half the men on guard at all times. Nick was awakened by Arturo and Angel at 2AM and gathered his gear to include his three barrel and his scoped automatic 7.62mm NATO rifle. He began to check the loads in all his ammunition and began to separate them for the coming battle. He told Angel to tell Arturo and the others that he would be attacking with two other men the front of the house. Arturo disagreed knowing the frontal attack was the most dangerous but then gave in. Angel reported in English that he and Arturo would be attacking from the front with Nick. Just before the attack, Nick would use the drones as a distraction and would try to fly them into the front doors of the house and barn.

Nick scanned the area during the light for any sign of disturbed soil that might indicate land mines that could be detonated from the home. He saw none, but that did not mean none were there. Also, land mines that are triggered by someone standing on them could be laid in the trees just before the cleared grounds.

The militia men were already chosen for each side and instructed where to position themselves before the attack. Arturo and Angel were waiting for

Nick to give the signal for the attack. The time was 2:26AM. Nick was ready to fly the drones in with the resulting explosions signaling the attack hoping the distraction would allow some to survive long enough to try and take the home. Nick was busy flying the drones when a large helicopter came up over the back of the home firing two missiles. The two explosions lighted the sky, making the two explosions from the drones seem like fire crackers, and most of the roof was ripped off with tiles and other debris flying into the fields. The militia men instinctively knew the attack was called off and were working their way back into the woods toward Arturo. Arturo motioned for the men to fall back farther into the woods and meet. Suddenly, there were red flashlights moving all around them. The police chief spied Arturo and said in Spanish that the police and military would take over now. Arturo looked both surprised and grateful. Angel looked meek and told Nick what was just said. Nick let out a long breath in relief and said, "thank you" to the police chief.

The police chief stopped right in front of Arturo and in the reflection of the red flashlights looked straight into his eyes and began to speak, "Angel's responsibility is to keep track of you. He is an undercover cop sent to infiltrate your militia. Did you know that?"

"No," Arturo said as he looked toward Angel with disgust.

"I did not think so," said the Police Chief in Spanish. "I am Police Chief Eutropio Morales. Arturo, I will no longer recognize your men as a militia."

Arturo dropped his eyes and said, "Sir, I ask that you take me but leave my men alone. Will you do that?"

"Arturo, I no longer call you militia because, as of this night, you are my deputies. I expect to see you at my station sometime this week to work out the details. Is that good with you?"

Arturo's smile could be seen in the dark as he replied, "It is wonderful, sir. But, we have others that are with Reverend Charles Dorgan."

"Angel informs me of everything, even your raids today to include the raid on the killing hole. As I said before, you are to go home now. We are taking care of this. You are to bring all your militia members to the meeting. I checked on your wounded man. I believe he will make it to the meeting too, but if not, you can explain everything to him. Arturo, the killing hole is destroyed. Apparently,

I lost two detectives in the explosion. Some of your men are suffering from minor injuries from falling debris, but none are hurt badly. Also, Reverend Dorgan is missing."

Chief Sanchez looked at Nick and said in very good English, "I do not want to know your story."

Nick looked back at the chief and reported in a sad voice because he recognized Charles name, "I am so glad not to tell it."

"Good, now go home."

Nick turned to Angel and asked, "What about Charles?"

"Missing."

Nick knew he had no time to grieve and immediately pushed the feelings that Charles was harmed or killed to the back of his mind. Besides, he did not feel Charles was dead.

Angel looked at Arturo and said, "May I go with you?"

Arturo looked at the men who were mere shadows in the diffused light standing in front of him and noted their shaking their heads in agreement. Arturo looked at Angel proclaiming, "We are all cops now. Of course, I want you to go with us."

The men loaded into the pickup and were leaving the area when a large red limousine passed them on the small road. Angel recognized the vehicle and reported that it could be carrying the main cartel leader. The police and Mexican military were busy taking the home with large and small caliber fire snapping in the distance with occasional explosions. Somehow, the people in the limousine had escaped. Arturo took off as fast as possible in the pickup slamming the men into each other and eventually the tailgate in the back of the pickup. Nick took the three barrel and stood up ready to fire over the cab when fire erupted from the right back window of the limo. Nick got down behind the cab after three pistol bullets scrapped the cab to his right. This was enough verification to completely ensure Arturo that it was a cartel vehicle. He rolled down the window and yelled to return fire. Angel interpreted to Nick who placed three rounds into the back glass of the SUV; the glass shattered, but the bullets did not penetrate. It was bullet proof glass. The vehicle began to drive erratically to make the target more difficult. Also, the slower pickup had problems following the increased horsepower limo, and it disappeared toward the main road where it would be impossible for them to catch. Arturo pulled to the side of the road and stopped; he jumped out of the truck scanning the pickup's bed with a red lens flash light while asking if anyone was hurt. Someone said in Spanish that nobody was hit by the bullets. Angel got out and walked around to Arturo and asked what could be done. Angel looked to Nick for new plans when Arturo reported their only chance would be if whoever was in the limo was going to the cartel yacht. It would be at the end of the main road ahead and would lead directly to the private pier near its mooring. The pickup might just make it to the pier before the ship sailed. They decided to move ahead down the road and head toward the pier knowing it would take time to get everything and everyone into a dingy to travel to the mooring and then to get the large engine powered catamaran ready to move. The ship was large but fast because of its two catamaran like hulls causing less drag in the water. If the head of the cartel was bugging out, it would be the perfect getaway vehicle. Angel called the chief on his cell phone for permission to pursue. Commander Morales reluctantly agreed but gave strict orders for them to retreat if the risks became too great.

Arturo had Angel drive, so he could watch the road and fire quickly if necessary. Nick asked the man beside him to hold the three barrel while he got his semiautomatic rifle ready. He banged on the top of the cab with his hand while yelling at Angel to watch for an attack at the intersection to enter the main road. Angel agreed and informed Arturo who ordered Angel to cut his lights. The moon was darkened but enough light came through once their eyes had adjusted to see the light gray gravel on the road. All the men were watching the road with weapons at the ready when car lights began to come into view from about a mile away. Suddenly, shots began to ring out but missing the truck sparking the road in front of them and also breaking limbs in the trees beside them. The amateurs had shot too soon giving themselves away. Arturo in Spanish and Nick in English gave identical orders to dismount the truck and begin to approach the ambush through the trees. Angel slowed and then stopped the vehicle behind as many trees as possible. The bullets were still coming but missing. Nick, seeing that Arturo took the right side of the road with three men, yelled for Angel to come with him on the left side with the remaining men. Then, Nick yelled for Angel to ask Arturo to move into a flanking position with the men on the road while he held his men back. Arturo agreed to the ambush plans and began to move around to the enemies right while bullets still peppered the area from the intersection. The cartel men were shooting wild.

The plan was simple and understood quickly; Arturo would begin firing from the side of the adjoining road at the attackers who would possibly begin running away from the fire right into the side fire from Nick and his men who had held back. If the crossfire was successful, the ambush would work perfectly.

Arturo made it to the black top beyond the cartel men and could see the road in the moonlight looking smooth and black like water. Car lights were in the distance as he whispered for his men to get down and wait. The car passed out of sight when he raised his weapon and began to fire. The men followed suit and a hail of bullets caught the darkened shadows by surprise scattering them down the road right into Nick's trap. Nick's men opened fire at the darkened silhouettes that showed black against the slightly lighter road with the shadows hitting the ground. Bullets were finding their marks and all would be over soon. Nick's right side was exposed; otherwise, he was well covered by brush and dirt; he was looking down his scope to pick off any strays when the AK-47 burst of fire set bullets hitting to his front right side, and a deflected, deformed bullet angled into the right side of Nick's chest. It was an unlucky one in the million shots by the enemy as the bullet caught Nick on his right side ripping out part of his rib cage rolling him suddenly upon his left side. Nick found himself gasping for breath and reeling from the pain. The men quickly returned fire in the direction of the shooter with three distinctive thuds occurring. Then, all was quiet.

The men assigned to Nick quickly ceased firing looking for any motion from the front, and then, the nearest man hovered over Nick feeling for a pulse. Arturo yelled that he was advancing to the edge of the intersection and that all should watch again for enemy movement. No enemy movement occurred. Angel moved beside Nick examining him as best he could in the dark. Nick's right rib cage felt like hot steaming wet mush with sharpened bones sticking out as he ran his hand over the area. Nick continued fighting for his breath as Angel yelled to Arturo in Spanish that Nick might be fatally wounded.

Nick managed to drive out a few words to Angel to tell Arturo, "Get them and leave me behind."

The men looked for enemy and then advanced forward with weapons ready. One enemy groaned, and three rifles were fired toward that area. Then, there was an eerie quietness again. Arturo's men searched for bodies and found four dead with all killed directly in front of Nick's men. Arturo and Angel returned to Nick while the rest of the men stood watch for any signs of movement at the side of the road.

Arturo asked if Nick had a chip embedded under his skin making it possible for his people to find him. He replied a groaning, "yes."

Arturo informed Angel to pick two men, to improvise a stretcher, and move him into the forest away from the road as far as possible and place him near a possible landing zone for a helicopter. The two men were to return to the intersection for pickup after Nick was delivered. With any luck, Nick might be found by his people. A makeshift bandage was made from a shirt with a piece of thick plastic set over the chest wound to hopefully restrict air from entering through the hole in the chest.

Arturo, Angel, and the remaining men went back to the pickup to pursue the cartel leader to his boat. It was getting toward 3:30AM when the pickup left the two men quickly stretching their battle dress jackets over two cut poles to make something to carry Nick to a possible pick up point. However, neither the militia men nor Nick believed he would live much longer. Nick gasped out in English with no understanding to the two men spoke only Spanish, "If I die, leave me."

Arturo and the remaining deputies arrived at the isolated pier beginning on the small beach just as the dingy was moving out toward the large fast yacht. The ship's running lights were on, so Arturo surmised this may be the last run of the dingy with the supplies. Two men were in the small dingy with what looked like no more than a six horse power outboard motor. The small aluminum vessel reached the ship, was tethered to a lift, and was being lifted on board. Arturo thought the eighty foot plus yacht had moved in to less than three hundred meters off the shore and may have been anchored while off the mooring that was farther out in the sea. No other boats were available, so he ordered his men to fire at will at the vessel.Everybody began to fire with two bullets finding their marks on the two men running the dingy lift. They fell back onto the deck.

Suddenly, the boat's motor came to life as the automatic anchor lift stalled that was feeding the chain into a hole in the front of the right catamaran hull. The dingy remained half way up and began to swing against the boat as it began to move forward. The lights went out on the ship except for faint lights from the console of the control room that gave just enough glow to show its location on the boat. Arturo and his men concentrated their fire on the faintly lighted area with the ship suddenly turning around toward the bank. Their fire intensified, but someone was able to right the ship and start it toward the open ocean. The men fired until the ship disappeared in the darkness. Arturo looked at each man while personally thanking them for all they had done that night and that this may not be over.

The new deputies and Angel traveled to the intersection where the men who took care of Nick were supposed to meet them. The two men were hiding and came out of the cover of the trees slowly but hid near the road with weapons ready after the pickup had been parked. Arturo sensing the possible danger of the situation ordered the men in a low voice to cut all lights and dismount. Arturo moved quickly to the two men who were crouching in the roadside ditch. One of the men whispered to Arturo, "Two trucks are down the road near where we came out. The people are in the forest. We think they are cartel and are looking for Nick."

Arturo had his men scout the area, and when all were satisfied they were alone, Arturo said, "The morning might bring more or less problems, and we are going home to protect our families."

The men disagreed; each felt much guilt that the head of the cartel had escaped justice, but the most guilt was felt leaving Nick without knowing if he was still alive. Angel came forward speaking directly to Arturo while the seven other men stood behind him. He said to Arturo, "You are our leader, and all of us appreciate all you do. But, we do not want to leave Nick vulnerable. I ask that you send four of us to check out Nick while the other five go back and make sure all our families are taken to a safe location and guarded. Also, the police are checking on our families per Chief Sanchez's communication with Angel, and our agreement before we ever went on our mission was that nobody would be left behind. Now, please split our forces?"

Arturo said in a calm voice, "You are all correct. Nick did much for us. Angel and I will take the two men who placed Nick." With that he turned toward the other men and requested, "Please make sure our families are safe."

Arturo gave the order to his four-member patrol to check their weapons and ammunition levels. Then, Arturo, Angel, and the other two men disappeared in the trees as the others moved toward the truck.

Juan approached Candice who was fighting back tears for Charles in the tiny communications cubicle as she was monitoring Nick's erratic vital signs on her super tablet. She knew he was badly wounded but could not discern other details from his embedded chip.

She sensed Juan moving toward her and said without looking around, "Juan, not now. Things aren't going well."

Juan continued to intrude to her right side, sat down, and said, "You know two are a straight line while three make at least a triangle."

"You know?"

"Been a part of whatever you are a part of now. They sent me in early to help you because the mission would be very difficult. Some parts, all of you made look easy."

"Yes, until Joyce Jamison."

Juan looked her straight in the eyes, and when he had her complete attention, he said, "The mission is not over. A ship is moving fast from an obscure area of beach. This ship is a watched vessel."

"Can the spy ship catch it?"

"No, but the Seahawk can. It can locate it and notify the proper authorities to include the local coast guard. It's on its way. Remember the ship has two helicopters."

"Of course, I know that."

Juan continued, "Before you say anything else, I want you to know that I have the civilian helicopter waiting for us to go and help Nick. Are you in or out?"

Candice looked at Juan and for the first time felt some affection toward him, "I am in. When do we go?"

"As soon as you get suited up. This is beyond most black ops, and I do not have to tell you what will happen if we are not successful, if you die in other words."

"Oh yes, the good old cremation and nobody will know."

"Yes. So, get suited up, and we will go. One other thing."

"OK?"

"Neither one of us is in charge. The pilot is, but most of the orders will come from the crew chief. Will you follow the orders one hundred percent no matter what happens?"

Candice looked at Juan with begging eyes, "As much as it hurts, I will. Please, just let me go with you to get Nick. I want him back."

They approached the civilian looking helicopter toward the port side after the crew chief signaled. The inside of the helicopter had been stripped out with a single mattress placed in the middle and a corpsman sitting at the head of the mattress with his arms folded. To his immediate right was a physician assistant. The inside of the helicopter was noisy and hot. The crewman signaled for Juan to sit at the right of the mattress and Candice to the left. Both were to hook themselves to the floor with the hook at the end of the strap that extruded from the webbed harnesses given to them. The lead crewman checked the 7.62 mm machine gun mounted to be hidden on the inside but positioned so that it could quickly be swung out the opened port door. Candice saw the pilot's lips move but could not hear him. Then she saw the crew chief move his lips, and the helicopter took off. It flew five hundred feet or less over the water and then the land going for the coordinates that Nick's chip had last signaled. They had about two hours before darkness engulfed them. The crew chief motioned for Candice and Juan to place the wireless ear phones with their attached microphones that were hanging behind them on their heads. The coordinates were correct, and the co-pilot spotted Nick's body lying in a small clearing with a workable landing zone nearby. According to everything on Candice's tablet, Nick was declining fast. The crew chief opened the port side door, and swung out the machine gun looking for any collateral movement. No movement happened, and no ground fire came. Juan was handed an M-16 by the physician assistant as ordered by the crew chief to be ready to jump to cover the medical staff. Candice began to unhook her strap holding her to the aircraft when she was told over the ear phones that she was to remain attached and in place. She was also handed an M-16 by the crew chief and told to cover only. The helicopter touched down lightly, and both the corpsman and physician assistant lined up at the door and jumped to the ground running with backpacks. The corpsman carried a rolled up stretcher while the PA carried a large camouflaged tackle box. Both men sprinted the fifty or so yards to the body.

The woods lighted with small arms fire against the helicopter as the two men began to kneel beside the body. The small bubble window near the co-pilot's right foot was shattered, but no one was harmed. The crew chief saw the rustle of leaves and movement and instantly placed the machine gun rounds into the area. Candice also fired at any movement that was not close to Nick. Juan asked to go out and protect the helicopter's right flank and was granted permission by the crew chief. He stood at the back of the helicopter making himself an easy target to draw fire away from the helicopter and medics and to return fire when needed if he survived. The crew chief and Candice continued to fire at movement, and for the moment, ground fire was suppressed. Suddenly, a shot was heard, and Juan grabbed his left arm as he was spun around. He quickly recovered and fighting the pain of a flesh wound in his lower arm placed half a magazine at the direction he thought the shots came from. Then, shots came from every direction for a few seconds. Quiet came again as the crew chief told every member to hold fire due to his hearing just now over his radio that friends may be in the area. No movement occurred except for Arturo and Angel stepping out of the woods with their rifles held over their heads with both hands. Then, they disappeared after a few seconds. Candice reported to the crew chief their names and that seven other friends could possibly be in the forest. The crew chief stood ready with the machine gun hoping the new friends could keep all shooting away from them. Angel came out of the forest again and asked by signaling with his arms to approach the helicopter. The crew chief motioned for him to come. Once at the starboard side, Angel yelled the story to the crew chief and to Candice how Nick was wounded and explained they had to mop up the area to keep the enemy away from him. He reported that some cartel members had parked on the road where the militia men had taken Nick to this landing zone to be picked up. Also, he reported there were four of them in the area and would watch and protect the landing zone and wished the best for Nick.

After a short time that seemed an eternity, the stretcher was being carried back to the helicopter. After Nick was situated, Juan jumped into the helicopter. As Juan moved to his area, his wounded arm dripped blood on Candice and the end of the mattress. Candice looked lovingly at Juan and said, "Thank you Juan and thank all of you for getting my Nick back." The PA made sure Nick was strapped on the mattress and then moved to Juan attending his arm as Candice looked on with sorrow that she ever had any bad feelings toward him.

Nick heard and felt the whirling wind as the helicopter came in to the makeshift landing zone. The two men with a stretcher approached as he began to pass out and then slightly regain consciousness in a cycle.He heard, "Breath out, now hold it." He felt something greasy and plastic on his right chest. He heard rapid gunfire and then muffled flapping as he breathed. Then, his breath came easier. He felt needle sticks in both arms and thought he heard the word "morphine". Then darkness came. Suddenly, he awakened while the helicopter was in flight finding himself lying on a mattress in the middle of the floor with a face over his face looking down at him. He could hear a man say that it could be massive blood loss and heard the words that he thought said "right flail chest". He imagined he heard Candice's voice and her crying. He thought her spirit was following him now. He imagined that he felt her hand touching his face as she prayed. He tried to hang on to reality, but half consciousness from the blood loss and pain came upon him. Then, darkness came again.

The Seahawk had to return to the ship once to refuel and then waited close to daylight to leave again. The helicopter crew found the cartel ship as dawn was breaking. Two wounded men laid on the front deck in large pools of blood while others may be inside the cabin. A man suddenly appeared on the deck waving his arms. The militia men had managed to wound all but one man on board who was trying to keep the other three cartel men alive while the yacht moved on automatic pilot. One of the wounded appeared to be the head of the cartel. The man from the cabin disappeared for a few seconds, and the boat stopped in the water as the helicopter called in the coordinates to the spy ship. The spy ship would report the ship anonymously, so the process of the pickup of the cartel personnel aboard the ship by local law enforcement could begin. The pilots and helicopter crew were not worried about the boat because it was full of wounded and definitely not going anywhere with only the healthy one-man crew. They turned the Seahawk away and returned to the spy ship.

Chapter 33

Nick's Recovery

THE INTENSIVE CARE unit was sterile and cold as Nick looked around for the first time since he was on the rescue helicopter where he dreamed Candice was touching his face and praying over him. Nurses scurried about as he looked out of the glass wall in his room toward the center of the round looking unit. As he looked out his large window facing the open center of the ICU, he could see rooms that seemed to be in a circle all with glass fronts, so the nurses could turn in one place and see all the patients through the glass inner walls. A young female nurse came hurriedly into his room asking him questions, "Are you OK? Do you feel you can breathe on your own?"

Nick began to answer and noted he had a tube in his mouth. He began to shake his head violently for yes when he realized the tube was blocking his throat. His ventilator alarmed as he began to try to breathe, and another nurse entered the room and stood by the left side of the bed.

Suddenly, a young man and an older lady he thought was a doctor due to her long white coat appeared in his room. Suction was held in one hand of the young man, and the young nurse disconnected him from the ventilator and placed a bag over the end of his breathing tube. The older lady in the long white coat turned off the ventilator, and the room seemed too silent.

He heard the lady in the long white coat say, "Now, I will remove the tube." He felt himself cough as the syringe was placed on a smaller tube lying beside the large tube that was in his throat and then pulling, choking, coughing, as the tube became longer and then appeared in front of his face slimy and with what looked like a flattened balloon at the end. He gasped for air as the young nurse told him to breathe slowly. His breath came difficultly at first due to the pain of his right lung expanding.

He squeaked out a question, "How long have I been here?"

"I'm Dr. Hardin, and you have been our guest in our hospital in the Orlando, Florida Trauma Center for almost three weeks. You have been conscious before, but your numbers looked too good this time to keep the tube in. Now, keep breathing, or I will have to put it back."

Nick's voice sounded a little less squeaky. "I'll keep breathing. I don't remember waking up before."

"That's not unusual Mr. Lippincott. Your parents came from Nashville to visit several times. Also, you kept calling out the name Candice. They said she is your wife."

Nick remained quiet due to being afraid of saying something wrong. He changed the subject quickly and managed to say between gasps, "Dr. Hardin, what are your plans for me?"

"Oh, to get you breathing well first and then, to see you get through rehab. You need a couple more surgeries for skin grafts to your right side. Do you remember anything? Evidently, your case is high profile because some FBI men came to visit you several times asking if you said anything. I notified hospital administration who is supposed to call them now that you are awake. The FBI men say you are the victim of a drive by shooting."

"Thank you, but my throat is hurting me." Nick felt uncomfortable suddenly not knowing what to keep secret. He said, "I promise to keep breathing, but I would really like to rest now." In fact, he wanted to do the opposite. He wanted to keep talking and visiting. He wanted to know his actual condition and what to expect, but he did not know what medication he was taking and other dangerous items that could cause him to say something secret or regretful.

The two FBI men came when the outside window showed darkness. He looked at the clock in front of his bed, and the numbers said 9:16PM. The two men, dressed in nice suits with white shirts and black ties, flashed their identifications and asked permission from the nurse standing in the middle of the ICU. Once approved by the nurse, they walked into the room, closed the door, and pulled the curtain blocking sight through the inside glass wall.

"Mr. Lippincott, we are agents of the FBI. We have good news for you. Your wife Candice is living in Texas and asked to see you when you are well enough to travel. Do you approve?"

"I would like that very much. What are your names?"

"I am Agent Stone, and this is Agent Rutherford. We have been assigned to your case since the drive by shooters were from another state, Alabama. Also, it is believed they robbed a bank prior to crossing this state line. What do you remember about the shooting?"

Nick looked at both the men's blank faces and instinctively said, "I do not remember anything."

"Mr. Lippincott, that is not unusual in trauma cases. We ask that you not discuss this case with anyone to include the hospital staff," said Agent Stone.

"That is not a problem. I will not discuss the case with anyone."

"You also called the name Charles while you were unconscious. Were you with someone named Charles on the day of the shooting?"

"I knew a Charles once, a while back. I really don't remember details right now. If I do remember anything, I will be sure and tell you only."

"Very good. Your parents visited you but needed to fly back to Nashville. We saw on your cell phone that they called you several times prior to the shooting."

"Will you tell them I'm doing better?"

"We will," said Agent Stone. "In the meantime, here is a new cell phone with our number already listed in the contacts. We advise you to call us with any problems or sudden memories." He laid the phone on the bedside table.

"I will."

"Thank you." Agent Stone pulled back the curtain as Agent Rutherford opened the door. The nurse nodded toward them as they left.

Nick's skin graft surgeries and rehabilitation took two months. His pain was decreasing now, and he needed less pain pills. He remarked that he did not know if his right chest or if the skin grafts from his thighs hurt more. His chest began to scar and take on a partial concave look where the ribs had been shattered. He forced himself to lift small weights, painfully stretch his right hand above his head, and to do anything that made himself better. He wanted to see Candice but knew that his scars, especially the star shaped scar on his left forehead, might make Candice run for cover. He attacked his rehabilitation sessions with determination not to let the pain or retracting scar tissue stop him.

For two months he did all he could do to get better while always saying that he remembered nothing about the details of the day of the shooting. Then, the two agents came to him with Dr. Hardin while he rested in his room after a difficult session.

Dr. Hardin spoke first, "Mr. Lippincott, you will have to continue some physical therapy, but you are well enough to leave my care. Agents Stone and Rutherford insist they set up transportation for you. If you will contact me with the Doctor and hospital you choose to follow your continued care when you get settled, I will send them your medical record."

"Thanks Dr. Hardin."

Agent Stone insisted they speak to Nick alone, so Dr. Hardin left the room.

"Are you traveling first to see Candice?"

"I would like that."

"Due to your case, you will be kept under surveillance."

"That would be good."

"Your flight will leave at midnight tonight. We will escort you to the airport. You will be taken by taxi to the hotel where your wife will be waiting to see you. Do you have any other questions?"

"Not right now."

"Do you remember anything about the shooting or the day of the shooting?"

"I am very sorry. I do not remember anything. Dr. Hardin said my memory loss was due to the trauma and possibly some of the drugs used to put me to sleep or to keep me alive."

"Speak with us first if you remember anything."

"I will."

Nick tried to sleep but would awake with fear. He wanted to see Candice but feared her response when she saw him. He was not a good specimen anymore with giant scaring on his right chest, pink skin graft patches on his thighs, and scars on his forehead and face. He had also lost a lot of weight and muscle from his prolonged bed time.

The day came to leave, and Nick was able to place on the khaki pants with the blue polo shirt, provided by the FBI agents, with moderate difficulty. His walking and moving into the cars and later waiting long hours at the airport in a special area flanked by the two agents was painful even when he sat in the padded chairs. He boarded the private plane sometime about 2AM and found himself a little short of breath as the plane gained altitude. After the landing, the taxi was waiting and loaded his luggage quickly at the destination, and his two agent escort quickly disappeared.

The taxi driver did not look typical and had a bulge in his left chest. Nick immediately surmised it was a 40 caliber pistol and that he was right handed.

The thought of rejection by Candice began to pain his chest. Fear began to encapsulate him as the taxi seemed to get closer to the destination. He thought about having some plastic surgery, especially on his face and possibly on his right chest. He could work out and get his strength back. His rehabilitation could continue. He wanted to ask Candice if he might move fairly close and maybe date her, or maybe they could be good friends. He decided he would inform Candice of his flaws and knew he could look at the expressions on her face to read if she wanted to see him again.

CHAPTER 34

Meeting with Candice

CANDICE AWAITED THE taxi bringing Nick from the Dallas airport. The Texas sun was dawning red. She would stay over in Dallas and then go back to her rock home on her small farm centrally located in the state. She was waiting in front of the hotel door as agreed upon by Nick and the FBI.

Candice saw Nick climbing out the right back door and approached him with open arms as he stood up from the taxi cab. Nick hugged her and asked her to wait while the taxi driver got his two small rolling bags from the trunk.

He looked a little worn and felt conscientious about the scars on his face. For some reason, he felt horrible about Candice seeing the small star shaped scare that was on his forehead more than the long scar on his left cheek. His dark hair was a little long, and he looked thinner than usual. There was also an indention in his shirt where surgeries had been performed on his right rib cage.

"How are you Nick?"

"Doing pretty well. Still, it's a little bit painful."

Looking Nick over from head to toe Candice proclaimed, "You look good. This is the earliest they would let me see you. You really look so good!"

"Well, when I feel better, I am asking if I can go back to find Charles. I don't believe he is dead."

Candice looked at Nick with serious eyes. "No Nick, you cannot do that. Besides, you can't bother them more than I am about finding Charles. They tell me that others will be assigned to find him. So, I need you to think about other things. For today, what are your plans?"

"To see you. Passed that, I have no immediate plans."

"Good, I have some plans for us if you do not mind."

"I was looking forward to spending some time with you. I figured you had things to do; I do not want to intrude."

"Nick, I planned the day for us. Is that OK?"

"I would love to spend the day with you."

"Well then, first let's get some coffee. There's a quaint little cafe with outside tables just down the street from here."

As they walked each pulled one of the small suitcases by their telescoping handles, Candice took Nick's empty right hand in her left and began to swing both arms as a happy little girl would do. Although the movements were painful, Nick seemed amused and rather enjoyed the contact.

They arrived at the small table for two, parked the suitcases beside their chairs, sat down, and asked the waiter wearing a long white apron for two cappuccinos. As the waiter disappeared, Candice leaned toward Nick and asked.

"Do you really love me Nick? I did not want to ask you that when you had hot coffee in your mouth."

Nick looked like he had been shot again. "Do you ever ease into anything?" Candice mesmerized Nick with her big brown eyes making Nick believe he was being placed into a trance. He could not come up with a better answer than "Yes, I love you very much."

"Good, because I really love you too."

Nick began to regain his countenance and managed to speak in a complete sentence. "Good, I would actually look forward to dating you and maybe do some real things as a couple."

"Oh my Nick, I was thinking marriage."

"Marriage!"

"Nick, keep your voice down. Besides, here comes the waiter. Now, don't be drinking coffee while I'm talking. I fear you might burn yourself."

"Are you serious? I have already had two gut jerks, and I have been with you less than five minutes."

"Fifteen minutes, Nick. You see, time goes by faster than you realize. I am thirty-three, and I want to have your children. I cannot be playing around with this."

Nick swallowed hard. "OK, I do love you and want to marry you."

"Now, was that so hard?"

"Yes!"

"And, you want me to have your children?"

"It was not on my mind while I was getting here, but yes, children would be good-very good now that I think about it." Trying to compose himself and not sound completely baffled, he sheepishly said, "I would like to discuss marriage and children with you."

"Let's discuss it. You want to marry me and have children with me and build a life with me. Yes, or No."

"Yes!"

"So, ask me."

"What!"

"So, ask me!"

"Ok, Candice or whatever your name is, I have loved you since I first met you in that run down shack in Tennessee. It is not the question that I thought of asking you because I could only think to ask if I could see you sometime or maybe even date you. But since you brought it up, the answer is yes; I do love you and want to marry you. I want to at least discuss having children, so Candice whoever you are, will you marry me?"

"Now see, is that so hard? The answer is yes; I will marry you." Candice reached into her purse and pulled out two small boxes. "Here are our rings."

"What!"

"Here are our rings. Yours may not fit well since you lost weight. Now, put it on and make sure it fits enough to not slip off your finger. Otherwise, we may have to put a small ring of tape on the back to stop it from coming off."

Nick took the platinum circle from the small brown box and placed it on his ring finger. "It's a little loose; I don't think it will slip off; we can have it resized," Nick said nervously and knowing that he was losing this discussion on every front.

"I see it is loose, but it will have to do. My ring fits perfectly and looks as simple as yours."

"You said it would have to do; what in this world are you planning?"

"Oh, I think we should get married today."

"Are you out of your mind? I just nearly got killed. My body is in pain. I fly here just to see you, and you want to get married today? Why not just take the other two functioning brain cells I have left and play marbles with them? And more than that, I have to keep telling two FBI men that I don't remember anything about my so called 'drive by shooting'. Also, I am visited in the hospital by two people I never met saying they are my parents. I need rest and to take some more pain pills right now!"

"Nick, you're not speaking well. Do you feel OK? I know the trip probably took a lot out of you."

Nick was not listening well and continued on his train of thought. "Do you know that my body has several scars now plus that big one on my chest. It looks hideous to me."

"Nick, you look so handsome to me. I can't wait to get my hands on your body and do some pretty pleasurable things with it. Oh, I need to tell you that Dr. Do is beginning to adjust to losing his right lower leg. I love him, and it hurts to see him limping around waiting on his third new prosthesis. Hey, he got his medical license for Texas."

"That is great; where is Dr. Do?"

"Living with us for a while or at least until he gets his prosthesis right. I feel sorry for the doctors, nurses, and physical therapists taking care of him. Also, the gray cat lives with us now courtesy of the strong man who had you sign the contracts.Gray Kitty actually kills scorpions that creep into the house. Dr. Do also says that he will stay and help take care of our baby, but if he gets permission to visit Cleveland, he is leaving."

"Scorpions!"

"Don't worry. Once you're stung by one, you don't fear them near as much."

It was no surprise to Nick that Dr. Do would be traveling to Cleveland as soon as he could, which might be a while, and suddenly, the most important part of the conversation hit him, "You said baby; you are not going to be using birth control tonight."

"You know how you restrained yourself all those months we slept together as fake husband and wife. I expect you to really put out on our actual wedding night, and no, I will not be using birth control tonight."

"Candice no name, you are scaring me to death. Will you slow down a little bit?"

"We can walk slowly to the church as long as we get there before 10AM. I have a suit for you and a wedding dress for me. I am sure the suit will be loose. Dr. Do is already there getting things ready."

"I can't believe this!"

"Honey, do you mind if we take the honeymoon trip later? I could only get the lady to watch our home for three days and to stop by and feed Gray Kitty. I can't believe you named him that. Anyway, we really need to get back home, but we will spend the first night of our marriage in Dallas."

Nick began to think and actually sound like he was giving a lecture, "I named him Gray Kitty because that was the most perfect name for him, and he got to answering to it very quickly. Besides, whoever owned him before probably described him as the gray cat or kitty. It was just logical to name him that. What am I saying! Now, are there any other surprises that I should know about?"

"I can't think of anything else right now. I'll let you know if I think of something. Oh, and I know you are still in pain honey, but I'll be as gentle as I can tonight."

Nick looking like a condemned man drank the last portion of his cappuccino and left money on the table for the bill and tip. He looked as Candice stretched backward after standing, slung her purse over her right shoulder, and straightened her clothes.

Each took the handles of a small suitcase again and began to walk on the sidewalk with Nick closest to the road and holding their free hands as they moved toward the church. Fear left him as they walked. Nick began to think about a real home, a chance for real love again, and even a chance for a family with children. He loved the idea of Dr. Do being around them and even loved the fact that his gray cat awaited him in an actual home. His heart began to overflow as he looked down at the perfect, freckled nosed future that walked beside him. The words slipped out as if he could not control what he was speaking.

"I do love you so much Candice."

"I love you too. Oh, I forgot. Our names are changed again."

"What!"